BETTY CRIES . . .

A Jake St. Johns Novel

JAMES A LEYSHON

authorHOUSE°

AuthorHouse™
1663 Liberty Drive
Bloomington, IN 47403
www.authorhouse.com
Phone: 1 (800) 839-8640

Published by AuthorHouse 04/01/2019

ISBN: 978-1-5462-6278-7 (sc)
ISBN: 978-1-5462-6279-4 (hc)
ISBN: 978-1-5462-6277-0 (e)

Library of Congress Control Number: 2018912284

Print information available on the last page.

Cover photo credit: Mackenzie Leyshon

Acknowledgements

Where to begin…? How about you!? Thank you for buying my book. Stay in touch… jim.leyshon@gmail.com

This one is for you, Jacque! Wish you could see the second edition.

Mr. Priselac, this is where you trust me and understand when I didn't take some suggestions. You're a brilliant man and great teacher—I have some vino on its way, big guy!

Easan, your ideas never fail to inspire me… to steal them.

Alex… Friend doesn't cover it, brother. Thanks for helping me get it right and keeping me true.

Thank you, Kenzi, for taking such a cute photo that I only had to invert to make scary.

— Jim

Prayer... The last refuge of a scoundrel.

- Lisa Simpson

Sunday

1

Sunlight beamed into the garden shed through a pinhole in the exterior wall and a sharp ray of light pierced the darkness within. Dust danced in and out of the beam as the stale enclosed air swirled in a lazy current. The summer heat was vicious and this single ray of sunlight intensified through the darkness to become a magnification point in the air that repelled motes into swirling smoke-like patterns around its needle-sharp laser beam.

The beam moved from the floor and onto the knee of a man. He jolted awake as the sunlight burned his bare skin. Jake St. Johns had been beaten bloody to the point of unconsciousness, lost his pants, and was duct-taped to a chair. His face tightened as he took in the situation.

Looking down, he found that his arms and legs were bound to the chair. He tested his restraints with a tug, but they were tight and would require a struggle.

A quick glance behind him told his eyes that the chair had been set back against a rack of hanging shovels. If he tried to rock the chair to escape his bindings, his movements would bump into several shovels that would hit against the wall of the shed like a kid beating screwdriver-handles on a five-gallon paint drum. Jake knew he needed to be silent and wait, he moved his knee out of the sunlight.

He didn't have to wait long. As his mind resolved to simply be still and determine a plan, there was the sudden sound of keys turning in a padlock on the shed door. Clink-click-clank. The bolt was turned up and pulled back.

The door creaked open and sunlight flooded into the dark interior of the shed.

Jake looked hard at the opening door—the intense light made his swollen black eyes tear-up and he could only partially focus on the shifting mass of a contrast-obscured man coming through the doorway.

1

Jake's tears flowed down his face when he closed his eyes. When he shook his head to rattle his brain awake, the tears snapped away in straight lines from his cheeks and jaw line.

"Is this how you planned it?," Jake said ripping his arms free of the restraints.

He stood up from the chair and said, "You can't stop me. This is your nightmare now."

With a smooth motion, Jake pulled free his legs and attacked the obscured man. The shed grew as if by magic to the size of a garage and before Jake could come within reach, his warden swung a shovel at Jake's head.

The loud PTANG echoed through what had become a vast warehouse.

Dazed from the blow, Jake's body dropped to the floor of the shed.

Creaking on its hinges, the door closed slowly cutting off the light. Jake looked and pressed his body up from the floor, but fell unconscious as the door closed again. Everything went black as the shed door shut on Jake.

THE DREAM SHIFTED ABRUPTLY from the shed's darkness to Jake blinking his eyes as he looked upon the backyard patio of an upscale suburban home with a tarp-covered in-ground pool. Trapped in a theatre of night visions, Jake turned his head and was projected into a kid's party that was well underway. The defused sunlight of a waning spring afternoon cast its warm colors onto the patio.

A clown-faced man opened his mouth and let out a loud laugh that startled Jake. Children were gathered around this laughing white-faced man. The clown had painted his eyes blue and accented them with tight black lines; his painted lips were big and red, outlined with carefully drawn white and black lines. The clown was dressed in a pudgy zip-up jumpsuit that had vertical yellow and white stripes. The costume was completed with big red shoes and a bright red wig.

Jake noticed that everything about this clown was a crafted subliminal message saying, 'You should laugh out loud with me as I laugh at myself.'

Staring at nothing for a moment, Jake examined his mind for all the reasons that he disliked clowns. He never understood why they had to hide behind makeup. To Jake, all clowns were all hiding something ugly.

Girls hide behind make-up.

Jake's stare became a grimace as the clown twisted an unnatural balloon animal until the balloon thing's erection was dominant. The clown smiled and handed it to Jake.

The balloon popped in Jake's face!

As if the inflated totem's demise caused distress in the heavens, a harsh peal of thunder crashed in the sky. Dark clouds gathered on the heels of an echoing crash of thunder and choked out the last rays of daylight.

Lightning flashed overhead and continued to pulse beneath and within the fast-moving clouds. The jolts of lightning were like electric fingers of a wanton man caressing the surface and insides of a full-bodied lover. Flashing with brilliance, the lightning created a stroboscopic effect on the clown and the on-looking children.

The clown disappeared, consumed within the total darkness of the weighty storm, and reappeared again with evil in his make-up streaked eyes. Malice danced on his lipstick-smeared smile when he jerked his head to stare directly at Jake! Everything went black, again.

When a flash of lightning flickered overhead, the clown threw back his head and shrieked a noise that could only be described as a demon's scream of tortured joy.

Thrusting his face at Jake, the clown peeled back his bloody lips to reveal sharp bloodstained teeth and spit out, "BOO!"

Before the first drop of spittle registered, Jake had pulled his arms up to brace against an expected attack from the clown that didn't come.

The sky opened up and rain pelted down.

Lowering his arms, Jake blinked the downpour from his eyes and looked at the children gathered around the clown.

This wasn't a safe place for kids and Jake had to do something.

The kids lowered their eyes from the freakishly tall and thin clown that now stood before them. They turned away from him and toward Jake. When their heads jerked in unison toward him, they had no eyes in their scarred blood-covered faces.

The clown blew up a new balloon as the children raised their bloody talon-tipped hands to grab the intruder, chanting in uneven rounds, "It's all your fault. You. All. Your. Fault."

The clown laughed and rolled his gaping mouth back and forth over his howling neck. His hands worked at twisting a new balloon creature.

Thunder crashed again as Jake turned to run from the nightmare under a flash of lightning that quickly waned leaving only the sound of rain pelting down within the oppressive darkness.

FROM THE DARKNESS, a little girl cried out for her 'Daddy-y-y!' It was followed by the short whine of defeat and a few child-like sobs.

The dark night was silent for a moment as the little girl inhaled.

Reloading her lungs, her next cry for 'Daddy!' was a horrible, piercing shriek of terror that echoed into eternity.

JAKE ST. JOHNS SNAPPED AWAKE with a jolt from his sweat-stained pillow. In his waking life, he was an unbeaten twenty-something pressing hard on thirty who wore wrinkled jeans and a black t-shirt. The t-shirt was silk-screened and said in bold red letters, *TheAnarchistBookstore(dot)com,* over a darker red 'Anarchy-A within a circle.'

He sat up on his bed in the center of a room cluttered with dirty clothes and piles of used books. The adrenalin generated by the nightmares faded with the memories as his sweat evaporated into the pre-dawn air.

Jake blinked himself awake and noticed his television blasting a heavy pop music video. He felt around on the bed for a remote control and couldn't remember leaving his office.

Scratching his head, Jake was surprised to find himself in bed.

Despite his drunken amnesia, he found the remote and pointed it with a shaky hand to turn off the noise. "Click," said Jake.

There was a brief moment of silence. Jake breathed in a new day through the haze of last night's self-abuse, he tried to piece together how he ended up his room.

Finding the lost pieces meant recalling, recalling meant he would find yesterday's self-feeding thoughts of Michelle and cigarettes. Mostly cigarettes.

Jake wanted—no, he needed a cigarette.

His mind had just started to fixate on smoking when the wailing sound of a little girl crying echoed from the walls and ceiling of Jake's bedroom. He rolled his eyes and sighed into the air above him.

Checking his alarm clock with irritation, Jake tossed it back down. He said to himself, "Five minutes earlier everyday." Standing from his bed, he straightened his clothes and tightened his belt.

Lifting his head, Jake shouted into the house, "Daddy used to smoke because you cry—"

To Jake's surprise, his alarm clock went off as the little girl's cries resumed anew. From every corner of his house her voice shouted for *Daddy*.

Jake groaned with frustration and bent down to hit the wake button of his droning alarm clock.

The girl's crying continued as Jake exited the room into the main hallway of his house.

"I hear you already," Jake said with dramatic stage projection into the house. "How about I get some breakfast and come back when you've calmed down and shut up?"

And, he walked on down the hall.

4

2

Even after Jake had stepped from his house and turned the deadbolt of the front door to silence the cries, the whimpering of the little girl echoed in his head.

There are things that you simply don't get used to hearing. You can try to ignore it or beat it out of them, but it's hard to forget a child's cries. The choice of action depended on the one hearing it, but when a child cried out, we all instinctively take action. Jake's choice was to avoid listening.

"On the road again," Jake said entering the half-acre lot of his beautiful century-old Victorian stone manor. The house was in one of the old money districts of Denver, Colorado. The neighboring lots had big old trees and big old houses bought using big old money. None of these trees were the elms of their northern and less rich neighbors.

In the summer, Jake lived in a magical forest of oaks, cedars, maples, spruce and willows where his neighbors sought to live up to a generational equation: more trees equaled more privacy.

While Jake had hired a crew every spring to maintain what previous tenants had left behind to bloom in the summer months, his neighbors lived all year to create hidden beauty within their walled estates.

A reoccurring thought came to him, this year would be the year that he told his grooming agents to go all out with invasive nut and fruit trees that rooted outward with suckers to create what would someday be called Jacob's Orchard. He smiled scheming about how after the trees matured, he would plant grape vines beside creeping fruit and vegetable plants to kill the area ground cover and force the trees to spread outside his walls and infect his neighbors' yards. For centuries after the fall of our federal governments, this orchard would attract the tribes and feed thousands.

It had been a frigid winter with little snow, but would likely be a heavy and wet snow-filled spring since the neighborhood trees still had bare branches and had hardly begun to bud. All the trees looked tired and cold except for the ever-green spruce trees.

The March morning air was a crisp slap in the face, but after a long cold February, it came with a breeze that had the warm promises of spring.

It reminded Jake of an especially cold February night after he had sent a card with flowers to Michelle and called on Valentine's Day. He even left her a concise and friendly message, but she had not called back.

Having thought long and hard, Jake still couldn't accept any of the reasons he had deduced for Michelle leaving him after eight months of what he recalled as good times.

Could it have been so bad that Michelle had to turn me away?, he said in his frontal lobes.

He tried to find other reasons, but knew it had been the night that she pressured him into smoking a joint with her. Jake remembered that night with regret as he walked patting down the pockets of his coat and jeans trying to find a pack of cigarettes and lighter that weren't there.

Stop it! No more looking for cigarettes, he thought stepping down a staircase that led to the street level in front of his house. At the foot of the stairs, he opened and passed through a wrought-iron gate that was riveted into the crimson brick walls. The crimson walls turned at perfect right angles to create an interior tunnel within the wall's womb. Jake closed and locked the gates behind him.

He was birthed again into the real world.

The gated tunnel led out of Jake's luxurious brick-walled estate to a square-curbed sidewalk where the brownstone walls became the dominant theme again and were trimmed to match the house's bloody trim. The walls of the estate stood 8-feet high beneath hedgerows that lifted Jake's residential barrier to a full 12-feet above his hunched shoulders and shuffling feet.

Jake shoved his hands into his coat pockets and hung his head fixated on Michelle. He had put on a peacoat and tennis shoes, but was still wearing the same clothes that he had slept in overnight.

His inner monolog droned on.

Michelle. Cigarette. There is no Michelle, need a cigarette.

As much as Jake would like to take it all back, their relationship had ended because Michelle heard the little girl crying after he asked if she wanted to know a secret. She did, so he helped her to tune into the right psychic frequency.

The moment she heard the weeping child, Michelle flipped out. Jake knew he had fucked up immediately and apologized for helping her to dial in to hearing the girl.

Nothing else mattered, she wanted to find the crying girl and demanded to know where Jake was hiding her. Jake said he understood, but it was no use to look for her. 'She's not there,' he had said. 'It's a ghost.'

His words just made things worse because Michelle hadn't spoken aloud any of the words of her concern that he had responded to. His words of understanding only served to confuse and agitate her.

Jake had kicked himself several times for not warning her about what she would hear and for not telling her that he had always been able to read her thoughts.

Damn it all. She expected an intimate secret, not a macabre surprise!

As far as she knew, they were going to play a little soul-bearing game of foreplay—Truth and Dare.

Cigarette.

When the girl's cries rang in their heads again, Michelle started to panic. Jake couldn't disconnect Michelle from their mental rapport because he was high from the weed they had smoked—his mind's neural pathways were sticky with THC-triggered cannabinoids. He couldn't let go of her mind nor grab hold of himself.

That was so stupid. God damned drugs.

Michelle was sure that he was holding a little girl captive and became very frightened. Then, she threatened to call the police.

When the words came out, she felt threatened and regretted saying them.

Cigarette. No.

Why had he apologized to her? Had he not told her several times that he shouldn't get high with her? But, she wouldn't let up and pressed hard against his manhood saying it was better than Viagra.

Cig— No.

At the corner of his affluent block, Jake lifted his arm to sniff an armpit inside his coat. Deep in the act of huffing his day-old musk to distract himself from thinking, he rounded the corner and almost collided with an elderly couple dressed in high-end matching Team USA Olympic jogging suits.

The couple was a complete contrast to Jake and looked like they belonged in this neighborhood.

Startled, the old man raised his cane and said, "Mind yourself, boy!"

Jake lowered his lifted elbow below his chin like a Dracula. "Mind yourself, sir! I am not armed or dangerous. But...," he said dropping his hand into his coat pocket. "I am, however, ripe with spring time, ma'am," said Jake with a wink to the old woman.

"I beg your pardon?" said the old man with an indignant tone looking from Jake to his wife.

"Go win the gold. Team USA, all the way!" Jake said fisting the air as he walked around the old folks without looking back.

JAKE TURNED A CORNER with growing purpose and strode down the sidewalk into an antique part of the city. He recalled how this city block had been re-urbanized from boarded up vacant buildings and returned to a shop-based small business district. Reflecting back, Jake remembered that the fifties-era diner on the corner had been there for as long as he could remember. What was once a diamond in the rough, this third-generation diner had become the centerpiece in an arrangement of lesser jewels.

The diner on the corner ahead was not one of those nostalgic chain restaurants where the staff danced on the empty tables to Elvis and Beatles songs. Nor did the staff gather in aisles to sing birthday wishes. It wasn't a cheap, small-town, greasy spoon leeching off the locals with low-quality hash, either. In fact, some of the regular customers drove an hour or more there and back each weekend to patronize the establishment.

Tom's Diner was a tried and true historic snapshot of forgotten times. The food was good and everything was clean and homey.

Several smokers stood on the sidewalk between Jake and the front door of the diner.

He considered asking one of them for a smoke.

Cigarette, no?, said a French-accented voice in Jake's head.

No, Jake declared within his skull.

He pushed through the chatty and laughing smokers in front of the doorway. They were so happy and reminded Jake of cigarette ads that they used to run in *Rolling Stone* magazine.

Jake knew that they were waiting for a booth. He also knew there was a spot for him at a short-end of the counter nearest the door.

THE PLACE WAS LONG AND narrow inside, the din of this busy diner echoed within its walls. It was packed to capacity with some forty diners coupled up at tables and booths drinking coffee or clicking plates with flatware. Only the staff was rushed, while the diners relaxed having casual-to-excited conversations.

Parallel to the long walls of the diner was a busy L-style lunch counter where the customers filled nearly all the stools bolted to the floor in front of it.

As Jake knew there would be, two empty stools for invited company at the short-end of the lunch counter nearest to the door. He slid onto an empty stool where everyone else was visible.

This was a bad spot for him to sit and he regretted it as soon as he looked around the room.

Jake began to hear everyone eating and they spoke in primal thoughts, he fought to not pull their thoughts into focus.

The diners beamed and bounced their mental signals around the room like radio towers on a mountaintop shooting their broadcasts into the sky looking for receptors.

To Jake, fighting the thoughts of the diners was like pressing the preset buttons on the AM band of a car stereo. They were all talking heads that were only interrupted by their personal endorsements and commercial propaganda.

If they weren't lying to themselves and yakking about nothing, they were selling themselves to their audiences.

Unless sports came up soon, Jake wouldn't know what day it was. Within a breath, he had learned every holiday and knew what local teams were playing each day this week. It was hockey and basketball season with a dash of fan speculations about spring training. Today was Sunday with only the Easter holidays pending.

Just thinking made him latch onto Michelle, again. *It was day thirty-three*, he answered.

They had watched hockey together every night speculating on the post-season contenders, even though Jake had to fake his suspense about the outcome of the season and play-offs.

They would root for the players she had picked at work for her fantasy hockey team. Worrying about her salary cap, she didn't draft a single superstar and had picked a very average team; Jake let her have her fun with it anyway. Hoping for the best was fun enough for her and it put her in the right mood for—

Cigarette…!

Jake tuned out the dining room with its overlapping multi-layered monologs and shook off his own looping thoughts of Michelle and cigarettes. He fought to bring his mental focus into the prep area behind the lunch counter where three cooks of mixed race and size hustled short-order meals on a large grill and prep table.

No thinking in there, just the mindless action and reflexes of fulfilling meal tickets that hung from clips on a shelf at eye-level.

Having been behind that very counter, Jake knew the routine; he watched the cooks in motion to distract himself from the thoughts of those around him and there, he sheltered himself from his own inner monolog.

Most of the time, Jake was psychic to the point of pain while in a group of people, but restaurants were a place that gave him the opportunity to hear the white noise of primal human thought.

Even in the overwhelming din of diners, he could regain control of himself again. If he could wait for it and adjust, the diner was ripe with the right kind of voiceless and primal impulses that made Jake feel at home.

Deafened for a moment and numbed by the diner's over-stimulating mental broadcasts, Jake again looked at the chatting couples that filled the seats of the lunch counter. The noise had become a buzz to Jake, except for a single man sitting on a stool at the end of the long counter.

The silence around this man was like a shout to Jake. The guy was a young, gritty punker straight from the early-80's with spiked jet-black hair that matched his black t-shirt and jeans. His T-shirt said in bold red letters, *The Anarchist Bookstore (dot) com*.

This guy was a thought-vacuum for Jake and stood out like the gold tooth in a decayed mouth.

The dark man flicked at his teeth with a toothpick and whistled spittle into the air.

Jake stared at the silent man's tattoos. The inky snakes slithered up and down his arms. While no one else noticed him spitting the food from his teeth onto their plates, Jake didn't take his eyes off of him.

The punk rocker started to get agitated and his eyes met with Jake's. He squinted under a brow twisted with dislike for being noticed by someone else.

The punker flicked his toothpick over the counter and plucked out a cigarette from behind his ear before moving up the aisle. Walking up the aisle, his eyes never left Jake.

Jake's eyes followed him as he lit up.

The punk puffed his cigarette hot and exhaled smoke through his clenched teeth and nose over the counter at Jake. He lifted his hand with an extended pinkie and forefinger saying, "May you choke, sir." He stopped for a beat and his face lost intensity. The smoking punk smiled pointing the index finger on his raised hand at Jake and said, "Nice shirt."

Jake looked down at his shirt and realized that he was wearing the same shirt.

Walking on, the punk rocker gave a smart-assed head nod to the empty register at the front door and exited without paying. He slid through the crowd at the door, which opened to let in the diffused sunlight of the chilly morning and closed as another couple entered Tom's Diner.

Looking back from the door into the diner, Jake's eyes scanned the clientele and rested on a large, framed poster mounted on the back wall. It was the enlarged black-and-white photo of a smiling man. The man was in his late-twenties, handsome with slicked back dark hair and a neat little mustache.

An old man with thinning white hair moved into Jake's line of vision crossing in front of the poster—it was the same man from the photo, only older and heavier.

The old man spoke first, "So, Jake, you want 'Scrambled Hash Over Easy' or the 'Hit-List Special' this morning?" He added on a wink of secrecy to punctuate his question.

Leaning forward with contempt, Jake looked to his left at the elderly couple nearest to him and rested his elbows on the counter.

Knitting his fingers together over the edge, Jake said slowly through clenched teeth, "Which one is the cold coffee, runny eggs, and burnt toast crap I usually get, Tom? How many times do I have to tell you that I want a 'Good morning, Jake,' with a cup of coffee? Unless you got a cigarette."

The older couple near Jake shared an uncomfortable glance in response to Jake's tone. Tom noticed their concern and showed a strong disappointment in himself. He turned his eyes again to Jake.

Jake gave Tom an 'all is forgiven' smile with a wink as if to say, 'Let's start over.'

Tom took the cue and said, "Good morning, Jake. I got a cup of black coffee coming. What can I get you this fine morning, sir?"

"Ah, it is a fine morning, sir," Jake declared. "And a very good morning to you, too, Tom. I'd love a smothered Denver."

Tom wrote on his order pad. "Sounds good, Jake. So, what're you doing later on today," he said with another wink. "I can give the low down over dinner."

"I dunno. I'm going to my dealer and have to box up some stuff," Jake said. He leaned in and winked, "Why, what's going on later?"

Tom looked around whispering, "You should come over for dinner. It would make Mama very happy. She'd feel connected to the family again."

Jake raised his eyebrows and leaned back. With an even tone, he said, "Is your squatter son still living in the basement waiting for you both to die?"

The anglo cook, Sid, stopped working for a beat and looked over his shoulder at Jake with contempt.

Jake raised his voice and projected it passed Papa Tom toward the cook, "That's right. I'm talkin' about you, Sid. You small-time little weasel."

Sid and Jake glared at each other for a beat. Jake broke their eye contact with a smile as he rolled his eyes.

"Look, Papa Tom, I just can't do it. I'm not telling you and Mama to make him go, but I'll keep reminding you until Sid gets his own apartment.

Maybe, you and Mama can come over to my place instead and teach me how to—"

Tom snapped closed his order book and held up his hand. "To cook for you? You know I don't do take-outs for you mooks. We already have dinner plans at our house tonight. The offer stands, Jake, and your place at Mama's table—across from Sid—will or will not be served at six o'clock."

Tom dismissed himself with a respectful nod and a 'sir' to make leave of Jake.

Jake and Sid exchanged eyes, again. Jake bowed a sincere apology to Sid and he followed with a shrug that looked more like 'You know how it is, Sid, so quit bustin' my balls already.'

Sid looked at Jake without backing down.

Jake was charming and said, "Come on, that was Emmy material. Whaddya say... still brothers, Sid? You know, I can't sit across from you at dinner."

AT THE END OF THE COUNTER, the uncomfortable old couple was still whispering about Jake's thuggish antics while a young woman with a round face and wide eyes watched in disbelief and interest as Jake acted like an East Coast wise guy. She couldn't believe the Mob had decided Denver was a good place to send one of their brightest stars.

Sure, there was a history of Chicago retirees moving to Denver and creating strongholds for themselves. *It was just like every other major city in the four-corner states,* she thought. He couldn't be Mexican Mafia? It just seemed silly to her because Jake looked like an underdressed Mormon out of salt water.

So, who is this guy? Vegas, she thought smiling to herself. *I'll have to find out more about Mr. Jake-sir.*

AN OMELET SMOTHERED WITH green chile and melted cheddar cheese was placed on the counter in front of Jake. He said thank you to Tom and began eating; the room grew quiet with only muted echoes from the diner's ethereal distortion of bodies in motion, emotional gratification, and physical stimulation. The world had become silent for Jake. Consuming was all Jake had to create a mental silence that made him feel like he was normal. So, consume, he did.

FLYING UNDER JAKE'S PSYCHIC RADAR, an extremely fit man in his late physical prime entered the diner.

Mike the Cop was a large guy with good legs and a barrel chest; he had made himself a timeless man of duty with his buzzed head and police uniform.

He parted the crowd at the door like a Greek hero and moved to the short end of the bar, he sat down between the old couple and Jake.

Jake was buttering a piece of dark rye that had already been lightly whisk-brushed with liquid margarine.

Neither man acknowledged the other, but both contracted their personal space out of respect. Jake moved his toast plate in front of him and out to the edge of the interior counter.

JAKE HAD FINISHED HIS meal and the empty plates were already bussed from the counter. He was relaxed, pulling in warm coffee with long sips. Jake reveled in the high of his breakfast and fought back thinking about how nice a cigarette would taste with his fifth cup of coffee.

Sitting beside Jake, Mike the Cop had just finished his breakfast when the waitress rounded their corner with a pot of coffee.

Wiping his mouth with a white paper napkin, Mike caught her eye and nodded her over to him. In response, she pulled a handful of tickets from her apron. She handed one to Mike and reached over to set another beside Jake.

Mike stood up with a smile so big that the waitress had to respond with her own. He moved to the register and waited behind two couples ahead of him.

Jake finished his coffee and set the cup down in its saucer. He picked up the ticket, it had been totaled for the diner's books and marked as <u>COMPED</u> by Papa Tom.

Looking at the ticket, Jake shook his head and he stuck his other hand into his pocket. He took a money clip from his pant pocket that held what looked like a nice amount of folded cash; he removed the clip and peeled off a couple of bills.

Setting the meal ticket down, he placed two fifties onto the counter and slid them under the ticket. From any other customer's point of view, the dollar value of the bills he pulled could have been of any denomination.

Jake whispered over the counter and said, "Hey, here's your tip, Sid. Get a real job. Remember that one, bro? You're the one taking orders now."

Acting like he hadn't heard Jake's barbed comment, Sid didn't look up from what he was cooking at the grill.

Jake glared at the cook reaching into his pocket again. He looked as if he felt there was a point to be made.

He peeled two more bills from his money clip and tossed a couple of hundreds on the counter beside the cup and saucer, so everyone could see the amount.

Standing from his stool at the counter, he looked around for the waitress and Tom to make sure both had seen him leaving. The waitress was coming, but Tom was taking an order.

Jake picked up the fifties that he had subtly slid under the ticket and stuck them into his coat pocket.

When Tom didn't look his way, Jake raised his voice over the crowd and said, "See you, Papa Tom. Buy Mama some flowers tonight and send her my love."

Papa Tom looked up at Jake's voice and gave a respectful wave to him. When Jake had turned away toward the door, Tom turned to Sid who was waiting for their eyes to meet. Tom nodded him toward Jake's coffee cup.

Sid went to Jake's spot at the counter, he took up the ticket and cash as the waitress picked up Mike the Cop's plates. Sid tossed one of the hundreds back down toward her and nodded for the waitress to take it.

She took the hundred-dollar bill with a grateful smile. Sid smiled back with a nod, while shoving Jake's ticket and remaining cash into his apron pocket.

"Take it, Doris," Mike said holding out ten dollars to the clerk.

Doris, a forty-year old woman, who had worked the register at Tom's for fifteen years, said, "I'm gonna tell you once again, Mike. You are good for business and you don't have to pay. It's been comped on the house."

He still held the cash out for her and said, "Take it, Doris. The meal was worth twice the bill. Put it in the tip jar, if you don't want it."

She took Mike's cash and hit a button, the bell rang within the register as the cash drawer opened.

The young woman at the end of the counter was watching Jake again and trying to figure him out.

Who throws around two hundred-dollars for a ten-dollar breakfast?

She wasn't sure what had just happened, but was certain something shady was going on. She couldn't believe the audacity of this guy to pull that behind a cop's back and looked on hoping to catch Jake's eye as he followed Mike to the register. The round-faced girl put on her prettiest face and watched from the corner of her eye, waiting for a chance to make eye contact and smile sweetly.

Her romantic interest would have been evident if Jake had paused from chewing his nail long enough to notice her.

But, Jake walked past without looking her way.

"Yikes. Our batter struck out looking," she said under her breath, disappointed. She bussed her flatware and napkins onto her plate, ready to leave in frustration with her tab in hand. A bell rang from the register.

JAKE EXAMINED HIS FINGER'S delicious cuticle waiting for Mike the Cop, who currently blocked Jake's exit with his bulking presence and he knew better than to pass a cop on the right.

Doris jammed Mike's ticket onto a cashier's spike while maintaining her eye contact with him and sent an electric jolt of attraction into the air.

She was lucky she didn't impale her hand on that spike, Jake thought. *Whore. Michelle. Cigarette.*

"Thanks, Mike," said Doris. "You are always welcome."

Nodding with closure, Mike moved to the door.

Jake, stepping up, smiled at Doris. He shook his hand with a thumb extended over his shoulder to say he had paid at the counter and grabbed a toothpick.

"So, you like that guy, eh," Jake asked thumbing toward Mike.

"No," said Doris emphatically. "Jake, I know it's not my business, but I wish you and Sid would patch it up. Do you really think this is good for your—"

Tammy moved into line and stood a little too close to Jake.

"Stop," Jake said with a polite grin. He held up a hand telling her to save it and said, "Doris, we're all counting on Sid to be there to take care of things. If Pops doesn't survive his next stroke, then I'll worry about Sid's feelings on how I handle my business." Mockery rang in Jake's voice as he said, "Until then, Sid's living the American Dream." He popped the toothpick in his mouth and turned to leave.

This close to Jake, Tammy overheard what sounded quite criminal to her. *Money laundering?*

MIKE HAD EXITED THROUGH the people at the door waiting to be seated inside and those smoking beside the door. Jake moved easily in Mike's wake like all of Israel behind Moses through the Red Sea.

The people in front of the diner talking on the sidewalk were hushed and had to step back as the people waiting inside backed out to make room for Mike's exit.

They were still standing at attention when Jake exited chewing on a toothpick.

In off-timed steps, both men stepped through the people to the sidewalk and split without looking at each other—Mike turned right up the sidewalk and Jake went left.

15

THERE WAS THE RAPID click of a high-speed camera as Jake and Mike exited from opposite sides of the camera's viewfinder.

JAKE HELD UP A step and paused a split second. He almost turned back to approach the smokers for a puff or two, but his resolve hardened on his face and he turned back to the sidewalk ahead. "No," Jake said quietly as he picked up his pace down the street. The pretty girl from the counter exited before the sea of people closed the gap and turned left up the sidewalk.

A HUNDRED AND TWO steps later, Jake paused at the corner and made room for a scruffy old man with wild hair and well-worn clothing.

As he passed, Jake heard Scruffy's thoughts in a less than musical resonance of distorted mental signals that pulled together into a rapid thought-speak.

Scruffy's thoughts echoed in Jake's mind, *Damn Blue Laws. Why can't I get a cheap bottle on Sunday? Politicians and their bar lobbyists, that's why!*

The same buzzing resonance of thought-speak happened another eighty-two steps later in the middle of the street as Jake jaywalked passed an angry laborer wearing a tan jacket and blue jeans. This guy said in his mind, *I'm gonna kill her. My money. I work hard for my money.*

Jake ignored Angry's random thoughts, too, and kept walking down the street.

3

Two men in the latest fashion of government-regulation suits were sitting in a late-model government-issued sedan parked across the street from the diner. They watched Jake and Mike exit the diner, while the rapid-fire shutter opened and closed in front of the passenger's face.

Joe was the senior agent in the driver's seat with Charlie beside him holding the camera to his eye.

Charlie said, "What's with this local cop? Think they were talking? Maybe we can get some leverage on him to spill the dirt on St. Johns for his pension."

Joe assured him that it was a coincidence. "That's our man there," he said pointing at Jake.

Jake had paused for a second to look back at the smokers. He said something to himself and left with resolve on his face.

Back to his onward path, he added a bounce to his step as he marched down the sidewalk.

"I dunno. He looks pretty happy," Charlie said. "Where do you think he's off to?"

"Think?," Joe said. "That nerd is going to a bookstore. He hasn't gone anywhere else this week. Eat, read, eat, read… crap. Buy books, eat, read, crap. He should by a big fatty."

Charlie rolled a thought round his head like a BB in a child's toy and said he didn't understand this whole bookstore angle they were still investigating. "That girl we talked to who works at the bookstore ID'ed St. Johns for us without thinking twice. I guarantee we can ask the owner to show us his books and prove that he runs a non-profit business. This is a dead end."

Joe replied, "Operating at this guy's reported losses isn't a crime, but it is evidence of not having brick-and-mortar business sense. So, it could be a front for something shady like money laundering through places like this diner. Maybe the books are a cover for shipping drugs or financing a drug business for someone else to do the crime."

"You can't launder millions like this guy does," said Charlie. "The guy gets his books on credit and is not a drug trafficker. My guts tell me to call the book thing a fetish cuz the guy has been killing on the stock market."

Joe continued, "We can follow him around, but we aren't going to find him guilty of anything more than petty over-tipping. I still want to find the fish he might be cooking through his gallery. This book nerd is working with people who know their stocks."

This conversation had grown stale to Charlie over the past week; he didn't have to listen to know Joe was going to rant about the hi-brow art pieces in a gallery show and how that was a solid way to launder money.

Joe would tell him again about how the high prices for art were nothing more than rich people passing play money back and forth. About how the art agent and buyer used the artist as a pawn for insider trading and then returned favors by creating a hyper-inflated local art market. When the dirty deals were done, the artist would disappear from the front window and wonder why their work stopped selling after three good months.

Joe stopped talking and they watched Jake jaywalk past the angry man, who planned to kill his gold-digger girlfriend, until he stepped onto the curb out of their line of sight.

Joe exhaled through his nose and started the car. "Those gallery bastards are all the same," he said putting the car in gear. "You want to get something to eat and take some down time, Chuckles?"

Grateful not to have to hear about Joe's hippy daughter struggling to make it as an artist, Charlie ignored 'Chuckles' and said, "What about St. Johns?"

Joe paused in thought before saying, "I am expecting a call from that Natalie-girl at *The Neighborhood Bookstore* within the hour. St. Johns will stop at one of the three places he goes to on his way from there and we'll be waiting for him when he gets home around sundown."

Charlie shrugged and said, "You're the boss." He almost asked where they were going, but decided to tell Joe that they weren't eating Chinese again or he could find a new fucking partner.

Drumming at the wheel, Joe said, "No Chinese. I know a place on the way that opens at eleven and it's the right type to help me flesh out some angles."

Charlie shook his head and sighed, he had heard that one enough to know its meaning, too. "It's your car, Joe," he finally said with a sigh.

"And don't you forget it," Joe said shaking a hang-loose gesture, "Cheer up or I'll buy you a lap-dance."

The sedan pulled into the street and turned at the corner. Slowly, Joe followed Jake's path up the street.

A brief moment later, the sedan rolled up beside Jake. This caught Jake's attention and he looked toward the driver.

Joe and Jake made eye contact, neither offered the other a friendly look. Jake heard Joe's thoughts, *I am so going to nail you. See you later.*

Joe smiled and winked at Jake as the sedan gassed up and accelerated past him.

Jake shook his head snickering at the forwardness of gay men these days and continued walking. He didn't get offended, but thought it was just funny to feel like an object of male sexual aggression.

At least, the guy didn't call me cutie or baby and whistle, Jake thought.

His dad used to do that when they were driving. Now, his dad just did his job and everyone was supposed to play the other parts. It was weird how things changed after his stroke.

Papa Tom was in the middle of watching Season Five of *The Sopranos* when the stroke happened. Currently, he didn't remember Jake and the doctors (yes, plural doctors) said that they should let his memory recover naturally. Hence, Jake couldn't go home for dinner until Tom remembered him. They were even afraid that Tom might see a picture of Jake on the wall at Mom's house and it would be like waking a sleepwalker. Tom couldn't afford any serious stress. The worst part was Jake having to play along and act like some goodfella until Tom remembered him.

Jake had become to his father, Jakey Good-Tip, and Tom thought he always wanted to hear about some criminal activity happening in the city. Jake disliked acting like a tough guy and making Sid the butt of his aggression, but he kind of felt honored to be some askew hero in his dad's illusionary life.

Nevertheless, Jake had always hated lying and felt stupid acting like some gangster rather than telling his dad the truth. How many times had Jake thought about digging into Papa Tom's mind to repair the disconnected neural pathways?

He couldn't feel good about doing that, either. It felt more wrong than just playing into his dad's delusions and lying to him.

4

After walking a few blocks, Jake approached a homeless man with salt and pepper hair in grubby military-surplus clothing. He stood beside a shopping cart in front of an inset doorway. The cart was packed with junk except for a comparably nice portable CD/radio unit.

The homeless man's head was static-filled and rushing as he thought, *Damn it's cold, man. Maybe this guy'll want the CD player.*

The man started to speak as Jake approached, but Jake lifted up his hand before he could exhale a voice.

"I don't want your CD player," Jake said.

The man looked at him oddly while lifting the CD player to display it and said, "You sure you don't want it for five dollars."

Jake looked at the CD Player and concentrated a moment. He saw a woman throwing the player into the dumpster; she thought, *That's the last CD you'll scratch.*

Shaking his head, Jake said, "Nope. The player skips and you should toss it back in the trash before it scratches another CD."

The homeless man, looking at the player in his hands, turned on his sales pitch and said, "Maybe the player skips, but I bet the radio works just fine."

Jake said, "Even worse... Radio in Denver is crap. Leave this stuff behind and go eat at Tom's." He threw his thumb over his shoulder and began walking onward. "There'll be an empty seat in the back by the black and white poster. If you tell them Jake sent you, someone will feed you. And, it's warmer there," he said.

Walking on, Jake crossed over the homeless man and the man was gone.

However, the same man was actually lying propped up in the corner of the inset doorway a few feet from the cart of junk.

Jake pressed on without looking back to see that the dead man's spirit had begun to move on, heading back the way Jake had come and leaving his cart behind.

JAKE WALKED DOWN THE sidewalk in front of a two-story storefront built at the turn of the century. The large display window had a painted art-nouveau logo on it that declared, *The Neighborhood Bookstore*. He climbed the steps and entered through its rickety over-painted door.

Inside, Jake carefully scanned the titles of used books stacked on wall-to-wall shelves in this ninety-year-old converted two-story brownstone-styled city house. Occasionally, he removed a book that caught his eye. Some books he opened to skim, others he only read the back-covers. With a mind on what he wanted, most of the books he touched were just added to his stack of books that grew from section to section.

After an hour of looking, Jake carefully carried two big stacks of hardback and paperback books to the tidy front desk. The stacks leaned against his belly and chest measuring up to his chin.

Standing at the desk at the door was an older man wearing retro-framed glasses with a casual sweater over his collared shirt that was tucked into his slacks. Jake recognized him as the owner, but had decidedly not remembered his name. He regarded Owner to be a prick to his employees, thus an enemy. He was especially rotten to the girl, Natalie, who was there on most Sundays, a single mom without an artistic bone in her body.

However, Owner was very friendly and said, "Hi there. So, did you find everything good I had in stock?"

Jake lit up a big smile and said, "Your books are all good, but I left a few behind for the other customers." He slid the stacks of books across the front desk toward him and made a lightning quick decision to ruin this clerk's sales quota for the day. Jake sang-said, "I'm a member and should have credits to cover this."

Owner's visage showed disappointment and his voice reflected it when he said, "What's the account name?" He turned away and toward a card catalog of index cards.

"Jake St. Johns," Jake said.

Owner opened the card catalog and fingered through it. He made small talk by asking Jake if St. Johns was British.

With a smirk, Jake said, "Probably, but I'm Scottish. Aren't you the owner? I don't see you working here often."

Feeling at a disadvantage, Owner turned around from his task to look at Jake hoping to see something familiar.

Jake stared at the owner with tense concentration. The owner's eyes moved up Jake's body before resting on his face, but he couldn't focus on its features because the target was nearly blank with over-exposure as Jake hid his face behind a mentally-created screen of psychic static.

The owner stammered saying that he owned the bookstore and usually only covered the sick calls as he adjusted his glasses, blinking, trying to focus his eyes on Jake's face. "I'll be in the next few days for Natalie," he said with a touch of inconvenience. "Funeral or something."

Jake smiled that he had decided to use book credits rather than paying with cash, this guy deserved a bad day.

Owner looked away to resume his looking for Jake's card and said, "What was the name again? St. James?"

Jake, relaxing his concentration, smirked, "St. Johns."

After tallying up and updating Jake's book credits, Owner helped bag up the books and said, "These are some of my best books."

"I'm working my way through the whole horror genre now and looking for someone else who understands. I just keep finding fiction and creative allegory," Jake said as a matter of fact. "King might be reaching out for a companion, but you can't just call him to ask if he is psychic without sounding like a kook."

Owner was confused by the statement and asked what Jake meant, "Someone else who understands what? You think the psychic stuff that Stephen King writes about is from a first-person experience?"

Jake shrugged and flashed a big grin as he said, "Did you know that this place is haunted?"

The owner hadn't expected a question in reply and struggled to say, "Haunted? By ghosts?"

"And your cologne," Jake said chuckling at his own joke. "I'm just kidding."

"Good, you almost gave me goose-bumps," the owner said with relief. "I haven't heard anything, but some of the clerks say they hear stuff, like—"

"Laughter, screams, women gossiping," Jake said interrupting the owner. "Yeah, Natalie has told me some of it. Did you know that the mob used to run booze and prostitutes out of this place?"

Owner beamed with pride saying he did know that historical fact and asked if Jake had also heard it from Natalie.

If this were a movie, the camera would pan-out to reveal three women dressed in 1930's lingerie positioned around Jake standing at the desk. Jake said dramatically, "Natalie doesn't know about the mob stuff."

He picked up the bags with a snide smirk and moved toward the door. Without looking back, he said, "Good-bye, ladies!"

Owner shook his head as the door slammed behind Jake, ringing a bell. He picked up the index card with Jake's credit record and felt very alone as he replaced it alphabetically in the catalog.

Thinking to himself, the owner reflected on the weird conversation he had had with Jake. He would have to ask Natalie about—

What was his name? St. George? He turned back to the card catalog to check the name on Jake's card, when the giggle of several women echoed fleetingly into the back of the store. Following his ears, the owner turned with concern toward the interior of the building and was surprised by the sudden thump of a body on the floor above him.

His eyes jerked to the ceiling as he heard the shriek of a woman crying out, "No! Don't touch me, you pig! Nooooo..."

The owner was frozen with shock as he listened, waiting for something or someone else to make a noise.

JAKE STEPPED OUT OF the bookstore onto the sidewalk and into the warm daylight that the sun had been slow in sharing with the northern hemisphere of its big blue neighbor. He breathed in a big lungful of spring-like air and smiled exhaling with sensual joy. He set down the three grocery bags he carried to take off his peacoat. Wishing he had room in his bags for the coat, Jake was resigned to tie the arms of it around his waist. Feeling full of life as he picked up the bags, he began walking toward home.

The sunlight reflected brightly from Jake's exposed skin and clothing. An aura of gold light trailed behind him and formed a set of vaporous wings. The energy wings ebbed and flowed from Jake's shoulders like the magnetic waves of the Aurora Borealis.

5

In a bedroom that was just large enough to serve as a boxer's home gym, Mike the Cop, dressed in a muscle shirt and sweatpants, began his workout by doing jumping jacks to settle his breakfast.

As his body went into motion, he engaged his mental gears. The past few days had pushed him to the edge of his patience regarding justice and politics. Mike pulled together a conscious argument that presented the facts so clearly that justice had to be served. He would serve that justice.

A speed bag smacked against its backboard in a tap-tap-beat-tap rhythm.

Politics had put his partner in jail and Mike couldn't let him take the heat for what seemed like an obvious setup. There was someone on the inside that had fed information to Sarconi and his partner wasn't the type to sit on a hot piece of dirt without looking into it. He was a man of action, a real cop.

Mike grunted in the middle of a set of fast ground-to-extension clapping push-ups.

When Sarconi showed up at that bar, he was staking it out for evidence to build a case. He was either setup or it was like they stated in the official report, Sarconi had just been there when a deal went south and stepped in as a vigilante. Sarconi wasn't the type to be at a dive like that in plain clothes with a firearm on his hip unless it was cop work.

There was the thud of fists beating a heavy bag as Mike threw a continuous series of combination punches, he then drove a thundering kick into the side of the bag that shook the house and rattled windowpanes.

Something had gone down at the bar, but it wasn't Sarconi's style to go on a drunken rampage. If he shot those two guys, there was a reason for it. He didn't shoot average street thugs, they were made men who shouldn't have been at this bar, either.

Now, the water cooler talk said Sarconi was a part of some big deal with these guys and had gone dirty. The whole thing was dirty in Mike's mind. Even if his partner had been tempted, it would not for be the petty shit they were accusing him of and not this close to retirement. He was setup and now they were talking about revoking his pension. With Sarconi and the other two guys in the ICU on life support, all they could do is wait and piece together what might have happened.

Lying with his back to the floor, Mike pulled his opposite knee to his opposite elbow over his chest in a series of scrunches.

Mike had weighed all the facts again. If this dirty deck had been stacked against Sarconi, there were only two people deep enough and dirty enough to put together something of this magnitude.

During the day following the shooting, it had been a media circus with state and local politicians shouting about Sarconi's action as being an illegal use of force and making criminal allegations before the ink had even dried on the detectives' report.

After an aggressive workout that suggested Mike could be a violent killing machine, he ended his workout by curling and pressing massive free-weights.

Sarconi was going down and his wife would lose the pension unless Mike could dig in and prevent them from framing an innocent and dying man. He knew he would have to reposition these two insiders if he was going to stomp down the leverage they were using to press charges on his partner.

What had Sarconi found out that would seal his death warrant? Mike didn't know, but he would find out soon enough. One thing he was sure of, Patterson and the Judge were hanging his partner out to dry for some power play. The first thing that would have to be done was to take down the Judge. Without the Judge's protection and influence, Patterson would get his due within the week. The trick would be to burn down the main tent of this circus, so the other tents would follow.

Mike moved to the bathroom and took a hot shower filling the house with steam from the opened door.

Sarconi was a good man and Mike wouldn't let this injustice go on. He had no leads and the footwork would call for some serious head banging, but no one was going to frame his friend without a fight.

Mike dried off, wrapped the towel around his waist, and moved from the bathroom into his bedroom.

He took a reinforced Samsonite business-travel suitcase from his closet and returned to the bathroom. From the way Mike carried it in both arms, the suitcase weighed as much as a bag of cement.

Do this job and then get on with the case, he thought. *It was time for justice and there wasn't much time to figure out a plan. Tonight, I take action on Patterson.*

Mike had lathered his face and was shaving with a premium disposable-head razor.

Wiping his bald face with a towel, he looked at his reflection in the mirror from side-to-side and then set the electric clippers to zero before shaving his head.

His thoughts had faded out before his hands reached for a pair of black spandex-like Kevlar leggings and the matching long-sleeved turtleneck. The material clung to his body like a wetsuit. The leggings were high-waisted and the shirt draped a foot over the waistline. He reached under the bottom hem of the shirt and connected it to the long Velcro strips sewn into the side of the leggings.

From a suitcase on the floor, he removed a shirt of tightly linked silver chainmail; it rattled like the shimmering hips of a belly dancer. The hauberk had rounded, metal, quarter-sized scales mounted down the chest and over the shoulders. The scales also extended to cover the top half of the shirt's arms, but without the added scales over the ribs and arms, the chainmail shirt would remain extremely flexible and allow for broad movements.

The spandex was slick and the tailor-made metal armor slid over Mike's head onto his upper body. The long shirt was loose at his waist and covered his hips.

He sat down on the floor with his feet sticking out the bathroom door and slid into a pair of similar chainmail pants. At the waistline of the shimmering pants were attached rings that clipped into hooked leather straps that were woven into the shirt. Mike secured the pants to his shirt.

Once connected, he stood outside the door of the bathroom and shouldered up the weight of the armor up to his ears and exhaled to let armor fall comfortably onto the places it was designed to defend.

Returning to the suitcase, Mike wrapped around his waist a garish white belt with a large gold buckle and a white loincloth trimmed with gold thread that hung down to about mid-thigh.

He flipped a huge white and gold cape over his shoulders and attached the corners to his neck using another ring and hook system like the one under his armored shirt holding up his pants. He clipped a thick gold chain across his chest to the top of the cape.

The huge white gloves that he tugged on were trimmed with gold lions and matched the design on the jackboots he pulled on over wool-socked feet.

Mike placed on his head a gold-trimmed silver Corinthian helmet and examined his face from side-to-side with approval.

He moved from the bathroom into the house where he took up a gold-hilted arming sword that was fitted into a white and gold scabbard. He hooked its steel ring into his belt and tied the scabbard to his left leg at mid-thigh.

As fast as he had tied the sword to himself, Mike growled pulling it from the sheath and performed a brief series of parry, block and disarming movements across his front room when he rested into an offensive stance. Mike smiled and slashed the air with three quick moves to replace the sword into its scabbard.

Those bastards were going to pay for killing Sarconi, he thought.

Mike stepped from the front door of his blue suburban ranch-style house into a bright spring day. He had transformed into a superhero knight and the late-morning sun gleamed from his shining armor giving Mike an aura of enchantment.

He moved with a fluidity that betrayed the hundred pounds of equipment he wore and set down a duffel bag on the porch. Mike pulled the door closed behind him and locked the deadbolt with a key.

After stepping from the porch into a neatly trimmed lawn, Mike carried his duffle bag toward a late-model dark green pick-up with limo-tinted windows while jingling through his key ring.

THERE WAS A PARTY underway in the backyard of a recently built super-sized McMansion with a tarp-covered in-ground pool. There was a happy couple in their thirties looking like typical catalog models at a barbeque cooking dogs and burgers for the adult friends and their kids gathered there.

At the opposite end of the pool-deck from the grill, Mike in his superhero outfit was especially agile wearing the big white gloves and twisted up a balloon animal for one of the younger kids. The young kids were in awe of Mike and had gathered around him, while a dozen other kids were running around the pool with squirt guns—more than half were too old for a superhero.

He towered over these little kids and was quite believable at playing the living symbol of honor and justice, *The Champion.*

Mike said in a deep heroic voice, "Here's a good joke. Knock, knock."

The kids replied half-heartedly and said, "Who's there?"

"Let's try it again together for justice. And louder!," said Mike. "Knock, knock!"

The kids shouted in unison, "Who's there?"

Mike said, "Interrupting cow…"

"Interrupting cow w—"

"Moo!," Mike leaned forward mooing over their final word.

The audience laughed!

Some of the older kids came over in response to the laughter seeking some of the attention and the rest followed.

The central birthday boy was named Gary, a lanky skater with long dirty blonde hair, and he stepped forward toward Mike.

Gary said, "I got a better one. Hey Champion, do you know the difference between you and other superheroes? Balls. Even Ocean Girl is tougher than you and all she can do is talk to fish."

The older boys snickered.

Mike said, "Don't be distracted by this young man, fellow citizens. I can assure you that I am much tougher than Ocean Girl, but that young lady is one of the smartest people I've known in three centuries. Only Merlin was wiser. Would you like to see some of the fire magic Merlin taught me?"

Gary looked around at his friends, who smiled at the thought of seeing some of The Champion's fire magic. He had lost his audience, so Gary piped up and said, "Here's some magic for ya, old man."

He held up his hands to reveal that there was nothing in them.

Gary cupped one hand and then reached into it with other.

He dramatically pulled out his middle finger from his cupped hand. He held it up with mock surprise and waved it proudly at the superhero. All the kids gathered around laughed at the naughty joke.

Mike said with disapproval, "Come on, friend, not in front of the little kids. You should cut me some slack and try to have some fun."

Gary took a step forward and Mike took a step back.

"Oh, I am having fun," said Gary as he moved in and jabbed an extended finger into Mike's armor belly... Mike didn't flinch.

Feeling like he had jammed his finger into a tree trunk, Mike tried to act cool and said, "Do your job, Champion, and entertain us with your flash paper fire magic."

Gary's mom, Jen, a trendy thirty-something that wore a baby-T and waist-high clam diggers, walked up and said, "So, are you guys having fun?"

Gary said in a snotty tone, "I guess. This fake told us we were going to see some lame trick." He nodded away to his friends.

As they ran off, one of the older boys shouted, "Come on, you guys. Let's play Freeze -Tag!"

The little kids who were Mike's audience followed the older kids, leaving Mike and Jen alone.

"Kids," Jen said smiling. "You should come over to the grill and show us adults some fire magic."

Mike smiled and said, "Ma'am, I can cook with the best of them, so please, not too close to the grill." He fanned his hands toward his chest.

Jen thought it was cute and smiled as she pulled Mike by the arm, she tucked her hand through his elbow and guided him toward her friends at the other end of the patio. After a few steps, Jen squeezed Mike's arm a couple of times and said with awe, "Hey, you aren't wearing some lightweight costume with fake muscles underneath." She tapped a nail on his chest, "Is that real armor?"

Mike was proud of his costume and said with a shy smile, "It is about one-hundred five pounds of authentic armor, if you count the sword."

Her face flushed in response to her mental impulses to say she only weighed one-fifteen and managed to giggle out a question instead, "How many push-ups can do with it on?"

Mike smiled as if the question had been spoken by a nine-year old and asked her if she meant straight or clapping push-ups?

She liked the answer and said, "Most guys would be lucky to do a jumping jack if they weighed three-hundred and fifty pounds."

Jen looked at Mike as they arrived at the grill and turned to her friends announcing, "Ladies and gentlemen, may I introduce you to who I believe is the real-life Champion?"

Mike smiled and nodded to the adults.

"He told me that if we would like to see some juggling, he would need three volunteers." Everyone laughed, including Mike who adjusted his posture to reset his armor. Mike's full height caught Jen's eyes, fanning the side of her head, she looked around and said, "See what I mean, you guys? Mr. Champion, you are too much."

She moved to the barbeque grill and closed the lid. Taking up a bottle of beer, Jen turned and smiled at Mike. "I thought I heard you say something about doing magic."

Mike made a sideway smirk, he knew it was time for the adult magic show and launched into his seasoned routine. It was his bread-and-butter and why the agency charged him out at a hundred dollars an hour. He was the best in the town.

AFTER THE PARTY HAD wound down, Mike was settling up with Jen in her immaculate kitchen. He dug into his duffel bag on the table to retrieve a business form, he tore off the bottom page and handed a pink receipt to Jen.

Mike returned the rest of the paper to his duffle bag and said, "So, what's your son's favorite meal?"

Pausing mid-step as she was turning to her purse on the counter, Jen said, "That's an odd question. Are you asking me out?"

"No-no," said Mike, who was surprised by the accusation. He bowed to Jen, "The agency's rules are clear about making advances toward clients and I didn't mean to sound forward. I'm sorry if I offended you. Knowing what kids like is part of my job."

Jen smiled coyly and thought for a beat before she moved to take something from her purse. Turning back to face Mike, she said, "Well, Gary loves corndogs, but I like cheese enchiladas and chile rellenos with margaritas." She closed the distance between them with something in her hand. "I hope I didn't sound offended when I thought you were asking me out."

Mike said, "I really—"

She interrupted, "Actually, I had hoped you were. Listen. You were well recommended by a friend who said you were single, a cop, great with kids, and in good shape." She poked him once in his iron stomach with an extend finger from her loaded hand.

Mike took a step back, "I think this is rather awkward."

"Well, if you're interested in getting together sometime when it's less awkward, give me a call," said Jen taking a step toward him. She held out cash in her hand toward Mike and said, "Gary and his friends are too grown-up for superheroes, but I had you here for little ones…and us adults."

Mike pushed the money back toward her and said, "Did I not say this was awkward?"

Jen shrugged, "You did, but I liked how you were the life of the party. Everyone had a great time because of you."

She extended the cash again and Mike pushed it back toward her. "Ma'am. I don't handle the business end of this. If I'm here, you were already billed through the agency," said Mike pointing to her purse, "That's your receipt, not a bill."

"I paid it on the phone with a credit card. This is your tip."

It was rare for Mike to be tipped by the people hiring him and her finality disarmed him. He took the money from her with a smile and said, "Thank you."

Running into the kitchen, Gary stopped in his tracks and interrupted the moment. He said, "Why are you paying him?" Resuming his path to the refrigerator, Gary groaned, "He sucked."

Mike was not shaken and actually smiled, "Kid, you have a great future in front of you."

Gary looked back at Mike and said, "Really…?"

"You'll make a fine comedian," said Mike with a wink and nod.

"Whatever," Gary said looking back into the refrigerator. "I'm going to be a rich lawyer just like my dad. You super-hero types might know him, he's The Judge." He grabbed a big can of Monster and said while moving past them, "We have a saying at Greenwood Academy, 'Be a hero, not a sidekick.' Mom, I'll be in my room. Call me when dinner's ready." He left the kitchen with a wave of dismissal.

Mike's eyes narrowed beneath his helmet as it all came together, he thought knew exactly how he would be taking down The Judge.

Jen was embarrassed, "I'm sorry. I told him that I wanted to meet you and he's a little—"

Mike held up a hand, clearly not interested as he picked up his duffle, and said, "No apologies needed, ma'am. I'm sorry. He said something about The Judge?"

"The Judge? Well, he's my ex," she said slowly. "Gary's father is a Denver courts judge. Judge Scarpella. Everyone calls him The Judge." She shrugged to release the sour feelings of not liking to talk about her ex-husband.

"Wow," Mike said. "The Judge, eh?" He couldn't believe that destiny had just come up and shook his hand. "Sorry to hear that."

Mike smiled at Jen as he dropped the cash into the duffle and zipped it closed. Mike moved toward the door with his mind on a plan that had really started to come together. "Thanks for the tip."

As Mike entered the chill of the spring evening, he chuckled at his unbelievable luck and knew that tonight would be all about fixing Patterson on his home turf. Tomorrow, he would be only days away from repositioning both of the dirty bastards and clearing Sarconi's name.

6

Still glowing with a golden aura of psychic energy, Jake walked up the sidewalk of an older neighborhood. The area was nothing like the grandeur of his subdivision, but grand in its own quaint way. He turned left at the corner and onto a broad side-street that served as a truck route. It was a tree-lined straight away with alleys in between the two quarter-acre housing lots on each block and had a stop sign on every other corner to mark each acre of road.

Jake always liked to think of this area as Arburbia because each street was named after a type of tree; Ash, Birch, Cherry, and various other alphabetical streets that didn't represent any of the actual trees. *There were likely crazies on Nut Street, but...*, he thought before judging that it had been a better marketing campaign than the subdivisions where streets were most appropriately named Cottonwood, Clay, Elm, and Pine. It was as easy as pitting Greenland against Iceland in the real estate market.

Knowing she would have liked that little bit of clever small talk, Jake's thoughts turned once again to lost love.

Instead of fighting the wave of thoughts that rushed at him, he fell into a dream-like mental slideshow of memories with Michelle. Realizing his lapse of self-control, Jake looked up the street trying to focus on something else and saw a dark man standing halfway down the block at an alley.

Jake knew the man too well and more than recognized the punk rocker. He loathed running into him and figured Frank felt that Jake had gotten off too easy when they saw each other earlier at the diner. Frank was the ever-present thorn in Jake's side. And, to make matters worse, they were dressed alike today.

When Frank saw Jake, he stood up from the wall and waved through an exhaled cloud of cigarette smoke.

Jake sighed and looked away, but this just caused Frank to shout and call for his attention, he extended his waving hand over his head.

The peaceful soundtrack of walking in the sunshine that played in Jake's mind was jerked off-track like a needle being dragged across a spinning record and replaced with a scratched and grainy eight-millimeter film reel of *When Frank Met Jake.*

JAKE WAS A HIGH-SCHOOL graduate at eighteen, two weeks after his commencement he had moved to Arizona and into his first apartment. Living alone for the summer months in the Arizona heat had taken its toll on Jake and he was very glad when he was finally allowed to move on-campus into the Sun Devil dormitories in mid-August. As if the heat wasn't tough enough on Jake, within a week of moving into the air-conditioned dorms, Jake had heard a little girl crying again. After moving from his apartment in town onto campus, he could only assume she was a ghost and had followed him.

He shared a room with a big jock named Carl, who insisted on testing their top bunk's structural integrity. Jake would lie below impending doom in the darkness listening to the little girl cry as his roommate's snoring vibrated the screws loose on the upper bunk.

Jake kicked the bed frame hard enough to shake the bunk-bed and whispered loudly, "Do you hear that, Carl?"

Carl snapped awake and groaned out, "Mom...," just like he said every time when jolted from a slumber. Jake smiled thinking Carl would have a tattoo on his forearm of a heart with MOM written inside it before the next semester.

"Your mom ain't down here—she left," Jake said, intending to anger Carl, so he would be wide-awake.

"What did you just say about my mom!?"

"I said, do you hear that? Listen."

A little girl started crying in long wails.

"Listen to what?"

The ghost cried out again.

"Can you hear that girl crying?"

Rolling over, Carl bounced around on the bunk above Jake and shook the bed. "I don't hear anything but your yapping," he replied.

Jake listened to the girl for several minutes, minutes that felt like they stretched on for hours. Like many mornings to come, Jake arose from his bed with a heavy sigh and started his daily athletic routine to get away from the tortured child's cries.

He had asked twice if Carl could hear her cries and he didn't, so Jake had carefully quizzed his psychology professor about his aunt who had heard a ghost crying. The professor described various conditions, like carbon monoxide poisoning or mold allergies, that led to hallucinations. When Jake forgot he was talking about his aunt and said that he didn't fit any of the diagnoses, the professor grew tired of the game and suggested that Mr. St. Johns enroll in Advanced Psychology, so he could interrupt someone else's class next semester with his silly questions about ghosts. The students all laughed with the professor.

AFTER EXHAUSTING THE SCIENTIFIC and logical resources available through the university to identify the source of the crying, Jake decided his lachrymose girl was preternatural and went to a psychic gypsy for a tarot card reading; he went with a young man's certainty that his hearing the little girl wasn't just a textbook mental ailment. If the supernatural didn't point him in a new direction, he had decided to then find out if he had a tumor. He had heard that psychic abilities, or delusions of psychic abilities, could be a symptom of a brain tumor and would ask the gypsy about it while he was there.

At first, the gypsy was confused by Jake and couldn't put her finger on anything about him. Whether she was psychic or not, it was the room's design and trappings that really switched on Jake's latent psychic abilities and he started to hear her panicked thoughts as he penetrated into her synaptic channels. The walls of the place had thinned and he could hear the neighbors exchanging snide comments about their mutually poor spending habits before he realized that the gypsy had become frozen with fear.

She could see a spiritual aura that looked like wings projecting out from his back.

Suddenly, Jake had an immediate impulse to piss and feared he might wet himself right there. His face grimaced with panic, "Can I use a bathroom?"

The gypsy blinked several times and finally pointed toward a dark alcove across the room telling him it was on the right.

When he returned from his overly urgent bathroom duties that yielded only a few seconds of a weak urine stream, Jake sat back down across from her card table, his brow furrowed in confusion.

The concern and fear in the gypsy's face had visibly subsided as she watched the energy that Jake emitted evaporate into the dark room.

"Will you give me a list of the incenses you are currently burning," asked Jake.

The gypsy nodded and reached for a pen as Jake's undisciplined psychic abilities grabbed at impulses flickering through her mind.

"Don't worry about the incense, thank you," Jake said. "It's dragon's blood and wormwood. Will you instead write down some books and tell

34

me some things I should know about meeting more people like you? I want to meet other psychics and learn about magic."

Despite of all the rules she had about not giving strangers access to her personal life, she wrote down her home number in awe of the glow she had witnessed coming from Jake and said, "We should talk about what you want to learn. Call me at home and we can meet at my friend's New Age bookstore. Then we can guide you to the books you need." Behind her words was a strong attraction for Jake and a lust to know more about him, she had never seen someone radiate so much life-force nor just turn off their aura; this triggered a deep curiosity in her.

With full knowledge of her feelings, but not sure of what she had seen radiating from him, Jake took the bait and rang her line the next day.

A couple of days later when they met at the bookstore she suggested, Jake liked her nervous attention and decided she was quite attractive without her gypsy outfit. They even dated for a few months after Jake had bought two hundred dollars worth of books on one of his eighteen credit cards.

In that short period of time, he tallied up a skilled charlatan's knowledge of basic witchcraft theory and its practices that included incenses, herbs, astrology and tarot. Jake had to fight (and fuck) hard to pluck the deepest secrets from her little dirty mind. Gypsy was quite aware of Jake's powers and pretty clever at guarding her mind...until they were naked. Jake didn't have to think about baseball as he tested his cross-country stamina because during sex her mind was an open, twisted book to him and when he learned to mimic the rhythm of her ecstatic physical reflexes, he was able to read the deepest parts of her mind and peruse through the chapters freely. Discarding any thoughts or concerns he regarded as ethical limitations on his powers, Jake became an extremely skilled psychic spending nights and days engaged in the calculated empathy of perfect lovemaking while raping the mind of another.

His journey with Gypsy led to another woman that Jake had met at an occult bookstore across town outside of her circle of friends. It was during what would become an eighteen-month relationship with a sexy and evil girl name Cheryl that Jake discovered magick. Because she couldn't see Jake's bio-magnetic energy bursts, Jake decided to not tell her that he could feel her thoughts and read her memories. His omission left Cheryl much less guarded mentally then she should have been and she taught him everything she knew about Tantra, spiritual tarot, the Sabian astrological symbols, planets, ancient runes, oils, potions, secret herbs for incense, and moon rituals with swords, wands, cups and coins... and oils... and Tantra.

When he broke it off with Cheryl, Jake first let her cat out into the backyard and then did it with special care because she knew some pretty heavy witchcraft. He worried about the effectiveness she demonstrated in the other facets of her daily life and didn't feel it was wise to test her or her damn witch cat. So, Jake lied and blamed the break-up on his not being able to really embrace the lesbian requirements of her coven, which was a huge lie, because he liked that the most about her religion. He sent a mixed emotionally positive message into her mind, which served to distract and empower her. He told her that her spiritual advancement wasn't worth his petty, but insurmountable jealousy.

Breaking up with Cheryl was tough on Jake's heart since he really liked her and it bruised his ego when she didn't seem to disagree that it was time to move on. Regardless of his strong feelings for her and his fiery spirit of competition, he had tapped her knowledge and needed to find a new lover with unknown secrets. This meant a permanent separation with her because there wasn't a chance in hell he was going to get caught cheating and fuel any spells she might cast his way.

Shortly after their separation, Jake found an interesting secret organization called *Thelema*. Its doctrine not only considered psychic ability and seeing spirits as skills to be obtained, but taught that true perception was a crux to their craft. However, the local master was a dreamer and his followers were not psychic, so Jake quickly advanced beyond the other initiates and became much more aware of the true secrets of their symbolism. His peers were not just non-psychic, but they were well-meaning fakirs who believed that magic was a way for them to be a part of something bigger and it added a sense of mystery to their lonely lives. They didn't see any of the spirits, angels, or demons that they summoned, let alone the impotent ghosts that hung around their temple, and would have benefited their lives more if they had joined a mystical-leaning Masonic Lodge. To Jake, the spiritual entities he saw were all just ghosts—he learned their names and they told him secrets. It was here that he learned non-corporeal spirits could only live through the mortals who knew their stories.

Ultimately, Jake learned that the beliefs and worship of people in the third dimension were actually fueling some vast divine comedy in the multi-dimensional universe. So, when he discovered quantum mechanical wave probability, he returned his whole focus to the world of human science and enrolled in a Quantum Physics class. There he exploited his psychic abilities by scanning his professor and other student's minds to learn everything he could grasp of the extra-dimensional world of superstring theory.

When he began to study speed-reading techniques and modern neural science theory, it grew quite easy for Jake to read volumes from people's minds within the seconds of a conversation's uncomfortable pauses.

One brutally hot day while he was walking across campus past the air-conditioned business school, an idea struck Jake like a lightning bolt—he decided to focus on his painting and artwork at home and changed his major studies to business and investment.

AFTER THREE YEARS OF picking and choosing his self-guided college curriculum, winning track meets, and cheating his way through the Dark Arts, Jake decided to apply several of the magick theories he had learned. He performed several banishment rituals that left a lingering mystical residue upon him that affected random ghosts and people for the remaining days of the lunar cycle, but none of the experiments he conducted would dispel the little girl's ghost and end her crying.

He left behind the practical magic with its garden-variety spells and will-imbued symbolic incantations to venture into the more complex planetary-powered rituals of conjuration.

However, none of the minor spirits that Jake summoned could be pressed into speaking about the crying girl...if they knew anything, they weren't talking to him about it.

In a final attempt to find the extra-dimensional child, Jake prepared for a supreme ritual. After researching the materials available through his occult resources, Jake had identified what he felt were the best accounts of an inscrutable process. As described, the recorded rituals would require three-months of gradual steps, daily purifications and a kitchen sink of arcane ingredients. Jake condensed the experiment down to its meaningful steps and reduced the invocations down to a few easy-to-remember rhythmic verses. When he identified the essential materials, Jake used his maturing, but sharply honed powers of persuasion to get what he needed for the ceremony.

It was a task to pull off gathering the required items and drawing the magic confinement circles before the solstice, but Jake was able to and got most of the required exotic herbs and heirlooms through bartering for "favors." He only had to buy the stuff he could afford. The only item he couldn't find was a lion skin apron, so he settled for lamb.

Jake knew going in that any item he got would have psychic impressions attached to it and planned to overwrite any previous enchantments on any of them; he also knew he would have to apply any necessary misinformation that was needed to conceal any of the missing items.

During the entire prep process, Jake knew in the end he would be required to kill a dove with a silver dagger in declaration of spiritual war in order to invoke the royal demon. The first and last thing Jake remembered killing was a bird that he had shot with a friend's BB gun. He was thirteen again and staring down at the bird's dead body, his heart was filled by the enormous uselessness of his action. There was no remorse, but the question of why overwhelmed him. However, Jake knew why this time and used the memory of his most profound violation of the Ten Commandments to fuel the arcane experiment he planned.

On the proper day after the final preparations and ritual were complete, Jake finished the last line of the incantation and put an enchanted dagger into the dove that he held in his hand. When the blood that poured from the dove landed in a silver chalice beneath it, the wormhole that opened within Jake's front room created a less than noticeable effect. However, the vague form that unfolded from it was a man-sized monster with three heads and a serpent's tail that coiled around the inside of a eight-foot magic circle drawn using salts and silica to form a mandala with symbols and candles positioned symmetrically.

Jake's spell was well-timed with the moon, but it required that he risk holding the demon overnight and would force him to sit in perfect meditation until the little girl began her cries. Facing what could be hours of sitting in the dark watching a candle without falling asleep or letting his mind drift into casual introspective, Jake cleared his mind and allowed himself and the flame to become one. He danced sucking at the wick of our universal wax.

In the early hours of the morning when the girl's cries began, Jake came out of his trance and asked the demon if it heard the cries. The monster's coils turned on themselves flowing against the containment field and it denied being able to hear anything. It grew more and more agitated as her cries bellowed on and Jake decided not to taunt the being by threatening to put it into a containment vessel when he asked if it could identify the source of the cries.

The demon was silent for a moment and its coils paused for a breath before it replied, "I don't hear anything."

In surrender and defeat, Jake concluded that his two-month endeavor was a lost cause and he offered the Archduke of Hell his release for a promise of truce in return.

The demon immediately stopped all motion and glared, "Clearly, you are a fool. A truce? I don't think that works for me."

"You heard me, Lord Asmodeus," Jake replied with strength. "I know the rules and I made no promises to be granted audience with you." He continued with the matter-of-factness of a lawyer, "Favor for favor. You favored me with your presence and I am honored. In good faith, I will return the favor by releasing you in a truce."

"Favor for favor, is it," the beast asked. "Your math is off. You summoned me, I came. One favor to me. You asked your question, I answered. Two favors, me. I recall your question being rephrased and asked again. That's three favors and not killing you makes four. Unless, you have a team of oxen to sacri—" The little girl called out for Daddy and the ghostly monster winced.

Seeing how the cries affected the captive spirit, Jake was quick to point out, "But, you lied in your responses to me. I asked if you heard that child crying and you said you did not. I saw that you clearly just did."

The demon sucked against the teeth of the central head and smirked saying, "Answers for favors, eh? Fine, Solomon, I can hear her cries, and no, I can't help you find her. The 'child' is your problem to deal with and that now brings us back to my four favors."

In frustration, Jake grimaced at being tricked so easily.

The demon was quick to reply to Jake's expression and said, "Hey, look, I know that wasn't fair and we could play this game forever. I know you are just a stupid monkey, so I'll promise a truce for three favors."

Knowing he was haggling from a disadvantage, Jake sighed before he said, "Two."

The demon laughed and roared, "Sucker! You civilized people know nothing about negotiations. Deal. I want your first born and—"

Jake was shocked by the cliché and interrupted, "My first born? Fuck you, that's two favors, ugly."

"This is getting exciting," the demon's ram head neighed to the bullhead.

Before they butted heads, the bullhead snorted, "Counter-offer!"

Seeing that the demon was enjoying every advantage, Jake was nonplussed and fought to think his way out of the terrible situation. He finally offered, "Sorry, setting you free is all I can offer for a truce."

"Deal," said the head of the man, extending a huge, stubby, clawed turtle hand. "We have a truce for my freedom now and a future favor on the table to be negotiated at a later date when you have something to offer to me."

Jake didn't like being trapped again and settling at a deficit was a terrible idea, but there didn't seem any other way out and he knew any additional haggling would lead to owing Asmodeus another favor. Reaching out his hand to the black candle at the bottom of the carefully crafted mandala on the floor of his front room, Jake said, "With the condition that we will negotiate the terms of the final favor, I accept your offer."

"That's a deal and I promise a truce," said the archduke of Hell and acted as though he was going to continue. Jake snuffed the candle with his fingers and interrupted any additional conditions that the creature might have had as amendments to their agreement.

In an instant, the other candles went out and the sand of the mandala was swept up into the air. The cloud of dust pulled into the form of a man that wagged an extended finger at Jake before it exploded when the demon jolted back into its dark realm of existence. Jake was knocked back against the wall and fell hard on his ass. He sat there wiping sand from his tearing eyes and tried to recall what had happened in the moments leading up to this and found it difficult to remember any precise details as if it had all been a dream.

He went to bed and slept through the rest of the morning into the afternoon. As he showered under cold water, Jake resolved to give up on the occult as a viable avenue of recruiting help to exorcise his ghost child and promised himself to use magick only if needed.

IN THE MONTHS THAT FOLLOWED, Jake excelled in his business classes and saw solid advances in creating his unique painting style. During the summer before his senior year, he started dating a lesbian couple that he had met at a music fest in Tempe; one was an art major and the other majored in lit. They had lived with him for about six months and paid their share of the rent by posing for him.

He learned something unexpected from these women; they were a portrait of Ecotopian relations and all about open communication based on empathy, emotional control, and a shared pack of cigarettes. Nevertheless, when the girls broke up, they broke up with him too and he never heard from either again.

A few weeks after their break up, Jake made his first sale through a local art gallery and he wanted to tell them he had sold their *Desert Nymphs* series. When he couldn't find anyone who knew them or a record of them in the administration office, Jake surmised that they weren't really co-eds and creeped himself out as he ran through the catalogue of possible explanations. None of the spirits he considered were the friendly kind, Jake was furious that he had been so seduced and didn't recognize them as demons.

Desert nymphs my ass, Jake thought. He smacked himself in the head for being duped and fought back the urge to recall the true form of the girls who had been living with him. His first impulse was to wretch, but he didn't succumb and was swishing his mouth with vodka as if it were mouthwash when he dialed Information to find the nearest Planned Parenthood for a complete STD test.

ON A COLD WINTER morning in his off-campus apartment, Jake sat up with a heavy sigh. His dream was just looping a string of mismatched memories from a journey that followed a gilded path littered with guilt and used condoms.

That morning, listening to the child cry again was almost a comfort compared to the memories marking the utter vanity of vanities in his pursuit of self-awareness and spiritual knowledge.

Nevertheless, Jake was tired of listening to her crying and had gone to sleep the night before deciding that he would use the rest of his college funds to buy a computer. His portfolio was good enough to get him an internship, and with his computer design skills, Jake would be hired a month before the internship would require his re-enrollment at the university.

After buying the computer and applying to the college's internship placement program, Jake dropped out of college and moved back to Colorado to get away from the little girl.

When he returned to his hometown, Jake attempted to work with several groups that he had found through occult bookstores and head shops in the Denver metro-area. Jake wanted to believe he could find another psychic to co-lead a local movement with him…a real movement.

After Jake got a job and had settled into the working life at an ad agency in downtown Denver, he realized that leaving the college town had left a huge vacuum in his life that was once filled with interesting people who had ideas and stories to tell. Bored with television, Jake decided to buy some books that he had always intended to read and not just know through someone else's memories.

Jake had fallen asleep after finishing Stephenson's *The Diamond Age*. Waking, he found the book on the pillow next to him and remembered deciding that he preferred *Snowcrash*. Suddenly, the sound of a crying little girl echoed from the walls of his new bedroom and Jake jolted awake with shot of adrenalin.

That was it and Jake had had it. Furious, he tossed back the covers and stomped from his bed. He looked in the closet and grabbed his least favorite pair of running shoes. He had grown tired of running and didn't have to keep his scholarship anymore. In fact, Jake had enjoyed sleeping in and hadn't bothered with a morning jog for over three weeks. With a fist

41

raised to the sky, Jake cursed the heavens for hating him as he jogged into the morning air to avoid hearing the unshakeable girl's cries.

ONE MORNING SEVERAL MONTHS later, Jake jogged past what appeared to be a little group of homeless men who gathered at the gate of the park. Jake said, "I tell you guys every morning. There's no fence, you can go around the gate."

The park-bound ghosts of the men turned and followed Jake at the sides of the path into the park with slow lumbering steps on the first lap of his regular eight laps around them.

He was tired of this park and turned at the next corner, cutting left to run toward another city-required park. Jake had run five laps around the next park's lake and turned back to loop around to the first park again.

Satan's magick and God's miracles played back and forth in Jake's mind as his thoughts jogged several steps ahead of him. Jake argued that evil and good were both manmade concepts, life was about energy and entropy. Manifest focus versus tangential disorder.

There was no placing value on either...life was simply activity against the natural state of the universe, he thought. *If the universe were to judge, all life would be evil; whereas if the living were to judge the universe, they would declare it guilty of murder. Relativity and truth were both based on the amount of symmetrical interference obscuring the observer's view of the asymmetrical. If there is a plan, where was freewill? If low entropy and rest are the natural order of the universe than the high entropy of life is proof of God erecting his preferred order against his nature. All creatures, great and small, fall as nature's casualty in God's war against the universe. The Bible refers to the Fall of Man as the breakdown of the natural order and could be inferred to imply sin created entropy.*

Jake turned a corner and thought on while he ran, *So, is it God who fuels the energy for life or is it Satan who is fighting to keep the universe from collapsing in on us? If God and nature are against us, who would stand for us? If in the Beginning, God established order from chaos and then sin entered the universe to start time, shouldn't we really be, as Jesus would say, what men call evil-doers and support the destruction of universe...?*

His sense of purpose jerked him back into focusing on the path ahead as he picked up the pace to finish his run like he should have finished the cross-country finals for State in high school.

Setting aside his internal thoughts about his place within the world religions, Jake tried to find his rhythm before turning down an alleyway.

Jake turned from the top of another alley and had to hurdle the front end of a car that had been parked over the curb. It was a clean hurdle and he didn't break stride.

There was one more alleyway to run before he would hit the main thoroughfare where the stop signs protected him from side traffic. He turned into that alley and picked up his pace again.

In the distance and overhead, the loud and laugh-like caws from several crows echoed down the alley. The laughing crows had gathered in a huge murder perched on the overhead lines and in the trees above the alley ahead of Jake. When Jake's eyes connected with one of the nearby crows, they all swarmed into the end of the alleyway closing it off and he had to slow up his steps.

The crows entered the alley and bounced like foot soldiers in a V-formation phalanx toward Jake.

Instead of slowing, Jake did one of those jogger high-stepping moves and reversed direction to resume his pace back the way he had come.

When Jake turned to run in the opposite direction, another bouncing and dive-bombing army of crows had entered the other end of the alley.

Jake slowed to a walk when he perceived that he was trapped in between streets. He wasn't as scared as he probably should have been and the humor of being cornered by crows had a greater impact on him.

So this jogger runs into an alley and no sooner did he get to the midpoint when two big flocks of ravens landed at each end blocking him in, chuckled Jake. It was just another joke setup looking for a punch line.

Jake stopped and put his hands on his hips; he looked back and forth over his heaving chest and shoulders at the approaching crows.

"What the hell is this," Jake asked the world in disbelief. "You want a piece of me, crows?"

He would not go down without a fight against these scavengers. Looking up and down the alley, he examined the dumpsters that lined it. He found a shovel handle without a head sticking up from a dumpster two houses ahead of him.

Jake sprinted to the shovel and readied himself for the kill.

When he had taken up the handle, the birds paused their approach. "That's right," Jake said taunting them. "Come get it. Let's play some crowball!"

Jake warmed up with a few practice swings and had set his feet for the first pitch when he heard a man shout from within the garage beside him. The voice shouted again and said, "Hey! Can you hear me?"

Jake looked to the garage door.

"I can hear you out there. Hey, can you hear me!? I am locked up in this garage," shouted the voice. "Come around the gate and get me outta here!"

Jake looked over his shoulders to estimate the time of attack from the advancing crows, but when he turned the birds were gone.

"Hey, retard," shouted the voice from within the garage. "If you can hear me tap the door three times."

Still surprised to find no crows, Jake kept an eye on each end of the alleyway as he crept to the garage door.

Despite his earlier lack of conviction that it was sane to be debating the logical conclusions of intelligent design, Jake now completely doubted his sanity.

He leaned his head toward the garage door. Right before Jake touched his ear to the door, something from inside hit it and startled him.

Jake called out, "Is there someone in here?"

"Y-E-S," the voice shouted. "Now, tap three times if you are going to help me."

Jake tapped the shovel handle against the door thrice.

"Right on," called the voice with glee. "Now come through the yard to the door and…LET ME OUT OF HERE!!"

Tossing the stick toward the dumpster, Jake stepped through the broken fence and moved into a backyard filled with lush weeds and sun-scorched grass. The garage's side door was six feet from the gate. Walking through the yard to the door, Jake opened it and let light into the garage.

Inside the garage, Jake saw an unbelievably immaculate shrine for ritual magick. Someone had taken a lot of trouble to follow the finest laws of summoning for confinement.

There was a horned and bloody altar near the wall. On it was the burnt offering of a dove and flies buzzed around licking at the remaining blood. A foot in front of it was a human-like figure floating within the confines of a carefully drawn circle with candles burning and symbols placed symmetrically. Jake recognized the Hebrew characters and knew exactly what demon they had planned to summon.

"Hey thanks," said the misty spirit inside the circle. "Okay, you can't just blow out these candles, you need to remove the chalk lines." The spirit pointed away and said, "It would be great if you could grab that broom and blow out a couple candles."

"Wait up," said Jake. "You are my captive for the moment. I get to give the orders."

"Wrong," said the spirit. "You knocked three times. I owe you my name and the honor of restoring my freedom."

"Courtesy should allow for at least a topical question."

"Courtesy allows my name, which is unspeakable so you may call me Frank," said the spirit.

Jake ignored him and said, "Frank, are the people who confined you here knowledgeable of the true science of this spirit trap? I am and I know your name."

"You know me, eh? Then I will speak freely, these candles will burn out and I will get free. At that time, I will kill them and you. But to answer you the obvious, I don't see them coming to stop you from desecrating their altar. No! These idiots picked me out of a list of demons as "the coolest one" and they got lucky, they don't even know they have me and when there was no wizz-bang magical explosion, they left to consult a friend. They won't be able to do this or anything else again, ever. Since we're all done with our buddy talk...Broom, monkey!"

"Using a broom could be dangerous for me," Jake shook his head and continued as he walked around the drawing on the floor and examined the altar. "I don't know if I believe you because this circle is pretty well crafted and the candles they are using appear to be a sealing wax. I don't think the candles burning out will help your escape, but I do think they can keep you here until they stop their daily sacrifice of doves. This conjuration required a lot of work and these guys look like they are going to try to put you in a genie bottle."

Jake lifted a rune-decorated decanter and wagged it at the confined spirit. "You don't remember me, do you?"

"Of course I remember you, St. Johns," the spirit hissed as it assumed its true form. The snake-bodied monster folded its scaled arms across his chest under the bull, man and ram heads, and said, "We have a truce and I thought you were using someone else to summon me to return my favor. Oops. Now, get me out of here."

Jake smiled and thought he had hit the heights of clever when he said, "I do seem to remember owing you a favor. Remind me."

The monster rolled its eyes and sighed, "Look, I can lie about everything, but that. You already paid your favor. Sorry. Can we just call this a condition of our truce?"

"The truce is under no conditions, Frank," Jake retorted. "In fact, the favor I owed had a condition of our negotiating the terms."

"Well, technically, we did that night," shrugged out Frank as the coils of his body flowed in unison around the edges of his confinement.

Jake narrowed his eyes and said coldly, "Remind me."

"You are being very clever not to ask a question," said Asmodeus the archduke of hell. "When I said I wanted your first born, you said that you would fuck me for two favors and called me ugly."

"That doesn't remind me of any negotiations," Jake replied.

"From your mouth to God's ears. I sent those two lesbians and gave you your first art sale as two favors. One of the girls conceived your child."

"What?!"

"How rude of me? Congratulations, Jake, you're a father. It was a binding deal offered by you, so I took you up on it. When one got your child, our deal was sealed and I sent them home."

"You are saying that I have a child," Jake demanded in doubt.

"No. I have a child. You got to live with two demonically hot girls for six months and sell their sexy, naked paintings."

"But, I didn't agree to those terms."

Frank's ram and bull head butted as the man's head said, "That's the nature of a favor. You accepted the favor and not only benefited, but also profited. I did you two favors as offered."

"If I let you out of here," Jake said as he began to pace. "You will owe me more than a favor."

Frank was slow to reply and finally said, "If you get me out of here, I will concede to you a favor of your choosing. As a second favor, I will even promise to help you choose a wise wish that cannot backfire."

"Not sure I want any favors from you. How about you give me something right now as a measure of good faith," said Jake, angling for an advantage.

"Fine," said the otherworldly beast. "Shortly, your child will be born on an Indian reservation in Taos, New Mexico. The names aren't coming to me, so maybe you can wish for that at a later date. Now, grab that broom."

Jake swished the words in his mouth. As he turned to leave, Jake said, "That's all I needed to hear. See you in Hell when you finally get out of your bottle."

Quickly, the monster changed its tune and sang, "I'll serve you until my debt is paid, monkey. Get the broom."

Jake turned back smiling and said, "First, I really don't like being called a monkey. Second, a broom is out of the question." He stepped up to stand about a foot from the chalk circle and symbols drawn on the floor. He smiled as he pulled down the front of his sweatpants and said, "The salt in my piss will protect me from making contact with the circle. Only two candles or do I have to go around the world?"

"Don't you piss on me," cried the spirit as urine squirted into the circle. "Oh you will pay twice the indignity, you son of a pig-fucking whore!"

Jake emptied his bladder exhausting two candles and carving a solid line through the lines between two symbols. He squirted a final burst at the five symbols nearest the lines on the other side of the circle.

When Jake looked up, the spirit was gone. He shrugged and shook himself a couple of times.

This was definitely a tumor, he thought.

He spun on his heel and turned to leave. Blocking the doorway stood a large man with long spiked hair and clad from head to foot in black leather.

"You shouldn't be in here and may I be frank with you," the man in the doorway said to Jake.

"I'd prefer if you just moved out of my way," Jake said pressing his will into the mind of the man. "So, I can run along and you'll just forget I was ever here."

Unheeding his psychic manipulation, the man moved toward Jake with outstretched arms, Jake raised his arms with a poised karate-stance he learned in seventh grade in a six-week karate class. The man ducked through his arms and bear hugged him!

The man lifted Jake from his feet and said, "Thanks, dude! I ain't your servant, but I sure owe you. Unto the Great Death and my debt is paid, sir!"

Frank jerked him up and down several times kissing his cheeks before Jake could break his hold. FADE TO BLACK...

JAKE'S DISLIKE FOR THE man in black was intense and he wished that he had left him in that garage. When he considered crossing the street and looked across the pavement, Frank was leaning against the corner of the fence at the opposite alleyway. He waved again, but with mockery. Jake changed his mind about crossing the street.

Before Jake could look back to the other side of the street again, the punk called out to him from the first alleyway where he had been standing and smoking.

Jake jerked his line of vision back to the corner where he had seen Frank.

Frank wasn't there. Jake looked back across the street to the other alleyway. No Frank there, either.

Was there anyone there? Why do I—

The man was suddenly walking beside him and said, "You weren't just looking for me were you, Jake?"

He had indeed startled Jake, who showed his irritation with a cold glare. The punk threw an unexpected arm around Jake's shoulders and gave him a few shakes.

"How you doing, buddy?," he said billowing out a cloud of cigarette smoke.

Jake shirked off the arm from his shoulder and said, "What do you want, Frank?"

Frank walked beside Jake down the street and snorted smoke from his nose a couple of times before asking, "Do I have to want something to hang out with my best buddy in the whole world?"

"You always do," Jake said.

Frank was silent for a moment. He then laughed, shrugging out more cigarette smoke, and said, "Okay, you win. I want...what do I want?" He paused for a second and blurted out, "I want to know why you are still playing bookstore?"

Jake walked on ignoring him.

"I mean, you're wasting all your talents on getting free books to give 'em to people who won't even read 'em. What's the point? You're a super-hero, Jake!"

Jake groaned in response and repeated, "What do you want, Frank!?"

"I want you to know that if you don't start righting some wrongs, the wrongs are going to start finding you. And, you won't have a choice then."

Jake stopped to confront Frank eye-to-eye and said, "Like I have a choice all of a sudden. What wrong do I need to right to get rid of you?"

Frank mocked him with a look that said, *Aren't you oh so very clever,* while smoke jetted from his nose. "Pick your wars, sunshine..." as he blew smoke from his mouth in Jake's face. "Not your nose. Oh, yeah, and your fly's down."

Frank pointed his cigarette uncomfortably close to Jake's crotch.

Jake looked down to check—his fly was zipped—but Frank was gone when he looked up. The golden wings of energy that earlier danced on Jake's back had also disappeared.

Jake said a little too loudly, "Good. Now stay gone!"

He marched onward without Frank.

JAKE TURNED A CORNER and nearly ran over the round-faced girl, who had watched him longingly from the corner of the lunch counter and followed him when he left. She was in her twenties and wore a baby-T with khaki pants under a long, red sweater-jacket. He dropped his book bags and grabbed her arms to catch her as if she were falling. Her sudden appearance had startled him and his aura shot out from him with flames of golden light when he embraced her.

"I'm so sorry. I wasn't paying attention," Jake said.

He pulled his head and shoulders back, consciously reeling his tangible aura back into his body.

"I was," she said. "I could hear you coming from a block away."

Jake couldn't believe what she said. He pulled her closer and said, "Did you hear me talking with someone else?"

She looked at her arms in his gripping hands and then lifted her face to meet Jake's eyes. He stood motionless as he tried to understand something.

The woman spoke up asking if Jake was okay. His eyes darted away from hers in a conscious effort to avoid reading her mind and said he was fine.

Leaning her head to meet his eyes again, she smiled and said, "I didn't hear anything bad."

Jake realized he was still holding her arms and let go of her. "Whoa! Sorry about the arm thing. But I thought I was going to clobber you—" he said waving his hands in the air to calm himself down. "You said you heard me talking with someone? What did you hear?"

"You sounded angry saying something about being left alone. Then another man said something about heroes and that your fly was down," she said looking down at his crotch. "Who were you talking to," she asked as she looked behind him for someone else on the empty sidewalk.

Trying to deflect the conversation away from Frank, he assured her that they had heard the same thing and told her some guys were in the alley behind him. He suggested that she not go that way and made a loco sign beside his head before saying, "Do you want to get some coffee? I know a place around the corner up ahead," pointing onward and over her shoulder.

Tammy stuck out her hand with a big smile and said, "Hi. I'm Tammy. You are?"

They shook hands.

"Tammy, I am pleased to meet you," Jake said shaking her hand. "Have you ever considered that you might be a little psychic? Cuz I'm surprised you heard that back there. In the alley, those guys, I mean."

She said, "Sometimes, I feel psychic, but most of the time it is just body language and stuff." Tammy took Jake's hand with both of hers as he continued to shake it.

She shook his hand with final closure and asked if she could have her hand back.

Jake let go of her hand with a laugh saying that she probably needed it and apologized again. He paused for a moment and said, "Ahhh, you don't want coffee. You're a sucker for dessert."

Tammy smiled. "Know a place?"

"Yeah, I know a place, but," he said making a face of closed-eyed concentration. "You like…? Fried ice cream."

"Love it," she said. "Who's the psychic now?"

Jake nodded onward and picked up his bags. He started to walk up the sidewalk and she followed beside him, looking at his bags.

"Whatcha got in the bags," she asked.

Jake acted surprised as if he just realized he was carrying books.

"These? Oh, I collect books. Well, I don't really collect them. I have this bookstore. It's just a hobby…nothing really."

Tammy reached her hands into her jacket pockets and appeared to be playing with something in her pocket. "That's interesting," she said. "So, since it's a hobby you must have an online bookstore or something."

Jake said, "I knew I had a good feeling about you. Yes, The Anarchist Bookstore (dot) com." He pointed at his shirt. "I'm trying to evolve humanity by selling better books."

Jake appeared to remember something important and stopped, he turned to Tammy like a blind man looking inwardly with no focus on her. "Wait."

He bent to set his bags down and said, "What're you reading right now?"

Tammy told him they were reading an Oprah book in her book club.

Jake looked back into a bag of books and said, "Baaah. Want to get them reading something good next month?" He shuffled through the books within. "I've got *1984*, Clarke's *Childhood's End*, and Bierce's *Fantastic Fables*."

Smiling with polite disregard, Tammy said, "I read *1984* in high school. It's a little far-fetched."

Jake looked up at her with a critical eye and said, "Really…?" He rolled his eyes before he looked back to his bags. "Did you know that you don't elect in a true Republic? The rich and sage are supposed to appoint leadership to elevate humanity through the arts and science. In this Republic for which it stands, since the sages are dependent on the rich for their continued funding…it's the rich who appoint and they force the citizens to go to war for their financial gains. It's just like *1984* and you're all slaves."

Tammy held her hands to her head and said, "Uh oh, my psychic powers tell me you have…" She dropped her hands to her side with a slap and said, "Nothing I'll like."

"I'll take that bet," he said chuckling and removed two books. "How about *Alice in Wonderland* and *Through the Looking Glass*?" Jake stood and held out the books to Tammy.

She was surprised at his choice of books. "How'd you do that?"

Handing her the books, he smiled and said, "I'm psychic."

She took the books, fighting back a big childish smile, and said, "I loved Alice when I was a kid. Been meaning to pick them up for a while."

Jake smiled with satisfaction and picked up his bags. "Now you have them. You might even like reading *1984* as an adult," he said. "Got to love the People's Gin as a perfect ending for the free-thinker."

Jake walked on mindful of Tammy's slowed pace as she returned to childhood flipping through the books to refresh her memory of the original drawings within.

Tammy was all smiles when she found the picture she was looking for and showed it to Jake. "I used to have nightmares about this one," she said.

He smiled as he looked at the image and nodded to her saying he knew she would like the books. Tammy focused on the books and moved a little closer to Jake.

"Hey," Tammy said. "You didn't tell me your name. You said you were pleased to meet me."

"Haha. Did I? That's why they call me, Jake St. Johns," he said with a coy smile. "Lady killer."

Their eyes met for the first time without shyness and she said, "Good books. What else you got?"

"Nothing that you'd like, yet."

Sᴉᴛᴛɪɴɢ ᴏɴ ᴏᴘᴘᴏsɪᴛᴇ sɪᴅᴇs of a booth in a cozy and clean Denver-styled Mexican restaurant with draped woven blankets, photos of Emilio Zapata, and Aztec faux-artifacts hanging on the walls, Tammy and Jake sat with large margaritas in front of them and their eyes turned toward a young man standing in the aisle.

Jake said, "Just one fried ice cream and two spoons."

The waiter, Juan, a tall skinny Hispanic kid with silver-capped teeth smiled with a wink to Jake, while taking back their menus. He said with a heavy accent, "If there is nothing else, your order will be right up, Jake."

When the waiter exited toward the kitchen, Tammy moved her books from the table to her purse. Jake's bags were already shoved in beside him.

Tammy said, "Thanks again for the books. But, since we're sharing ice cream, I should ask, you don't have any diseases, do you?"

"No worries," he said. "As a gentleman, I planned to finish it, not share it. You know you don't finish your meals. Which reminds me of finishing, I started to talk about the bookstore. How did you know it was online?"

Tammy acted coy as if she were psychic. He watched her body language for boredom and hurried his story before she could change the subject. He needed to tell someone and she was there. She was a woman and he really needed a woman's ear. They seem to listen better if there was drama and he was damned if he couldn't hook her with his story. He would take it slow and project a secondary mental dialogue over his spoken words. He needed to see if she was psychic and could hear him.

Is this what my life had become? A series of irritating psychological profile test questions to find out if someone was psychic, he thought.

Jake said, "Here's what's up with my bookstore." Meanwhile, he thought-spoke and said, *I had five hundred orders.* "You wouldn't guess how many orders I had when I got home yester—"

Tammy was hooked and interrupted by saying a dozen.

He said, "Nope, not even close. Have you ever heard of Thelema or Aleister Crowley?"

"Thelma and Alice Turk-who?"

"No. Aleister Crowley. He was a magician. Jimmy Page bought his house."

Recalling the impulse of a memory, Tammy said with concern, "Wait... wasn't he a devil worshipper?"

"Close enough," he replied. "Anyway, some of the members of his group loved my bookstore and their national website featured me." Jake snapped. "BANG! Two days later, I can't keep up. I had 500-orders when I got home last night. That's like 4-weeks of full-time work."

She took a drink of her margarita before she said, "Four weeks full-time? So, you don't work otherwise?"

"Hell no," said Jake with a sharpness. "Like I told you, I'm a real psychic. So, I get to be a philanthropist, who plays the stock market and re-invests the earnings into the local community, the arts, and education. The books are a hobby. But, don't tell my mom, she thinks I'm a financial analyst," he quipped.

Tammy grinned and said, "Ahhh, so, you're a trust fund baby."

"Oh no," Jake laughed. "Not no, but hell no. My dad has a restaurant that only makes a profit because I launder my cash through there."

"I never understood laundering cash," she challenged.

Jake told her that it wasn't really laundering cash in the organized crime sense and said, "I just dump cash back into the local market because I can afford it. It's your basic community welfare system in return for perks I enjoy. Like this place."

Tammy was interested, but was still confused. "I thought you laundered money to put it in the bank and avoid having to claim or declare it," she said. "So, you don't pay taxes?"

"You are killing me," he said. "I shouldn't have said 'launder,' it has confused my whole point. Of course, I pay taxes. I make a lot of hard money and pay a hell of a lot of taxes, something like forty percent of my earnings because I invest and it is all capital gains. But, that doesn't mean I think it's right for other people to have to. Our tax system's bullshit and only oppresses the working poor." He took a huge pull off of his drink like a desert-parched man. "I over-tip everywhere I go and no one else has to claim it as a wage."

Tammy sat forward and whispered, "You aren't worried about the IRS?"

Jake gave her a coy smile turning his glass to get at the salt on its rim and took a drink of his margarita. "Not at all. I keep my receipts and manage several clean corporations. If anything, I am only guilty of being wasteful and paying myself obnoxious salaries. I mean if someone were to follow me around, they could probably shut down some of the small businesses that I visit, but I operate with cash only, so no one could prove anything and I would fight for any of my people. It would just be another one of my many write-offs. Without stockholders, it's easy to create hard losses using petty cash." He smiled and said, "So, what do you use your 'psychic powers' for…? Besides charming book nerds."

"Well, I read tarot cards for friends and try to prevent bad things from happening to them," she said.

Jake said, "Sounds like we are both on the side of noble causes. But, why not apply some science and try to live up to your potential. You play cards, but have you ever tried to play stocks with your cards?"

Tammy was surprised and tried to voice it, "That's an interesting transition. This whole thing is…Jake. Jake, right? I am terrible with names."

He nodded an affirmative as she sipped at her drink.

After her sip, Tammy said, "So, what is your story? I mean, why have a bookstore if you can cheat on the stock market?"

Jake took a big slug from his margarita and set it down. "Cheating is a strong word since you couldn't prove I am psychic. Someone would have to prove that there is another psychic who can do it, have them act as a witness to my psychic activities, and then rewrite the law to say I can't do it. I told you I'm clean-clean. Let's go back a step, you asked, 'Why the book store?' I'm ashamed to say it out loud," he said. "But, I'd call me a recruiter for the occult. I only sell books that have substantial matters for people who might get it."

"Get what? Playing the stock market to create financial anarchy?"

"That's a good one. Can I use that?," Jake said turning his glass to find more salt and took a sip. "It really doesn't matter though," he said. "It's all pearls before swine cuz people really like being slaves and no one wants to evolve or live up to their potential. Fear is powerful and self-imposed weakness even more so."

"You totally lost me. Why do you have the bookstore?"

Jake sighed and said, "The bookstore affords me electronic interaction with every weirdo in the world. Weirdos who want to believe that fiction is real. Weirdos like to talk about weirdo stuff. If there is another real psychic out there, they are going to be sorting through other weirdos if they want to find another psychic."

Tammy slowed it all down again with her hands and asked Jake, "So, you have met other psychics through your bookstore?"

"No. I've only found other weirdos, but I can't give up. I mean you aren't a weirdo, but you play with your cards to be a little psychic and more interesting. I don't think you are really psychic."

Without really meaning to, Jake had plucked a feminist cord in Tammy that always seemed to cause her to rise up in defensiveness. But, she was still coy when she replied and said, "How do you know? Maybe I've been hiding my true self to see if you are the real thing."

He couldn't help but chuckle when he realized what he had done. Jake knew there was no way to stop the vibration of this woman's humming neural pathways that were singing out, EQUALITY. So, he continued the course and turned up his pace to head it off.

He leaned toward her and whispered, "Okay, if you are psychic, may I ask if you've seen a ghost?"

This not only intrigued her, but it seemed to dampen her emotional resonance. Tammy smiled as she drifted into thought before saying that she had not seen a ghost.

Jake said, "This doesn't disqualify you as being psychic, but I'm not surprised. People all talk about ghosts, but no one's ever really seen one. We all feel them when they feed on our emotions, but then we go to therapy to feel better about being slaves to our emotions."

"Back to slaves, huh? You have this all rehearsed."

"Yep. Ignorant slaves are a monthly feature in *The Psychic Journal*."

She shook her head with a smile. "So, are you saying you have seen a ghost," Tammy asked with a tone of challenge again on the edge of her voice.

He leaned across the table and looked around. "No, I see them all the time. In fact, this place has one."

Eavesdropping, an old woman swept the floor beside their table.

Jake continued, "Elna lived here upstairs and took care of this restaurant until she died fifteen years ago. It used to be a real high-class joint, well, from what she says anyway."

When Elna abruptly stopped her sweeping and leveled a wry smile at Jake before saying, "It was very high-class, Jacob." She leaned close to Tammy, "She's so pretty. But, she's hiding something. Beware, Jake."

She reached out and touched Tammy's hair, Tammy shivered and set down her drink—

Elna was gone as if she was never there.

Tammy's voice croaked with emotion when she said, "Really...?"

Jake shrugged and finished his drink, "Yeah. Elna just touched your hair cuz you're pretty and said you are hiding something. Ghosts always act like there's some story to tell."

Tammy was uncomfortable at the statement and looked around as Jake tilted up his drink to finish it again. She said, "I swear to God I just felt a coldness on my neck like someone had touched my hair."

"That was Elna," Jake said. "Wanna hear a real ghost story?"

Tammy said, "Better make it a good one after that creepy feeling." She made an ick-face with a shiver and rubbed away the goose bumps that had arose on her arms.

Tammy's statement made him think about Michelle and how he should have told her the secret before he helped her—

Cigarette? No!

Was Tammy a second chance to find a woman? Should I take a peek into her head—No!

Yes... Cigarette!

Before Jake's thoughts and inner struggle could betray him on his face, the skinny waiter returned with their order of fried ice cream. Jake grew sick with himself for not knowing that Juan had approached. Maybe he should just start smoking again, one less thing to distract him—

Michelle...

Juan set the large bowl in between them and placed two spoons on napkins on each side of the bowl.

Jake ignored the fight raging in his head and smiled, "Thanks, Juan. Would you bring me another one of these?" He lifted his empty drink. "Tammy, ready for another?"

Tammy looked at her half-full glass and shook her head.

Jake said to Juan in Spanish, "Please bring another one for me, but make it a double, no, triple shot of tequila and as quick as possible, brother."

Juan smiled too broadly and said, "Pronto."

"You know Spanish?," asked Tammy with surprise.

Jake laughed and said, "I know a little Mexicano and he just walked away. Did I talk to him in Spanish?"

She said that he had and Jake chuckled to cover up that he tripled up his liquor. No woman tolerated a drunk upon first meeting, but he needed to slow down the battle in his head.

"I never noticed that I did that," said Jake. "Maybe that's why I get great service here."

Tammy grabbed her spoon and said, "So, you were going to tell me a ghost story."

"Ah, yeah. This isn't a real ghost story because it is about the only ghost that I can't see," Jake said with the depth of passion that he still held for Michelle. "Unlike Elna, this ghost still haunts me."

7

In a small apartment north of the old candy factory in Glendale, Arizona, an eighteen-year old Jake slept soundly in a messy bedroom cluttered with boxes and wearing nothing but his long hair, which was cut in a long grunge bi-level that still qualified as a mullet.

Suddenly, he had awakened with a start. He had thought the voice of a little girl crying had awoke him and he was about to write it all off as a bad dream when the soft voice of a child rang out again crying, 'Daddy...!'

He jumped out of bed and showed concern at hearing a girl sobbing.

Jake moved around the room, listening at the walls and looking around for the source of the crying.

The little girl cried out for her daddy again.

Jake looked out of the bedroom door and listened for a moment.

When she first came to Jake, he was terrified for the crying little girl. Her fear became his fear and he had to help her.

He tiptoed out of his bedroom and passed the bathroom into the front room, listening with concentration at walls and vents to locate the source of the sobbing. The crying girl's voice seemed to be coming from everywhere.

After a week of this crying and looking around his apartment, Jake decided that he had to do something to help the girl.

For the next few weeks, he sat on the second step of the staircase leading up to his weatherworn three-story apartment building and acted like he was reading Stephen King's *Firestarter*. As a college kid on an academic scholarship with an out-of-state summer housing allowance, he had all the time in the world until classes started in six weeks. And, it seemed like a better idea than getting a job, so Jake decided he would wait and watch.

An attractive mother who maintained humble dress, with pre-teen twin girls in identical dresses passed by Jake several times while sitting on the left side of the stairs. They didn't look at him and walked away looking forward. Though there didn't appear to be signs of any abuse, he couldn't help but watch them as they moved in a tight group up the sidewalk like a family of ducks.

It was the same thing for several families that traveled from the building as pedestrians. He was a young dreamer finally out on his own and couldn't help being interested in the family units that moved in and out of the building as a group. They moved in packs or herds together as a family and he reflected often on how he and his family would do the same thing in his younger years. He remembered how he, his mother and brother would leave their house in the afternoon and walk off to the market in preparation of their father's return home in the evening.

One family unit that really caught his attention was a round grandmother in stretch-pants, who always wore a hip-length blouse in the lead of two teenage girlie-girls and their skater-punk brother in his pre-teens. Whether they were exiting or coming back up the stairs, he had to smile at them either way. Jake looked over his book at this family while pretending to read. The boy caught his eye and lifted his hand giving him a sneaky two-fingered Satan sign.

Little did Jake know, but he was exercising his maturing ability to psychically "feel" people. However, they also were unconsciously aware of him prying into their minds and private lives. A few years later, Jake would have known the mental impulses behind the young rebel's salute, but he hadn't found his key to the art of mentally connecting to people and would have never suspected that the boy's openness was due to being warned to avoid the punk at the foot of the stairs and his Devil books. The boy hated going to church and his thoughts would have been clear and direct to Jake, *If you scare old Granny, you are all right with me.*

A FEW WEEKS LATER when the summer sun was blazing like the beam of a boy's magnifying glass and had the natives hiding in their holes like smart little ants, dripping sweat and without distraction, Jake sat on the steps of the building caught up in reading the story that Stephen King had crafted in the decade before.

The building manager was a short, overweight man in his fifties with thick slicked-back hair, wearing a short-sleeve collar over a T-shirt and jeans. He walked with a stout uniformed officer with a dark crew cut. They crossed the street and approached the steps of the building. With unknown purpose, they directed their attention toward Jake.

Instinct told him of the approaching men and Jake looked up from his book with perfect timing. The bioelectric fields that danced around the men were like wild static electricity. Thinking that his eyes were playing a trick on him, Jake blinked and squinted his lids.

Both men narrowed their eyes in response to what appeared to them as a challenge, he could smell their courage as they closed the distance to him.

The manager was first to speak and said, "Hey, kid, I was concerned that you was a predator or something, so I asked my brother, Dave, to stop by." He paused to describe the most obvious thing in the neighborhood, "He's a cop."

The manager stepped onto the sidewalk into the forward position to say, "So what's your problem, kid? Every other day, I find you sitting out here acting like you're reading."

"Is there a problem with that," Jake asked.

"There wasn't for a couple of weeks," the manager said with some hesitation. "Look, kid, every mother that has a child over three has been in my office this week."

"They don't like me reading?"

"They don't like you lookin'. Please hand Dave your book with your eyes closed."

With a touch of surprise, Jake said, "With my eyes closed?"

Dave stepped up and snatched the book from Jake's hands. He said, "Gimme the book, shitbird."

"Okay, kid, you've been reading the same book for the past month," said the manager. "D'you know the title of the book you are acting like you are reading?"

Jake sat looking at his empty hands and then toward the men. It might have been a good question, but this was the only novel he owned at the time. Having stolen it from his high school's library, Jake said with confidence that it was his favorite book, *Firestarter*.

Manager said, "Right. And, you don't think it's a little weird that you stare at children while you sit outside all day holding a book like this." He pointed at the book, which Dave was flipping through as if looking for clues.

Dave snapped the book closed and held it up asking if Jake was a molester or a pyro?

Before he could answer and without meaning to, Jake remembered why he was there and with surprising strength, the memory of the girl's cries pummeled into his belly like a boxer's ungloved fist. There was a little girl out there that no one else was going to help and he started to break down. "Neither," he gasped out.

Jake stood up and snatched the book from Dave. His feelings for the girl hit him hard again and tears welled up to overflow his fighting eyes as the truth fueled the lie that came out.

"My dad died last month and I'm not handling it well," Jake said. "This was his favorite book. Pardon me for looking at families. I'll st-stop—" Choking on the words, Jake turned to walk away into the building.

In shock, the manager said that this didn't go as he planned and looked at his brother with pity for Jake. Dave shrugged with what could have been sympathy. Regardless, Jake had disarmed the situation by unconsciously playing on their family's loss and the men's hostility was gone.

The manager called after Jake as he reached the top of the stairs and said, "Geez, kid, I'm sorry. Our dad just died, too. I didn't mean to…hey, look, my door's always open, so come talk to me if you need an ear. I'm sorry."

"I," Jake stammered. He waved over his shoulder and said as he entered the door, "It's okay. I just flipped out." He entered the building thinking about his lie and the little girl who would wake him tomorrow morning.

The brothers shook their misled heads and grabbed each other's shoulder deciding to walk back in the direction of the bar that they had come from in the beginning.

Later that day, Jake sat in his apartment reading *Firestarter*. As he reached the end, Jake finally closed the book and began to cry in spurts.

The next day after Jake had finished the novel, he cried off and on because there was a little girl knocking at an unknown door and he couldn't find it. He was consumed and just wanted to hold her and tell her, 'It's okay. It's okay now, I found you…'

Jake moped through his apartment and sat hard dropping onto the couch. For days, the phone rang several times, but Jake didn't move from the couch to answer it. He just stared at the television, which wasn't on. He sat waiting for the sun to fall and come up to chase him once again.

When a couple of days had numbed him to the book he had finally finished reading. Jake walked down the hallway toward the twin's mother from the front steps. As they passed, she smiled with sympathetic pity and concern. Jake smiled back as he moved to his mailbox and accidentally heard her thoughts. Her head rang with scattered thoughts that came to Jake with chiming resonance that focused in his mind to say, *Poor guy…I heart daddy. Daddy hearts Patti.*

Patti continued down the hall walking away from Jake. He opened his mailbox slowly while making a face that was full with a feeling of guilt and shame. He looked after Patti down the hall and closed his mailbox door. Jake said, "Thanks, Patti. I appreciate your kind concern."

"Our prayers are with you, Mr. St. Johns," she said from the stairway beyond Jake's view. "Sorry about your daddy."

On his way back to his apartment, another neighbor woman that Jake had passed in the hall gave him a sad and shy smile, *Dad. Dead. Sad.*

Jake forced out a smile and friendly nod as he turned to enter his apartment. He opened the door and entered. Jake quickly closed the door behind him and began laughing. It was muted crazy laughter.

Every woman he passed in the hall, even the round grandmother of the Satan-sign skater kid, offered him a head full of weird poems and sad smiles about his dead dad. His dad was hardly dead and living quite well in Denver.

The next morning, after the girl had stopped crying, Jake heard something outside his door and moved toward it. When he opened it there was a fruit-basket sitting outside, but no one was to be seen at either end of the hallway.

Living with his 'dad lie' had given Jake a heart full of regret. He couldn't stand how everyone cared so much about their Dads and he started to miss his own father more than his sanity.

The next day, Jake arrived home from class registration and found two greeting cards from his neighbors wedged between the door and frame of his apartment. The cards said that these neighbors cared and were praying for him.

He was happy to be moving into the dorms next week. He had to get away from what he had decided was a haunted apartment building.

When he moved to the dorms, the crying started again. Jake was about to lose his mind and give up on college. That Christmas, Jake came back home to Denver to eat breakfast with his Dad and he almost didn't go back to ASU.

AFTER THE FIRST YEAR, Jake was allowed to move off campus and he leased an apartment in Chandler, Arizona in the Silk Stocking neighborhood. He thanked God that his bunkmate, Carl, had helped him move. It had been more than a fair trade of labor, Carl had been accepted into a frat house closer to campus in Tempe and Jake was happy to help him. The best part was Carl had some upper-classmen friends who were happy to buy them some beers and vodka.

Carl left after a few beers and Jake's stuff was all moved into his new apartment. While unboxing his things, he found his copy of *Firestarter*. Memories of his early college experience came back to haunt him and Jake polished off what was left of the liquor. Jake was pretty drunk when he fell asleep on the second-hand couch he had bought with the TV. The TV hummed with the loud F-sharp tone of the Channel-15 test pattern.

A few days after he'd moved, the crying started again. A child cried out and Jake snapped awake in a new bedroom that was once again cluttered with garbage sacks and boxes.

The little girl cried out, "Daddy...!"

He jumped out of bed.

What was there to do?

Left with no untapped option that would get rid of this ghostly child, he did exactly the same thing that men have been doing since the dawn of reason: When one has exhausted every clear course of logical action, we deny there was ever a problem and avoid it.

8

Tammy and Jake sat in the booth with empty glasses, the ice-cream bowl was empty in front of Jake. "I have been running from her ever since," Jake said. He licked the spoon, tossed it clanging into the bowl and continued, "Now, I don't jog so much. I just leave and see every other friggin' ghost. As the only expert in my field to consult, it drives me nuts that she still cries every morning and will not just come to me. It's like she's waiting for something. Or someone. I don't know.

"But, there's no point in trying to find her because she knows where I am and has followed me six times and through two states this decade. Instead of looking for her, I choose to be annoyed and leave every morning. Mostly just to eat breakfast before I go to the art school."

When Jake shifted out of his storytelling mind frame he saw that Tammy was looking at him in a whole new way. He could feel the weight of her concern and affection for him. Her empathy toward him overwhelmed his senses and his eyes welled up with years of bottled up defeats and he looked away to blink back the tears.

Why hadn't I told this to Michelle?, Jake thought. *If this stranger cares, wouldn't she have understood? No, this is what strangers do and lovers avoid.*

Smoke a friend, said a voice in his head.

Seeing that Jake had disappeared into himself, Tammy asked if he was okay in the most sincere way and focused her eyes on him. He felt a flare of warmth between them and sniffled with shame, avoiding her eyes.

Jake said he was fine and sniffled, "Maybe we should talk about something else."

"Whatever you need to say," Tammy said. "I'm right here, right now. You look like you still need to talk about it."

Jake wiped his nose. "Tammy, you're going to think I'm crazy. Hell, I think I'm crazy. But—"

Tammy interrupted, "You're not crazy. Has anyone else heard her crying?"

"Look at me. I don't ever do this," Jake said pointing at his weepy eyes to sell his next lie.

"Well, maybe you should. Has anyone else heard her?"

"I've had a couple of girls over when the crying started. But, no one else has heard her."

Just Michelle.

Tammy reached out to Jake and took his hand. "I don't know if this will help. It might even sound stupid, but hear me out. I was watching this show on the Discovery Channel and they were investigating haunted houses."

Jake said, "I don't have a haunted house. I have a gho—"

"I listened, now you listen," she said. "So, they interviewed one couple that had named and basically adopted their ghost."

"Named it. Like a pet?"

"Sure," Tammy replied ignoring Jake's sarcastic tone. "Think about it in whatever way you want."

Jake gave up on the conversation and decided that Tammy was jerking his chain. "You're joking," Jake said. "I get it. Ha-ha. You almost had me picking names for my neurosis. You are as bad as the Satanists. Name your spirit guide and cope with your demons. How come no one ever tells you that vodka stops the voices? And cigarettes... Sorry, you were saying? Something about naming my ghost."

Tammy said, "I am not making light of this or teasing you. If I didn't feel... Believe... Whatever." She became very serious, "Jake, if you really have the crying ghost of a little girl following you, you should name it."

Jake said, "Her."

"Right," she smiled. "Her. Name her."

Jake smirked as he said, "Just asking, but, should I use a dog or cat name?"

"No, goddamn it," she said. "You should name her Sally or Jenny. Christ, I might be taking this more seriously than you are. I mean, why's this little girl following you?"

"Maybe Betty's just lost and wants someone to care for her," Jake said.

Tammy said, "No, you can't call her Betty." She pulled up her sleeves to rub her arms. "You need to stop now. Betty was my Grandma's name and you just gave me super goose-bumps. I am sorry I asked now. Don't tell me how it turns out."

The liquor and sugar was affecting her, making her loose and animated. "So, are you really psychic or just trying to scare me," she asked.

Feeling free for the moment, Jake smiled broadly and reached for his bags while saying, "Yep. And, you're ready to go, but not in a bad way. May I walk you home?"

Tammy said, "Very funny. How do you know I didn't drive?"

Jake held his ground and said, "May I walk you home?"

Tammy leveled an odd look at Jake. She nodded with a smile while taking her purse in hand and said, "You may walk me."

They stood up and walked together to the cashier desk.

Tammy continued, "However, if I am going to sleep tonight, we're going to talk about something else, okay? Ever travel?"

Jake handed a single hundred-dollar bill under the order ticket to a round and short Latina cashier in her fifties that was wearing a flared blouse and skirt. He said without looking back to Tammy, "Not really. I traveled some with my parents when I was a kid. Does going to college in Arizona for three years, Disneyland, and the Grand Canyon count?"

The cashier saw the hundred-dollar bill as Jake winked at her with a nod. When Jake told her to keep the change in Spanish, she smiled and nodded her thanks.

In response to the cashier's bow, Tammy looked at Jake oddly as they moved toward the exit.

"Disneyland wouldn't count," said Tammy. "You need to stay in question mode cuz it's my turn to talk about the world, Chatty Jake." She paused for a moment before asking, "So, how much did you tip her?"

Jake ignored her question and opened the door for her. "Where did you go when you first traveled out of the country," he asked.

Tammy smiled as she said, "I went to Europe. France, Italy and Spain. I was in high school and it was so awesome."

Tammy exited as Jake followed her voice out the door into warm daylight.

THE WALK WAS LIVELY and the early-spring day lifted their spirits and conversational intensity. Tammy asked questions like, 'You know what I mean?', 'Can you believe that?' and 'Are you sure you set your watch ahead from daylight savings?' Jake asked his own novel questions and laughed with her at his own punch lines.

Michelle had disappeared from his thoughts as the sunlight, tequila, and Tammy melted the cold loneliness of his long winter. Nevertheless, he was thoughtful of encountering Frank on the street and gritted his front teeth on an imaginary cigarette in bitter anticipation.

There had been the typical silence of all good conversations when Tammy out of the blue asked when Jake had his last cigarette. She told him that she wouldn't judge him and it was fine if he smoked.

Jake was taken aback. "I haven't had a cigarette for three days," he said. "How did you know?"

"Easy. One minute you are fine, the next you are on edge," she said. "When you get passionate about a point, you use two fingers to make it. When you drift into thought, you lift an invisible cigarette and hold it up to pause the convers—"

"Okay, I get it," Jake interrupted raising two clinched fingers. "I didn't give your visual gifts enough credit."

"Visual? You also inhale in sharp gasps and tend to exhale into the air before starting sentences."

"Really?"

"Yes. There is this whole smoker control thing that you all seem to have. Your smoker thing is this 'power over others' mechanism that begins from your point of personal weakness. Smokers all act like they have something to say and project it from some moral high groun—"

"Okay! I get it," he said, interrupting again. It was the same thing he had said about ghosts telling their moral stories and wondered if the ghosts were some neurotic and unconscious cry for help from his psyche. Jake raised his free hand to plea from mercy and said, "Have I told you that I quit smoking a few days ago?"

Tammy chuckled and said, "That is exactly what I mean. If you face the problem, it draws you back in or you get mad. Smokers prefer being angry."

Tammy's talking about smoking fueled his ego and Jake was consumed with the self-willed desire to smoke if he goddamned well pleased. The wrestling in his mind drew to a climax and Jake rose above his internal rules of 'to smoke or not to smoke.'

In his recovered state of self-awareness, Jake took the reins of both the feuding ego and id from the seat at the bench of his super-ego. He consciously willed the tobacco's self-generating impulses from his emotional mind-space and into his eyes where the cravings were cut off from internal energy resources.

Jake inhaled his personal freedom deeply and the world's ever-present free electrons rushed into his body to replace themselves in the gaps left in Jake's neural conductors.

If Jake had his way, biophysics and psychotechnics would be the big industry for the next two decades. He hadn't figured out a way to patent his techniques, but when he did, it will be trumpeted as 'psychovoltaics.'

Having to explain to the general public, 'photovoltaics,' and how the sun's infrared radiation knocks loose the extra electrons built into a man-made silicon crystalline structure, he knew he would have a long way to go in explaining to the general public how the mind can consciously loosen the atomic bonds that held the extra bio-electrons we attract and then transmit them through our body's bio-electric nervous system into the mind's psychic transistors.

Tammy asked if Jake was listening. He smiled and said that he was not. "Let me guess," Jake said. "You were telling me about the techniques used to stop smoking."

"I was."

"Drink water, put it off and procrastinate about your smoking urges. Stay determined knowing the urges to smoke will pass," Jake said counting on his fingers.

"You were listening," she said with a smirk.

Jake smiled, "Well, I suppose, if you could fly then you could come up with clever little techniques to help everyone gravity-bound in their struggle to quit that, too, eh?"

Tammy looked at him with an insulted look that made Jake laugh at his own joke, she didn't laugh. He shrugged and said with a whine, "What? Are you having some struggles with flying, Tammy? I know I am, but believe me, it's nothing compared to not smoking."

And with that they dropped the subject of cigarettes.

After a few silent steps, Jake broached the question of Tammy's current relationship status and she said she was single. She responded asking the same and he found himself eager to say that he had been single since late-January. Maybe there was something in the smoker pamphlets that was worth considering: To stop an old habit, one should find a new habit to replace it.

He fought back a strong urge to peek into her head and read her mind for secrets. He gritted his teeth and spoke through a clinched jaw, "My ex-girlfriend was named Michelle and we broke up after about eight months just before Valentine's Day."

"Sorry," Tammy said. "Holidays are overrated and create unrealistic hopes. Be glad she didn't wait to break-up until after receiving your love offering. Did you know Valentine's and Easter were originally the feasts that began and ended the Spring Rites? May Day was for those that didn't conceive in the spring to offer indulgence and their first blood offerings."

Jake didn't know if that was true, but he really liked what he heard and said, "I am trying so hard not to reach into you and read your mind."

Stopping, Tammy closed her eyes and flooded her voice with cuteness as she said, "Go ahead and try, if you can. Once you get in, I will feed you disconnected random thoughts and change my mind to leave you stranded."

"Nice technique," Jake said. "I like it, but it is like your smoker jive."

"Oh," she said. "How so?"

"Once you'd changed your mind, it would send impulses through neural pathways and leave a blazing chemical trail that would lead me in so deep, you would think my thoughts were your own. Well, unless your mental development was challenged." He turned to her with a big smile and said, "Don't worry, though, my urges have passed."

Her face revealed that she was really thinking hard about it and surprised at how he turned the tables on her.

Jake could see her mental actions work across her face and said, "So, are you going to invite me up for a drink? Or are you going to send me home dry?"

Knowing her apartment was within smelling distance and that his double-entendre was clever enough to get an internal reaction from her, he enjoyed watching Tammy's gears turn without knowing what she was thinking. Not knowing was as enjoyable as actually lifting open her skull and peering inside to see all the naughty gears grinding against the sensible ones. Jake could tell that the close interaction and alcohol had lubed up her naughty gears.

Tammy disliked being at a disadvantage with him, so she returned Jake's back-handed volley and said, "If you can lead us up to the door, then how can I resist the company of our generation's greatest stalker?" She pulled a set of keys and jingled them as if to mock him.

He enjoyed her challenge to a game of Blind Man's Bluff and asked for her hand. She offered it, but snatched it back again; she asked if he was going to try to shake her hand or just take the keys.

When Jake took the keys and her hand, he quipped not to tempt him to shake her again.

He felt a strong tingle of misdirection, but as he had warned her, the misdirection led him straight to the scent that he had sought. With her true scent locked in his mind, he smelled her hand for show and kissed the back of it.

He released her, she smiled and nodded him on.

"Okay," Jake said with the air of a magician. "I will need complete silence for a moment while I go into a trance to channel my spirit guide. I ask you to please be still." He closed his eyes and lifted his arms with his palms up. Holding the pose for a moment, he then touched his thumb to his middle finger, and brought his index finger to his nose while he smelled the air.

Turning his eyes, Jake opened them to look at the entry of an apartment building—

Frank was standing there and clapping his hands.

"Bravo," Frank exclaimed. "Encore-encore… FREEBIRD!"

Jake's face said everything that was needed to express his dislike for Frank offering his unsolicited assistance.

"What?!," Frank said jerking a thumb. "It's right here in three-o-nine. Pray to Christ you never have to help her move. Fuck! Only girls live on the third floor in this shithole town."

"I'd already found it," Jake said. "Why don't you beat it, Frank?"

"Don't worry about me, dude," Frank said. "I won't be here any longer than I have to, *your Humanness*. I just needed to make sure you found this place." Frank acted drunk and mocked Jake as he drank from an imaginary glass. "Tsst-tsst, you've been drinking. Drinking impairs your judgment, doesn't it?"

"I'd already found it," Jake grunted. "So, go."

"Look, jackass, you're the one who needed to channel your spirit guide," Frank said. "Don't get creative in there and forget what I just said. It's apartment three-o-nine and you need to go up there."

To Tammy, Jake said, "Are you sure you heard me talking to someone up the street before we met?"

Through a smirk, Tammy said, "Someone told you your fly was down."

Jake nodded and slouched to open the foyer door for her.

"So what happened to your Vegas flair?," she said snapping her fingers like an Aristocrat.

Jake rolled his eyes over his shoulder at her as she entered the building. "In the future if you want my Vegas flair, remind me not to channel my spirit guide."

He stuck her key into the security door and opened it.

"First try. Very good," Tammy said. "So, is that who you were talking to before we met?"

"Yes. I was just talking to him, again."

"Really? I didn't hear anything this time," Tammy said walking through the opened door. "Did he tell you that you have something in your teeth?"

Jake was on to her and said, "I don't have anything in my teeth. Nice try, though." The door slammed behind him as he followed her into the hallway.

Tammy asked as she turned to him, "So what did he tell you?"

Jake moved past her to take the lead and said, "He told me that you don't have an elevator and that I should pray to Christ that I don't have to help you move."

He walked to the stairs and led Tammy up to the third floor.

You might think this chance encounter was all some cheesy romance novel setup for a lust-driven fantasy leading up to an undeniable passion that burned in the young couple until there was a shirt-ripping, seam-tearing, and button-popping meeting of sweat-drenched bodies slamming into each other until the sub-atomic fabric of reality strained and burst open like the clothes they had worn.

But, you would be wrong.

It would be a lie to say that very long run-on sentence didn't go through Jake's mind as he climbed the stairs to Apartment 309, but it was very close to his thoughts.

Tammy held up and asked Jake how many keys it would take without his spirit guide. She wondered aloud if his spirit guide was an animal.

Jake stopped at 309 and set down his bags at her apartment door. Sighing as he stood, Jake said, "My spirit animal is this tall skinny weasel that has spikes growing out of his head." His description of Frank rolled off his tongue, but it sounded like a terrible phallic symbol to Tammy.

Jake rubbed the keys in his hands and touched the deadbolt. Within him, there was the spark of connection and a light feeling of home when he set his fingers on a key in the ring. Jake held them up and looked at the keys, he saw there were three house keys on the ring.

He looked at her with a question mark over his head pondering on how many different house keys she needed.

Tammy interrupted his thought and said, "Don't think about it too long or you'll talk yourself into a different key."

"Come on. It's the shiny one with the imprinted feelings of failure, dummy," Frank said from behind Jake. "Dazzle her. I already unlocked it."

Jake said nothing to either of the people mocking him and reached over to the door. Under his grip, the knob turned and the door creaked inward.

He handed the keys back to a shocked Tammy and said, "Keys? We don't need no stinkin' keys."

"How'd you do that?" Tammy stepped passed Jake and looked at the lock. "Really. How did you do that?"

"If I told you, it wouldn't be—" Jake said before Frank bumped into him and entered the door stepping over the book bags.

"Magic?," Tammy said. "I thought you were psychic."

"Read all the books and talk to enough people, you'll still be asking the same question. Magic/science, alchemy/chemistry, shaman/psychic; both sides of the coin. May I come in?"

Tammy laughed. "So, what are you a vampire/lawyer now?"

"No. Just being polite," Jake said as he picked up his bags and came into the apartment.

From inside the apartment, Frank said, "Ask her for sex instead of a drink. You are neither psychic, magic, nor polite when you drink."

Jake closed the door and locked it behind him. "Tammy, will you offer me a drink? A tall one."

"Sure, Dracula, I always wanted to live forever," Tammy said as she lifted her head to expose her soft, long neck. "Drink."

Jake almost kissed it as she stood so close and vulnerable, but instead touched her arm and said, "Blood's too salty. How about some wine?"

She looked at him with a smile, "Do you like merlot?"

"I do."

Tammy's smile broadened and she turned away toward a kitchen saying, "Me, too. I'll open a bottle." Leaving him alone, she called from the kitchen, "You aren't a wine snob, are you?"

"Nope," Jake said. "But, if you are, do you have anything else to drink while you let the wine breathe?"

Tammy projected her voice over the clanking of cabinet doors and said, "I don't need to let it breathe, but I do have Maker's Mark, Smirnoff Citrus... Want a beer?"

"Open your wine and surprise me with a double of whatever's clever."

While Tammy attended to drinks, Jake went to snooping around her front room. He of course went to her bookshelf first. Jake scanned the titles and scoffed a bit before finding a copy of *Firestarter*.

He called out to Tammy, "Have you read *Firestarter*?"

"I haven't," she called back.

"You should, it is the only book you have worth reading."

Tammy projected, "I have read half of those. Look on the third shelf for *Perfume*. That's a crazy book. I read it in German and they've made it into a movie."

Half listening, Jake moved around the room surveying her knick-knacks. He picked up a hand-sized statue of Ganesha, the Hindu elephant god of success. He closed his eyes. There were no psychic impressions from Tammy on it and he felt no emotional connection. How did someone have a statue like this and not look at it long enough to attach some kind of thoughts to it?

"What did you expect?," Frank said over his shoulder.

Jake ignored Frank and set the statue back down. He moved to a nearby incense tray and picked up the incense package to smell it. He sniffed recognizing it as dragon's blood and turned to Frank, smiling. "If I had a lighter, Frank, I'd light one of these up to send you on your way."

He turned his head and called out to Tammy, "May I light some incense?" He waved the incense sticks at Frank as he spoke.

"Ah, fuck you, Jake. I've seen enough and you have, too. This place is full of deceptions and you have other things to do. Burn that novelty incense, dummy," Frank said. "If you were smart, you'd bone her drunk ass, peep in her head, and leave her wanting more."

Ignoring him, Jake removed a stick of incense and placed it into its holder. When he turned back, Frank was gone, but Tammy was standing behind him offering two beers.

"This winery uses plastic corks in their bottles, so I better let it breathe. You like dragon's blood," she asked.

"It is good for love and banishment," Jake said. "What do you use it for?"

"I use it to cover up my weed," she said holding out the bottles. "You said to make it a double."

Jake smiled in spite of the rushing memories of Michelle and he looked into Tammy's eyes deeply as he took one of the offered bottles of Fat Tire. She smiled and looked away to the stereo.

"Want to listen to some music," Tammy asked as she glided on socks to an old-fashioned stereo component cabinet. Before he could offer a suggestion, she clicked on the radio, which was tuned to a Boulder station that played album rock. A song from Paul Simon's Graceland vibrated the air warmly with the rich harmony of a South African choral troupe. It reminded him of grading papers as a teacher's aide in high school.

TIME PASSED AND MUSIC played as they drank their beers and another two glasses of wine. Jake noted the warm, syrupy effect that the wine was having on her.

They exchanged their old stories to new ears with voices that ranged from secretive whispers to excited shouts. Everything was lovely until Tammy asked him about college. Jake was just drunk enough to become overly passionate, he told her he had hated college and dropped out.

He said, "College is bullshit and really only about unified specialized conformity to avoid responsible mentorship. The humanities, my ass! Jocks are taught to make money and exploit, while the geeks are made to be so specialized in a microscopic field that they have no relative value to society."

Tammy said she agreed in an effort to calm him, but then asked why he didn't finish and just do what they expected.

Jake's silence was his answer and it stood. This had become a replay of every bad night he had spent with Michelle. *Who cared about a place where they tell you what to read and teach you how to think?*

He set down his glass and said, "This has been a blast, Tammy. So, I apologize, but I have been here too long and I need to get home to my book orders."

Tammy showed her confusion and stood, "I thought we were having a good time. I'm sorry if I said—"

"Stop. It isn't you, it's..." Jake paused in an effort to shut his stupid mouth, but said it anyhow. "It's me."

He reached behind him and removed his wallet. "Look, you can call if you want," he said removing a business card. "Your best bet is leaving a message with my secretary. I'm sorry, but I have to go."

He stuck out the card. She took it with a confused look.

Putting on his coat, Jake turned to the door and grabbed his books in one hand, "Thanks for the wine. This was fun and I'd love to do it again, when we aren't talking about college. Sorry, I really do have an assload of work to do tonight that college didn't teach me how to manage."

Tammy followed and said, "I don't want this to end on a bad note and I'll give you a call. Do you want my number?"

"It doesn't have to be on a bad note, but it needs to end for now," Jake said. "Call and leave your number."

"Okay," Tammy looked at the card and said, "I'll call and I am sorry if I said—"

Jake forced a smile and said, "Really, don't be. I had a great time and just need to go."

He stopped forcing the smile, "If I taught you anything today, it was to chain your door. Thanks again."

Jake was gone from her door and into the hallway.

Tammy closed the door and locked it. She then paused before securing the door with its chain lock. Abruptly left in a world of solitude, she looked at the card and asked herself what the hell just happened. *What the hell had happened to her today?!*

9

Boiling with angst, Jake exited Tammy's building and hit the concrete remembering how he started smoking with the lesbian demons. As his psychic talents developed, he turned to drinking and partying with anyone who would have him. The more shitty they got on booze, the less he found himself reading their minds and being concerned about the little girl crying.

He remembered exactly how he decided to drop out of college, he found less and less to support him in his immediate problem of finding the ghost. Sure, he could have bucked up for another year and just done what was required to get by. However, what the fuck was he really getting by?

The problem with the collegiate systems for a young man maturing into a psychic freak was that it started off with the same fucking basics that he had just spent the prior four years hating. Why don't all colleges start with electives that give you something enriching to create a drive that leads to self-education? If students were developed to have a true sense of self in something that they sought to explore, they would be driven to go and claim what they needed to get where they wanted to go.

How can one identify the stumbling blocks between them and their goals if they have no goddamned tangible goals? How does anyone live to survive another course of shitwork that they can't see applying to anything that fires their undiscovered passions?

Jake went into a liquor store on the way home and bought a half pint of vodka. He hit the sidewalk gulping at the bottle before noticing it was dark. The fire in his throat fueled the anger in his heart. He was eight steps away from the liquor store when cigarettes crossed his mind, he fought the undesirable inclination by feeding his internal flames.

He took another big drink of vodka and fumed inside himself saying that when it all came down to it, the only thing most major colleges taught in the first two years was drowning youthful passions in booze and preparing students to cope with the bullshit they would be fed for the rest of their lives. Why not, everything still worked like it had done for the thousand years prior. Come on, really, what were they teaching at Oxford nine hundred years ago? It's teaching the same flat world status quo crap now.

In college, when you completed a task, you learned to celebrate with liquor.

Failed in an endeavor? Find comfort for your ego with your good friend, Booze.

Get a shitty middle-class job and commit suicide by dumping your soul into a career that gives back nothing in the end.

DRINK! And Jake did.

In his raging mind, our college system did nothing more than create expensive crack-whore consumers, who pimped themselves out to the highest middle-income job for a withered carrot dangling at the end of a stick as the Illuminati drove the masses into the ground for billions of dollars. The educated middle class piled up debt into the hundreds of thousands thinking that they were superior to poorer peers as the ruling elite laughed at and encouraged the strife against their brothers and sisters.

When someone wise asked the question, 'Why I am I doing this and who is profiting?' The answer was the most ridiculous rebuke, 'It's the market, dummy…get in line and punch the clock, wage-slave.'

Fuck that, Jake thought. *Punch yourself for being a dummy!*

Jake stumbled from a curb and crossed the street as he finished his bottle. When he was done, rather than littering, he stuck the empty bottle into his hip pocket.

Jake turned up his street and resolved that he would never fuck over anyone poor. If the rich fuckers wanted fresh meat, he would give them their own. But to feed the rich their own, he would have to be richer with an army of middle-class workers tired of being goddamned slaves to an inhuman system. He needed an army of people who wanted to live life by following their passions.

It was time to raise an army of people to take lives, so they could give life to a new humanity. When two percent of the world has taken ninety percent of its wealth, it was time to feed the rich their own children. Just like the snake eating its own tail, let the rich feed on their young and themselves rather than the masses that propelled them to their slovenly indulgences.

Jake was a few steps from home when he seized up under a piss shiver. Completely drunk now, he staggered backward from his gate. Instead of searching for his keys to get into his estate, he set his book bags down behind him and reached for his fly.

Out of spite toward himself, Jake pissed all over his front walk. He knew he was no different than everyone that he hated.

10

At the top of Jake's block, there was a black sedan parked with an unblocked view of Jake pissing on the gate of his house.

The two G-men were watching for activity at Jake's house through the windshield.

Charlie, in the passenger seat, lifted a camera pointing it toward Jake's front gate.

Through the lens of a night-vision camera, there was the snap-snap-snap of an auto-advancing shutter capturing close-up photos of Jake swinging his hips back and forth as he finished pissing on his own entryway.

Jake had moved through his gate into his yard. Snap-snap-snap!

He struggled with his keys on the doorstep before he entered the dark house. Snap-snap-snap!

Charlie said without lowering the camera, "I guess our guy has some other friends. We should have stuck with him today."

Joe sat watching and showed his irritation. "Ease up. So, he meets with a contact we don't know about yet. Good, that's a lead."

Charlie stopped taking pictures and looked at Joe, who shrugged his shoulders at the enquiring look from his partner. "Welcome to criminal investigations, Charlie. If it was an exact science, they wouldn't need us humans."

BACKLIT BY THE YELLOW sodium of his streetlight, Jake opened his front door and stood swaggering at the threshold. After a good struggle with returning the keys into his pants pocket, Jake picked up both bags in one hand and entered his dark house. He dropped the bags inside and closed the door behind him.

Click went the deadbolt.

It was black for a moment before Jake turned on the overhead track lighting racks.

The hard wood floor reflected a warm light into the room. The large front room was empty of basic furniture essentials and served as a stately book warehouse. Two towering double-sided bookshelves were set side-by-side on top of a billiards table. Books were stacked on the top of that same table. Most of the books were the same edition and organized together.

Jake took off his shoes at the door.

Near the billiard table was a large ornate carved marble mantel with twin Atlas figures on each side holding up the mantle over a fireplace that looked like it hadn't been used in years (with more books on top of the mantel). The windowless wall space of Jake's front room consisted of beautiful matching bookshelves that were filled with books. The track lights were pointed at each bookcase around the pool table's towers.

Jake picked up his bags and switched hands as he removed his coat, moving across the front room of his book-filled mansion.

Opposite of the front door were two elaborately carved wood-railed staircases that led up to more bookcases, the bookshelves were original and built into the walls of the stairwells during the construction of the century-old house.

On the wall between the twin staircase libraries, with its own track light beaming on it, hung a large cross with a dying Jesus in his final ecstasy. Jake crossed himself and bowed his head to the unusually bloody effigy before hanging his coat on the head of one of the wooden lions guarding the staircases above from its perch on the banister of the stairs.

Jake patted the lion's head beneath his coat and stepped into the darkness of a hallway that he had always considered, The Path of the Servants. He turned off the front room lights as he walked into the hallway.

AFTER A QUICK VISIT to the kitchen, Jake entered his home office and flipped on the lights. The converted servant bedroom was decorated with overwhelming visual noise. The walls were covered with pages from Jake's sketchbooks, neon-colored band flyers and comic book hero posters.

A male devil/angel super-hero stood proudly in his cape, briefs and fancy boots with glowing eyes on a poster hung over a huge Apple theatre-screen monitor mounted on the wall above a white, round-edged, leather-top desk with a matching white rounded leather chair.

The furnishings on this side of the room were matte-finished gray and white alloy without sharp edges; both blinds on the two oblong, circle-topped wall-windows were white with matte-gray alloy handles and mountings.

Jake carried his book bags in one hand and in the other was a less than filled semi-opaque plastic cup half-full of purple Kool-Aid and ice. He set the bags on the stylish desk and sat into its matching chair.

He tapped the keyboard spacebar twice and grabbed his mouse, clicking it like the trigger of a semi-automatic pistol before the monitor flickered to life.

Even drunk, Jake knew the routine of his computer waking up, so he opened a refrigerator that was inset into the desk. He reached in and pulled out a big plastic bottle of vodka. Jake poured it into the Kool-Aid filled glass and set the bottle on the floor.

On the opposite wall of the computer desk was a worktable of unfinished wood that was full of raw sharp edges, postal equipment and supplies. There were also more books stacked under a corkboard having pieces of paper tacked onto it.

After a big gulp of the vodka-laced Kool-Aid, the computer fired up and executed several program windows. An Internet browser window opened and loaded a website, which touted itself as being *TheAnarchistBookstore(dot) com*. Jake's voice, amplified with bass and echo, came over speakers and declared, "Welcome to the new world order..."

This announcement was one of many random clips that his web guys had used to welcome users to his web site. He smiled that it was one of his personal recordings and clicked the mouse a few more times before being prompted for his password.

Jake spoke a command and the password, "HEY! Empathy."

The computer screen flickered in transition and ground out a hardware song.

A website loaded the book order window. He held up a two-fingered Satan sign and said, "HEY! Hail, Satan!"

The computer replied, "Hail Satan. Welcome back, sir."

Jake took a quick swig from the glass of Kool-Aid and shivered.

He smacked his lips and shivered again before picking up the bottle. Jake poured more vodka into his purple Kool-Aid.

He said, "HEY! How many new orders today?"

"Two-hundred and seventeen, sir," replied the computer.

He looked into his swirling drink and to his imaginary friend, he said, "Wow, that's a lot of orders." He was silent for a moment staring into his glass at the spinning liquid.

Maybe I should look into Thelema, again. They have great taste in books, Jake thought.

He swirled the cup again before taking a big swig of the jungle-juice. Jake gagged with shivers before taking another drink and setting the cup down.

He looked at the glass on the verge of nausea and said aloud, "Whoa! That's a proper tincture. HEY! Print new orders and call it a night."

The computer started the printer and said, "The orders are printing, sir. Will you request a song?"

Jake stopped in mid-action and lifted his glass in pride to the computer, "HEY! Thank you, Big Brother, for the People's Vodka, cuz I hate gin. Play Freddie, Miles. Cheers!"

The computer replied, "To the People's Vodka, sir. Cheers! Will you request a song?"

Jake returned the vodka-bottle into the desk's refrigerator listening to the printer buzz on its rod.

"I should call Michelle," he said. "She wouldn't believe this day. HEY! Play Watermelon Man, Hancock."

He then thought that maybe he should call Tammy, but remembered leaving her in a fit because she had started in on him about college like Michelle always did.

Jake sighed and thought, *What is it with girls and college?*

He took a sip from his cup in defeat and Herbie Hancock's *Watermelon Man* started to play.

Jake shook the alcohol around in his head and decided to read that book on quantum mechanics at the top of a pile next to his bed.

I will pass out without calling anyone in the warm embrace of another dimension, he thought.

MONDAY

1

Ding-ding! When the bell rang, Jake, gloved and wearing only trunks, danced out of a corner and around the ring moving toward a huge clown. Jake was springy, lithe, and ready for a battle. The clown stood like a tree waiting for him without fear.

* * *

A POLICE SQUAD CAR pulled up to a red-light district.

Mike the Cop, wearing his police uniform, stepped from the squad car and moved directly toward a young flashy pimp, who was heavy-handing a hooker in her late-teens.

Mike stood there for a moment watching the pimp like he was waiting for something. The pimp wasn't comfortable with his being watched nor was he impressed with Mike.

The pimp said, "Sorry, big guy. I already gave to the policeman's other ball. Whatever you want, I gave it to Patterson. Beat it or I'll have him sic the Judge on you."

Hearing everything he had needed to, Mike smiled and said, "Wrong answer." Mike attacked him with brutality.

* * *

JAKE DANCED AROUND THE ring as he punched the clown in the head and body, combo after combo, over and over again without visible effect. Jake couldn't hurt the clown and he got angry, his attacks becoming more intense and directly accurate.

* * *

MIKE ENTERED A DIRTY dive with a long bar that had tall stools and a scattering of tables in the coffin-like room. He moved down the bar past the trashy, but silent, female bartender toward an old grizzled drunk man sitting alone at the end of the bar and watching a TV. Mike stood there looking at the souse.

The guy noticed Mike and grunted, "What do you want, pig? This is Patterson's beat, so beat it."

Mike shook his head and said, "Wrong answer."

Mike grabbed the souse from his barstool and slammed him to the ground.

Mike shouted in his face, "Want to tell me about the Judge?" Mike pulled back his fist ready to strike.

The souse said, "Fuck you! If I talk, he'll kill me. You ain't sh—"

Mike rifled his fist into the guy.

* * *

NOW, JAKE HAD RESORTED to just punching wildly and the clown was now blocking, punch for punch, everything he threw like he could read his mind. Then...

The clown started his assault. The audience became faceless bloody children chanting—

"Kill! Kill! Kill!"

* * *

MIKE LOOKED AT THE male bartender in another bar, and said, "I am just sending a message and I won't be causing you any more trouble."

The bartender said, "You know how to make a message clear."

"If anyone hassles you, you tell him you were in the backroom and only heard shouting."

"I was in the backroom and we never had this conversation. Were you anyone I know?"

Mike slapped two hundred-dollar bills on the counter.

"Keep it. In fact, I owe you a drink," said the bartender. "That bastard kept other customers from coming in at night and would refill his beer every time I turned my back."

"Just doing my job, then," said Mike smiling. He held up three more hundred-dollar bills and said, "Call the police and tell them that the guy said something about Sarconi killing the boss and that someone named Patterson had set them up."

At that, the bartender took the five hundred dollars and said, "Sarconi, that guy on the news, was setup by Patterson?"

Mike nodded and said, "When they ask you about the guy, tell the truth. The drunk was working for Patterson. But, the guy who took him looked like one of the Smoldones."

The bartender's voice notably reflected his increasing stress-level as he repeated it all back to Mike. He had just walked into a very serious game of life and death for five hundred dollars. Pointing the finger at Patterson and the Smoldones was signing his own death warrant.

Mike felt the bartender's fear and reassured him that after tonight, there would be no one left alive to fear. "By the end of tomorrow, Patterson is going to be all over the news and the Smoldones'll disappear for greener pastures."

He bent to his right and lifted something from the floor with one hand. Mike left the bar dragging a bloodied man across the room to the door knowing the bartender wouldn't call the cops. Pausing with a sigh, he left the body he had dragged and returned to the bar with a revolver in his hand decided that the bartender would never call anyone again.

* * *

JAKE BEGAN TO TAKE an endless battering from the clown and was hit by a thunderous uppercut that lifted him off his feet. His body fell in slow motion and then sped up. Jake hit the mat with a BOOM!

In the darkness of early morning, Jake jerked awake in his bed to the sound of a crying little girl.

She wailed out, "Daddy..."

He checked his alarm clock, it was 4:38 and he lied back with a hangover groan. He closed his eyes knowing that any deep sleeping was over.

Jake sat up with a jolt that shook his bed. He was thinking hard as he listened for the sobbing cries.

"Daddy...!"

He leaned back on his extended arms to project his voice into the house. "Betty...! Come lie down and I'll tell you a story about another little girl! Patti loved her daddy, too."

The long cries of Daddy began wailing again.

Jake's voice dropped in volume as he leaned forward to drop his head over the middle of his mattress.

Irritated, he shouted again, "Come on, Betty. Come hear a story about Daddy."

The crying stopped.

Jake's body language showed his shock and he looked around. "That's right, Betty! Come 'ere, I am here to help you."

Jake waited for a silent breath. Then another longer moment passed. The seconds dragged on into what felt like years. Silence. She had stopped crying.

After years of chanting and conjuring beings with unspeakable names, he shook his head in disbelief at not considering the simple idea of naming his ghost to summon her.

Jake was waiting for the shrieking to begin again, but the house was eerily silent. He was almost thankful in the thought that talking to her could be useful for getting to sleep in.

Why hadn't I tried to talk to her like he was trying to calm a stray animal? Because talking aloud to imaginary friends means you are crazy, he thought smiling.

"Come here, Betty. You can get on the bed if you quit your whining," Jake grunted out as he laid his head back on his pillow. He clicked off his alarm and closed his eyes as a pattering of rain started falling on the roof.

The sound of raindrops increased in volume and took on a peaceful rhythm.

Down the long hallway and rising above the sound of the rain, Jake heard the fleshy patter of a child running barefoot toward his bedroom.

An arctic wind blew through his heart. Immediately, Jake recalled his forgotten primal fears of the unexpected. The surprise had shot a muscle-seizing electrical shock up through the small of Jake's back and into his eyes. His skin pulled tight into bumps and every hair of his body stood out on end.

Betty appeared in the doorway of Jake's bedroom as the cold fear condensed into tears that obscured his vision. He blinked and sent a tear down each cheek.

She had back-length blonde hair and bare feet under her long nightgown, the little girl who had been crying for years was now standing in Jake's bedroom doorway. He was frozen with inaction.

Betty tilted her head with a royal nod, "Please, do not summon me as if you were beckoning for your pet." Keeping with her manners, she curtsied with a tight-lipped smile and said, "Hello, Jake. I have been waiting for you to call me to you."

Jake could barely stammer out, "I'm. Sorry. I didn't—"

Betty beamed an angelic smile that revealed a mouthful of baby teeth and skipped into the bedroom, she maintained her curtsy grip on the nightdress hem skipping toward Jake.

"Why didn't you call me sooner," Betty asked as she sprang onto the bed leaping into Jake's frozen arms still extended in his gesture pleading his ignorance.

His arms closed around her and pulled Betty to him.

Jake started to speak, but only the sobs and tears of disbelief came out. He squeezed her and she was real. He couldn't believe it and began to cry with gulping breaths, wondering if he had finally lost it.

Betty said, "It's okay. Don't cry." She rested her head on Jake's shoulder while hugging his neck.

She patted and rubbed his shoulder as he wept before hugging him hard while saying, "It is okay now. I have found you... Shhh... It is okay, I found you and you are no longer alone."

Jake wept harder as Betty comforted him.

2

Jake walked at a brisk pace down a city street with his hands in his pockets. The morning had a chill that reminded Jake of his winter without Michelle, but that novel of romantic memories had ended and was greatly eclipsed by the present moment.

He had cried himself back to sleep in the security of Betty's arms and slept late. Betty was gone when he awoke. This left Jake in a most discomforting mental space; he had found Betty, slept late, and was now late for class. Currently, he didn't have the ability to really take hold of this new reality. He had not been late for work in years because of Betty's crying, but was her not being there really evidence of his finding her or had the drinking worked as a sedative. It had worked before.

However, the stress of being late or the doubt of really finding his ghost couldn't dim the overwhelming feeling that something had changed.

Had he really found his little ghost or was it another dream?

Had he really wept himself back to sleep to wake up on his own?

Had his little ghost stopped crying?

Was she gone…?

JAKE SHOWERED AND chewed endlessly on what had happened like it was a big bite of a Slim Jim. Mentally masticating on the unchewable skin of these events, Jake refused to just swallow it as he dressed for work.

Before he left the house that morning, Jake called into the school and requested that his administrative assistant meet his morning class. "Helen, please let them know I'm on my way, but I have to eat something and will be an hour late."

Helen told him that food could wait until after class and he should really attend to his duties. She relished in having the upper hand on Jake for once and reminded him of why he had hired her to handle things when he wasn't there. She was an old prim bitch and the students hated her, which made them all love Jake even more.

Jake knew he had been dealing cards to her position of weakness from a stacked deck for several years, so he smiled knowing she had been waiting patiently for his hangovers to create this moment. He let her words roll off of his back as she heavy-handed him with a moot lecture about promptness and his responsibilities.

"Helen, they are adults and studying with purpose. You have nothing to worry about. Please tell them that until I arrive, they should arrange themselves to pose for one another or render portraits of their classmates who are drawing their posing classmates."

Out of spite for her lecturing, he stressed the point that there should be no nude posing. She gasped and he could see her grasping at the high-collar of her blouse in his mind's eye.

"I will critique their drawings one-on-one when I get there and close class with a brief lecture. Just too sweeten the deal, Helen, tell them their pay for this class will be doubled from the salon's normal rate of compensation. And that I'll expect miracles worthy of gallery space in next month's line art show."

She had begun a reprisal of his being irresponsible in his business affairs when he hung up the phone.

HE WAS OUT THE front door having forgotten to shave and brush his teeth, but by unconscious effort had clicked the deadbolt.

Jake smiled and said to himself, "You slept in late, Jake!" He was ecstatic. This being late to school business was new compared to his not being awoken by a crying little girl who would bawl until he left. He wondered if a decade qualified as an era. To him, it felt as if an era had ended. It was a new day and he was free. What did this unknown day have in store for him? He had an interesting woman on the line, had found his little ghost, and was late for work! Christ, the world had been rolled from his shoulders and he felt like Atlas when Hercules took his burden from him. Freedom at last, sucker!

On his ten-minute walk to the school, he took a two-block detour to Tom's Diner where the morning rush had ended.

The visit was like a rerun from Season Two of The Sopranos. Jake ate a hearty breakfast of pancakes with two eggs on top while Papa Tom told him about a couple of thugs from across town who had disappeared last night and about a couple of cops nosing around for info on him.

Sid wasn't there, so Jake simply played his part and told Tom to have Sid call him later.

Tom became indignant warning Jake to stay away from Sid and ended the conversation. Jake groaned at Tom's insanity and looked around the room as he finished his coffee; Frank was nowhere to be found, but the old homeless black man with the CD player was sitting at the end of the bar with a few of the regulars. They exchanged a wave when Jake left his seat with the ticket.

Jake took the ticket to Doris at the register and over-tipped her. He told her to make sure Sid got the money and a message that said he needed to call Jake when he got in.

Tom was not in his right mind today and only Sid would be able to translate. It wasn't that Jake couldn't dig around in Papa Tom's head, but it was a mess in there and he didn't feel like traveling the neural pathways. Everything eventually led to Tony Soprano's heart attack.

Jake belched walking down the street to his class. He glowed with a golden light as he moved down the sidewalk and was unaware that he was floating about an inch above the ground.

His mind lurched his hand toward an empty pocket for his phantom pack of cigarettes and found two fifty-dollar bills. Jake shook off the urge to smoke looking at the money and focused on the feeling of his feet being firmly connected to the ground. He felt his weight return and auto-associated the gravity to Michelle. Jake shoved his hands into the coat's pockets as he recalled how she hated his books. He wished he could call and tell her that the books were selling like hotcakes. It was another successful self-righteous venture from the boy without a degree or a job. Not the mention the art salon that fed artwork into a successful gallery or the battered women's shelter or the environmental marketing agency. *Bitch. What did she know?*

Cigarette? No.

Jake lowered his shoulders and walked on. He would be in class in eight minutes. Just enough time for a cig—

No cigarettes.

Turning the last corner of the walk, he prayed that his students had followed his instruction to draw and had not decided to smoke at the building entrance instead.

Effing cigarettes.

Michelle.

Tammy?

I found Betty, so stop it. Nothing else matters.

Did you really find your ghost or just dream it?

Stop thinking!

Stop eating. Stop living. Stop shitting. Smoke!

STOP THINKING!

Jake grew nauseous and paused a step to punch himself in the head. "STOP IT!," he said.

When he opened his eyes, Frank was standing in front of him, smoking a cigarette. Frank puffed a cigarette and snatched it from his mouth as he exhaled smoke. He said, "You alright? It's not like you to be late. You look like you need a cigarette. Take mine."

"Go fuck yourself, Frank," Jake said.

"Go fuck yourself, Jake," Frank said. "Why are you late?"

Jake stepped through Frank and pulled himself together upon entering the courtyard of an old church called St. John's Cathedral. He thanked God that the students were in class because he didn't have the strength to not bum a real cigarette. Perfect bliss to total crap in seconds.

Frank called after him, "I'll be waiting for you after school. We need to talk."

"Feel free to call. Leave a message at the tone," Jake said before he snapped his middle finger over his shoulder to Frank. "BEEP."

Frank watched Jake through eyes that had become merely slits and he took a drag from his cigarette. "You have a friend who needs a favor," he said.

Jake didn't turn back nor slow his pace. Frank drew in a hot lungful of smoke and with supernatural precision flipped the butt past Jake's ear.

He felt the heat and smelled the smoke as the cigarette whizzed by him. The butt hit the doors in front of Jake and the cinder exploded into sparks. Frank said, "We need to talk about Betty."

Jake jerked his head around at the mention of Betty, but was too slow— Frank was gone.

His face displayed a growling frustration and he looked up the street. His mind was spinning and it pulled him in deep. Too much had happened this morning and he was drowning. His face twisted tighter and his sightless eyes squinted off into the distance. He shook his head and willed one foot forward after the other to enter the building.

3

In their sedan, Charlie and Joe had followed Jake from his house to the diner and were outside waiting while Jake ate his breakfast and talked with Tom.

Joe was first to break the silence when he said, "Good food in that place and that Tom guy seemed like a real character. I understand why this guy eats here every day. Good coffee, too."

"It was alright," Charlie said. "That Tom guy is crackers, Joe. He acted like he didn't even know his own son."

"Hey, if you had a kid like that would you admit it to a couple of cops?" Joe shrugged, "If families weren't a mess, we wouldn't need Dr. Phil."

"There you go interrupting again," Charlie said. "It was just weird. He didn't know anything about the books, the art school, the gallery, the non-profits, or the money that his son has, but he knew everything about the shady stuff that never makes the news."

"Cops are in there all the time," Joe said with a scoff. "Sure, locals all like telling their stories. Just like criminals. This Tom knows plenty about Jake and is probably laundering money for his kid. St. Johns makes too much money to not show heavy gains at the end of the year, yet he continues to show a loss of capital while growing his stock accounts through trades."

Charlie said in a sharp response, "Everyone is hiding something, eh?

"We are here to find the simple route to a conviction, everyone cheats on their taxes. The guy is not just cheating on his taxes and we just caught him. Charlie, you need to learn that it isn't what they say, it is what they don't say. Papa Tom said he doesn't know anything and hasn't seen anyone with Jake. He's lying."

"I don't know man," Charlie said. "I thought it was a mistake to even go in there."

"We just went in to investigate. Heck, if he had asked about it, I would have told him we were looking into a counterfeiting ring and asked him to tell people to watch out. I didn't know he was going to act like that when

I asked about his kids. When he didn't mention Jake, I thought it wouldn't hurt to show him a picture. Who knew he would flip out? Maybe, we got the wrong facts and Tom is innocent of being this scumbag's daddy."

"My facts are right," Charlie said. "It was weird and I didn't like it. That is how we blow our cover."

An unexpected hand reached over and clapped Charlie's shoulder. Aggressive play never sat well with him and he was beginning to hate Joe. He just wanted to get back to the office and the next assignment.

"You got to stir the pot or the best stuff gets stuck to the bottom," Joe said beaming with wisdom.

"So, what's the stuff we are stirring up? That cook looked like he knew Jake and kept looking over his shoulder when we were talking to Tom."

"That is called stirring," Joe said. "I want St. Johns to know we are following him and asking questions. If he thinks it is the cops, maybe he'll act rash and forget about the IRS. We aren't here to track down criminals, we're here to collect taxes and make criminals of those who don't pay."

Charlie hated that part of his job and Joe's statement ended the conversation. He didn't like hating so much. Being on this case had cost him two weeks from home, Mass, and time with a new girlfriend. The guys at the office thought it would be funny for Charlie to take a flight with their very own Untouchable. Since junior high school, Charlie had learned the facts about peer pressure and yet here he was with some quixotic X-File nut job following around some guy who made a bunch of money playing the stock, paid his taxes, and was now spending as much as he earns. Joe wasn't just some clever office novelty to laugh about in the hallway, the guys were trying to send Charlie a message. He realized, they were the outcasts of the office; Charlie talked about his church and salvation, while Joe thought every case was leading to Al Capone.

Right on cue, Joe said, "How many times I gotta tell you, Charlie? It was the IRS who took down Al Capone."

In silence, they followed Jake as he left the diner and walked to the top of the street where Jake's infamous art salon was.

The sedan was at a less than noticeable distance when it parked at the top of the street and the agents watched him walk into the churchyard. They had pictures of him entering and leaving, so they didn't bother with more today.

However, after a moment they both wished they had had the camera clicking when Jake stopped in front of the doors and jerked his head back to look for Frank. He looked right up the street and his squinting eyes rested directly on the sedan.

Jake glared with a tightened brow at the two men through the windshield. Jake shook his head twisting more tension into his face. He turned his head with purpose and walked toward the building.

Joe and Charlie were silent, holding their breaths in fact, as Jake turned away from them and entered the building. It was as if a magic spell was broken and Joe exhaled a burst of laughter. "Holy shit," he shouted. "I swear to God that guy just made us."

"Saw it," Charlie said sharply. "I don't know what's so funny about it."

"It isn't funny. Don't you know anything about irony?"

"I guess not. This isn't funny."

"Oh no, it is funny. Tom is in on this and has moved up to next on our list. I told you that he knew what was going on. He told Jake, since there was no record of a phone call to him—he delivered our message in person this morning. Come into my parlor said the spider," Joe said. "What did that old bitty say today's schedule was for St. Johns?"

Charlie flipped through a notepad and said, "Today, his schedule has two classes and he isn't available until three. St. Johns has a three-thirty meeting and will not be able to meet for a local paper interview until Friday. The old bitty, Helen Reitzer, will call if something changes, but not before checking with the Director about his schedule for this week."

"So we know that he will be here until he leaves, right?"

"He isn't driving and teaches until two. She said, he might have time to talk," Charlie said. "But, it's no guarantee, since he is often quite busy after their sessions until three."

"He hasn't left early, yet," Charlie paused before starting the car. "Let's go."

Charlie sighed in disagreement and said, "Not so fast. He's an hour late, Joe. Maybe—"

"Don't give me any of that crap about losing him yesterday. One in a million," Joe said as he pulled the sedan into traffic. "Besides, Sunday's my day off."

"We did lose him and now I believe he has made us as a tail," Charlie groaned. "This case is unraveling, Joe."

"Like hell it is," Joe snapped. "I'm a pro and we have angles to flesh out."

"Goddamn it," Charlie said. "The last thing we need—"

"Shut it! No Chinese, titties, or pool tables needed for these angles," Joe said while gunning to make a yellow streetlight. "We are turning up the heat on St. Johns."

"I think you are jumping the gun. Let me say it again, we lost him yesterday and he has just made us, Joe," Charlie pleaded. "We can't do anything right now but watch, or we will be turning the heat up on ourselves. It isn't a crime for his dad to not talk to us nor is it a crime for him to tell St. Johns about cops coming around asking questions."

"Wrong again. That is obstruction," Joe said. "When we get back to the office, you will give me your notes and I'll type up the report. Meanwhile, you will arrange with the locals to get us a cop for the rest of the week. We need someone seasoned who knows the underbelly of this area." Gasping, Joe continued, "Get on the phone to the State Bureau for a full copy of their file on this Jerk N. McJohnson."

Charlie was confused and said, "A local? For what?"

Joe shook his head and heavy sighed like he was finished with this conversation. When he finally spoke, he said, "Would you stop distracting me? In fact, there is no reason for you not to get on the phone with the Colorado Bureau of Investigation right now."

As far as Charlie's next question and thoughts were concerned, Joe said they should be saved for the person who answered the phone call and the supervisor he was going to request being transferred to.

Charlie had started to speak, but thought better of it. He instead dialed a number on his cell phone and organized the reasons for needing that file today. Only Christ knew what his partner was playing at with this one, but he was the boss. Instead of opening his mouth, he opened his notepad and wrote down—

We need to be back at the school at 3:00 to see whom St. Johns is meeting with at 3:30.

He had just finished drawing a box around the note when an operator picked up his call at the Bureau.

4

Had Jake not been distracted by thoughts of cigarettes, Frank, Betty, Michelle, and being late, he would have entered his office at the school with a full knowledge of the tax agents, who were following him and plotting his downfall. Instead, he entered his personal art world and focused his mind on figuring out what the hell he was going to lecture about at the end of this class and later in the one following.

Jake smiled and thought, *A lack of planning in the art world creates opportunity for inspiration.*

He removed his coat and shoved his gloves and scarf into its pockets as he walked through the halls. As the warm air started to reach his skin, his mind's gears locked into place and his teacher mode engaged.

For this first class, if they had drawn their classmates as directed, a critique and wrap-up was in perfect order. If not, this would be a brief lecture on embracing the artist's passion they were being paid to use. Would he have the guts to say that he had a homeless shelter if they weren't up to competing for studio space and sponsorship through his gallery?

Either way, his teaching method of inspiration and instruction always started with a bang to get the student stimulated internally and churning mentally, so he could pull the questions from their minds to give them what they needed to hear. You might consider this cheating, but Jake looked at it as a fragile burden and his greatest responsibility.

Being psychic or otherwise, it is one thing to tell a lover or friend privately what they needed to hear in a time of crisis. However, his having a room full of eager minds seeking their own personal triumphs was not a raging sea that Jake liked to swim in and he never tread lightly in these waters.

Jake had barely entered the headmaster's office when Helen entered to apprise him of the recent happenings. She listed off the deadline for the next round of applicants, the next three shows, and two calls.

Helen said, "One from a woman at the local NPR radio station about your regional campaign against smoking and a reporter from the Denver

Post regarding the school's upcoming application process and open enrollment."

Without any regard to what she was saying, he hung his coat on an antique wooden hat rack. He turned to exit the office shaking his head, but he was not able to shut out all of Helen's thoughts and had heard as much as he wanted this morning about his lack of self-respect.

So, he held up his hand and said, "Look, Helen, I've never been late and it's a full morning to catch up on. I'll be back!"

Helen acted offended for a moment, but quickly resumed her update of calls and appointments.

Ignoring her, Jake exited his office and the front office area with Helen in his wake. "Helen, Christ gave us email for a reason. Please sum it up in a format that I can delete later," he said entering the hallway. "However, do expect a call from a young woman named Tammy, please take care to get her phone number."

JAKE WALKED INTO THE classroom and was greeted by a chorus of 'Jakes,' 'heys' and 'wazzups' from roughly fifteen students. There were even a few cat-calls and projected questions about what happened last night. Jake couldn't help but laugh.

"Sorry I'm late," he said. "No, I did not have a hot date last night. Yes, I met a nice girl. She might even be a psychic witch."

Several students gave out a collective, "Woooo!"

"Wow, you are a lively bunch this morning. I hope to see this reflected in your work." He motioned with his hand to bring the drawings to him. "Bring your best work up for critique.

"I have to say didn't expect to be giving a critique today when I got here," Jake said. "I was very clear with my instructions to Ms. Ironass about no nudity and thought you rebellious little animals would be having an orgy when I arrived. So much for my lecture on your hedonistic passions.

"Set up your best work from today, so we can all learn from your failures."

There were shouts of 'whatever,' 'do your best,' 'I'm not taking off my clothes again' and a chorus of laughing chatter as the students brought their work and arranged the drawings at the front of the room upon a long counter top above the room's waist-high supply cabinets.

Jake waited until everything was arranged and then paced the line-up of artwork. While inspecting the drawings, he was listening to the classroom's broadcasting thoughts that sought approval, but offered little else for him to exploit.

The class was well-trained in his style and watched him, waiting for him to start the critique.

Jake got his mental ping and stopped at one drawing. He turned back to face the class. He smiled focusing on one girl and then looked at another boy before he said, "Lisa meet Mark. I believe he has a little crush on you."

The room all snickered and Mark blushed as Lisa looked over to him and then back to the drawing he did of her.

"Let's start this off with this spark of potential to save something from my planned passion lecture," Jake said. "Mark, can you put emotion aside and tell us about your drawing? Or should I invite Lisa to discuss this incredible drawing?"

The class chuckled as Mark stood saying that he would talk about it. It was Lisa's turn to blush as he moved to the front of the room and started to describe his shortcomings in capturing the visage of the young woman. Jake coached Mark along with questions about what he had drawn verses what he had seen.

Jake asked Mark if he could add a few touches to the drawing. Standing by, Mark gave his approval to Jake, who had picked up a piece of charcoal and moved to the drawing. He threw Lisa a side-glance and squinted at her.

"Something that Mark missed, and all of us miss if we aren't truly seeing our subject, was the truth," Jake said as he touched the paper with the cinder. He spoke as he drew, "I am not giving Lisa nor Mark a bad time, but he wasn't seeing her for what is there. Instead, he was picturing her through his internal mind's eyes."

Jake worked on the drawing for a few more seconds with sharp and decisive strokes, smeared his lines with his pinkie and then blew on the paper to remove the scruff. When he turned back to the class, the drawing had become an exact likeness of Lisa in Mark's style.

He smiled and said, "Beauty is in the eye of the beholder. Lisa is quite charming, but art isn't about the mind's eye. It is about the beholder's artist eye, which doesn't editorialize in visual prose. Adding beauty creates a cartoon."

Jake set down the cinder and clapped the dust from his hands as he said, "I only had to add a few strokes to pull this drawing back into reality. I love you, Mark, but you missed the subtle dent in Lisa's chin and her higher cheekbones. Lisa, may I ask the class to look at you?"

Lisa smiled feeling a bit uncomfortable and nodded.

"Thank you," Jake said. "If you look at Lisa with an eye free from the person that you think you are seeing. You will see what draws our friend Mark to her. The truth of her unique beauty."

This made Lisa smile and she matched the drawing that Mark and Jake had crafted. Jake smiled and said with a wink to Mark, "I don't intend to change Mark's mind, but I wanted you all to see Lisa for what she is, not who you think she is. It's not about how you think you see her. Lisa is. And, Mark captured a good deal of it, now look at her and feel her with your eyes. Did I help Mark capture her?"

Lisa sat on her art room stool and felt the class looking at her. She could feel the weight of their judgment or acceptance. She could identify Mark's sympathy for her being on the spot.

Missy said as she raised her hand, "What? Wait. You want us to feel her?"

"Yes. See her truly," Jake replied. He smiled, "Now squint. She just becomes shapes and points on a grid."

Jake was never just teaching them art. Most lessons were guided toward group empathy and strong energy exchanges in hopes of triggering a psychic spark. He felt the class's exchange of free thought was a successful lesson and he brought it to an abrupt end by clapping his hands. He told the class they had learned enough from this drawing.

He moved to another one and asked Don to step forward. "Donny," Jake said. "Please tell us about your rendering of Peter, so we can help you capture what you are seeing next time."

Donny nodded and approached the front of the room.

"Hey, before he starts, I want to thank you all for really nailing this assignment. These are all great drawings. And, Mark, thanks for being so honest and helping us to see creativity in action. And thank you, Lisa, for inspiring him."

The critique continued as Jake helped his students see the people around them without prejudice.

AFTER AN HOUR, Jake concluded the class and thanked them again for saving his day from his personal failures with their great efforts. "Once I got out of the way, this was a great critique," he said.

As they filed out of the room, Jake pretended to be arranging his notes for the next class while he broadcasted a loop of his thoughts on a psychic level.

If you can hear me, please stay behind. There is much we can discuss. If you can hear me, you are psychic. Please stay behind. There is much to discuss. If you can hear me, please stay behind—

One student stayed behind and instead of packing up, he was working on unpacking a set of paints.

Mark paused at the door and acted as though he had forgotten something. When the last student exited, he moved to Jake's desk.

Jake looked up at Mark and said, "Is there something you wish to discuss, Mark?"

Mark was wrestling with an internal foe and grimaced before he spoke. "Jake," he said. "I wanted to thank you for picking me first today. It was like you read my mind. I've heard you often, but this time you really made your point and I had to stay after."

"You really heard me clearly today and had to stop," Jake asked. "I'm always available and you are not unwelcome. How can I help you?"

"You already have," Mark said as he turned his glance back to the other young man in the room. He whispered to Jake, "I am going to ask Lisa out, I drew that picture to impress her and to get her to notice me. She didn't just notice me, you broke the ice." Mark stuck out his hand and smiled, "Thanks, man."

Jake took his hand and shook it, "Is there anything else you that you wanted to discuss?"

"Nope," Mark said. "See you after lunch and I'll let you know how it goes. Thanks again, Jake."

Jake told Mark he was welcome as he walked him to the door and closed it behind him.

The lone student remaining in the room broke into laughter as the door clicked shut and said, "Man, I told you that Alfred Bester shit ain't ever gonna work." He rolled with another peel of laughter. "You really thought you had a new psychic. Damn, that's funny."

"You heard me," Jake said. "So we know it works."

Tim stood up to his full height of nearly six-foot three-inches. He was a lean black man with a long slim build that made him look taller than he was.

"Just cuz I heard don't mean anything," Tim said. "I think you cheated that day."

"Cheated?," Jake said.

"Hell yeah. I only hear your 'broadcast' part of the time and I ain't sure if I hear you or think I'm hearing you because I know what you are doing."

Are you hearing me now? Are you going to be done with the painting for the opening?, Jake said on a psychic bandwidth.

Tim laughed again, "I can't hear you, Jake, but your face is saying something. Am I done with the clown painting, yet?"

Jake said, "You're right, so maybe I didn't cheat. Maybe you just aren't trying hard enough to consciously manifest my signal on an ego level."

"I really do try, Jakey. I feel you, but I ain't hearin' ya."

"So, are you going to have the painting finished in time to be my featured artist at the gallery opening?"

Tim stretched his back with his hands on the small of it. His face twisted from a pressure in his spine and said, "Yeah, man. It's pretty close to being finished now. Do you really think you will be able to sell it?"

Jake laughed, "Are you losing your mind, Tim? Worry about selling the others. If someone else tries to buy it, they will have to compete with me. Are you ready to show me, yet?"

Tim smiled a big, warm, tooth-filled grin and said, "Let's do it."

He moved from his spot and crossed the room, stopping at a large canvas in the back of the room. Jake followed Tim's lead and stepped across the room.

The canvas was covered with a thick and stiff piece of brown paper taped at the top and bottom of its frame, it arched away from the painting to keep the paper from touching the oil paints on the canvas surface. Tim grabbed the top of the frame from behind.

Jake stopped to wait for Tim to return to his easel.

Tim set the frame onto the easel and removed the tape at the bottom. He was careful to remove it and not touch the painting's surface. When the painting was revealed, Jake stared in awe.

In silence, they stood looking at a painting of the clown from Jake's worst nightmares. When Jake could finally speak, he said, "It is finished. What else do you feel you need to do?"

Tim twisted his mouth looking at the painting and wagged his head back and forth squinting his eyes. "There is something important missing, but I can't put my finger on it. Look at it real close, man. What's missing, Jake?"

Jake squinted at the painting and started to speak when an unseen critic voiced her opinion and said from behind them, "I tell you what is wrong with it. It is an evil unto the Lord. Monsieur Marquez would not approve of this idolatry in his church."

Jake turned back and looked down at a fierce little nun wearing a Catholic sister's habit. "I'm not surprised," he said. "That's why I always liked Father Rodriguez, Sister Mary Celeste. Does the Monsieur not like clowns?"

"Bah! Your sacrilege knows no boundaries. You have defiled Our Lord's Altar with your sin and multiplied it by taking our Lord from this House of God."

Jake turned to Tim and said, "Do you feel her?"

Tim shook his head to say no.

"May I help you see her?"

When Tim nodded his head, Jake's body flared with golden light. The light jut out from his head into Tim's and enveloped his head like a halo.

Tim was profoundly unsettled by seeing the ghost of a nun and looked at Jake for confirmation with big shining eyes.

"Yes, Tim," said Jake. "This is Sister Mary Celes—"

She interrupted, "Thou shalt not address me nor make a spectacle of me, Mr. St. Johns. You and your friends are sin weavers and your work here is an abomination."

"Sorry to tell you this, sister," Jake said with a tone of sarcasm. "But, you are the abomination. Saith the Lord, 'Thou shalt not seek the council of the dead'."

Sister Mary Celeste turned red and swelled with fury. She began to expand and grow as her body and habit stopped responding to gravity.

Feeling Tim's fear rising to panic, Jake flared again with golden light, but the aura had a multi-faceted intensity beyond anything Tim had imagined. This affected him more than the raging specter, who had become a nightmare creature from his most demonic dreams. Fear gripped Tim so violently that he froze with his eyes on his teacher.

Jake's aura reached into the air around the nun. The golden light from his body grabbed hold of her with tendrils of fluid-like energy. He pulled backed his fists as if he were jerking up and snapping down the reins of a team of horses, the light around the menacing ghost seized her and threw her to the ground.

Sister Mary bounced from the floor hard and darted away like a cat that snuck under foot and took a surprising kick in the side.

"I always hated that bitch," Jake said. "Are you okay, Tim?"

Tim responded with two blinks of his eyes.

"Two blinks means okay," asked Jake.

Tim blinked his eyes twice and turned his head into the room where three children were facing into the corner. He tossed his head for Jake to look in that direction. Following Tim's unblinking eyes, Jake looked at the children in the corner.

Jake said, "Okay, I am turning off our connection right now."

Tim nodded with an urgent plea of, 'yes.'

Jake closed his eyes and jerked his head. The golden light floating in the room was sucked into him so fast that it was as if there was never any light emitting from his body. He looked at Tim with concern.

"Are you sure the connection is off," Tim asked.

Jake looked back and forth a couple of times and wagged his head. He said, "I can't find a connection, so I'm sure."

Tim inhaled through his nose with his eyes closed and looked into the corner again. He exhaled for a long time and said, "Well, I can still see those kids in the corner."

Jake grabbed Tim in a strong hug and shouted, "I knew it!" His eyes welled with tears and he didn't try to hide his excitement, "Tim, you are the real thing! We aren't connected and you are seeing on your own."

Tim patted Jake's back twice and broke the hug. "Muthafucka, I love you, but I don't want to see any goddamned ghosts. Can you make those kids go away?"

Jake looked like he had been broken inside and frowned. He put a hand on Tim's shoulder and said without looking to the corner, "You've already turned them off."

Tim looked into the corner and there were no children.

Jake said, "I could go for a cigarette right now."

Tim frowned and said, "I thought you quit?"

"I did," Jake said. "But, we need to go outside. You want to smoke, right?"

"I do, but I'm not giving you one," Tim said.

"That's fine," Jake said. "I don't need one."

Cigarette, Michelle, Betty, looped through Jake's mind and to the unending distraction had been added, *Frank, Sid, Tammy and Tim.*

5

Joe and Charlie walked into the Denver Police Department headquarters and flashed their badges to a dominating officer stationed on the dangerous side of the metal detector. He nodded them through.

They passed through the machine setting off an alarm.

With the fluid pantomime of an experienced SWAT teamster, the officer who had inspected their badges pointed at an older officer, pointed back to the IRS agents and gave a thumbs-up. The older cop nodded his understanding in reply to the other officer's gestures.

He approached the agents and extended his hand, "Sgt. Bill Douglas at your service. Thanks for calling ahead and being prompt. You guys saved us all some time." The men introduced themselves as IRS Special Agents Charlie Stillford and Joe Gaines during the handshaking.

"Call me Bill, if it serves ya," said Bill as he led them to the supervisor's desk. "We already have you logged and you only need to flash your badges again to sign in."

Joe displayed his badge and expressed to Bill his surprise that they wouldn't be waiting for approvals.

"Well, you called and gave us time to check your credentials. It's only right to return the favor," Bill said and paused to examine Charlie's badge. "You'd be surprised how many armed G-men still walk in here without calling ahead. If you come in here armed and unannounced while we're in an orange security advisory, we will make you wait before we send you home for the day. Denver isn't a little cow town anymore."

They chuckled. Joe winked at Charlie and said, "That's why I keep this kid around. He dots his i's and crosses the t's. Even when they're capitals."

They all chuckled again.

Joe and Charlie both signed in and were given visitor badges.

"So, tell me what's so special that you guys made a trip over from St. Louis," Bill said.

"Sgt. Douglas, I sent a fax of our report," said Charlie clipping on his visitor badge.

"Really, call me Bill," he said. Bill nodded into the interior of the building suggesting they proceed. "I'm a people person and have a stack of faxes on my desk, so get me caught up as we walk. I can review the fax later, if necessary."

As they waited for the elevator, the agents reviewed how the state bureau of investigation had not been able to track down any leads about St. John's activities related to some anarchist plot, but were able to dig up some evidence of money laundering for purposes of tax evasion. Joe said, "So they called us in."

The men waited for the exiting passengers in silence and entered the elevator. When the doors closed, Joe moved the summary forward. "In fact," he said. "Their last report to us said that they had found this guy to have a potentially terrorist agenda. However, there has been nothing related to the basic question of tax evasion.

"The guy has an online store called The Anarchist Bookstore. I've been there and seen what he's selling, it's a bunch of books we all know.

"Selling *1984* is not an actual crime any more than some of the 1950's science fiction crap he's hocking. I searched for The Anarchist Cookbook and the other books floating around the underworld, but I could only find mass-market novels and limited run collectables.

"I could have dug a little deeper into the books being offered, but from what I have seen, the Colorado Bureau is off on some McVey goose chase."

Bill chimed in, "Well, unless he is mailing out cash to fund his McVey customers. Anyone looking into that?"

Charlie replied, "Nope. That's going to require a warrant and the Postmaster General."

"What about correspondence," asked Bill. "Any reports of standard terrorist techniques like large purchases of materials for explosives?"

Charlie said, "Nope. We've bought several hundred large orders of books under a Satanic church front, but he hasn't approached any of our customers. This guy's prone to rant about working for The Man, magic, and being psychic, but it is in no way an indicator of recruitment." From his notepad, Charlie summed up his scribbles, "The last report from CBI indicated that he is trying to evolve humanity into psychics.

Bill said, "So, is this guy some kind of scientist?"

Joe took control of the conversation again and said, "We're getting side-tracked. This St. Johns character is showing huge profit during the year and showing nothing at the end of it."

The elevator dinged open. They stepped off into a hallway.

Joe continued, "If he is an angel of the community, great. But, if he isn't, I want to force his hand and find that hand dirty with green ink."

"So where does the DPD fit into this?," said Bill. He looked at Charlie, whose face displayed that he didn't know either, and then back to Joe.

Joe smiled and said he thought Bill would never ask. "We need a scary cop to lurk around as he tails St. Johns," Joe said. "Some big dummy who looks like the Law to motivate our perp into doing something rash."

Holding up a step, Bill smirked and held his tongue waiting for the bombshell to drop that would not come.

After a few silent moments, he asked if that was it. Joe nodded in agreement.

"So, you just need a big scary cop," Bill asked Joe.

"That's it," Joe confirmed.

"Can it be a smart, big cop," Bill asked. "Not too many dummies under my watch."

"That's too bad. The bigger and dumber they can act, the better," Joe said from the internal place from which he was plotting. "But, it needs to be a 'he' and I'll say it again, this 'he' doesn't have to be smart.

They turned the corner and Joe elaborated, "Bill, the dumber your hulk, the better it would be for my approach to getting St. Johns to go into action."

Bill looked at Charlie to check if he had heard Joe correctly. He laughed when Charlie shrugged in ignorance.

He said to Joe, "I have someone available in mind, but she is a petite black woman who is smart as a whip. Is that okay?"

Joe looked frustrated and almost started to explain again what he was looking for, when Bill said, "I'm just teasing you, Joe. I do have someone in mind, but he is pretty sharp."

They arrived at Bill's office, he spoke to his administrative assistant and asked her to send notice to Sgt. Jackson that he was requesting Officer Michael Straka be assigned to special duties until further notice.

Then he turned and said, "Agents, thanks for bringing me up to date. Anna will be able to finish this up for you. My requests are gold and Mike is your hulk with brains." He extended his hand and said good-bye. "If you just needed a big dude, you should have said so in your fax, Agent Gaines."

Charlie said, "Sorry. I didn't know what we were looking for exactly."

"I know," said Bill smiling as he turned to Joe. "I was just giving you a hard time, Charlie."

He turned and continued, "Joe, Mike is your guy. But, don't tell him what you told me. His partner is under investigation for an off-duty shooting and his sense of humor is a little strained. We'll just tell him that you need him to be an unavoidable physical presence in this St. Johns's path."

Bill turned, disappearing into his office with a farewell wave.

"We should have called this guy when we got to town," Joe said. "I like his style."

Charlie nodded to Joe in agreement.

Joe turned to the assistant and said, "Anna, Ms. Baca, if you prefer. Here's our cards. Please have Officer Straka call us after he receives his assignment."

The agents were in mid-reach of extending their cards when Anna told them that she had their information and smiled saying Mike Straka would call on his next shift. They shrugged and replaced their cards before thanking her.

They left the office and were waiting for the elevator when Charlie's phone rang. After a short one-sided conversation on the phone, Charlie disconnected and told Joe that the entire CBI file had arrived and was waiting for them at the office.

The elevator arrived and Joe said, "Let's go see what those clowns aren't doing."

6

The sun had dimmed as wispy clouds danced before its brilliance in a jet stream parade of white and gray. Tim smoked a cigarette while Jake exhaled vapor into the arctic front that had moved in to disrupt the spring-like weather of the day before.

They made small talk about the change in the weather to forget the ghosts Tim had seen. With each puff that Tim drew from his cigarette, Jake crept into his mind and indulged in the nicotine smoke-filled enjoyment that he experienced.

The conversation moved around in the rants that only smokers and drunks enjoy. Tim talked about his thankless night job at the warehouse and Jake asked questions about his love life. Tim said things were going real well for them—his lady had started a new job and she was making a good wage as an executive secretary to the Commissioner of the Land and Water Department in the State Energy Office.

However, when the conversation turned back to Jake and his jobs before becoming rich, Jake frowned not wanting to talk about it and changed the subject back to love.

"Ahhh, working is all thankless. I met a girl yesterday," Jake said. "And I think she might be a jewel."

"Man, that's your problem," Tim said. "They're always a jewel. Remember that Michelle?"

Jake did. He moved the dialog forward and said, "I am not talking about her being a new girlfriend per se, but I think she has the gift."

"Dude! They all have the gift and it's right there every time. Just reach down."

"That isn't what I mean," Jake said. "I think she's psychic. Just before I met her, I was talking with Frank and she heard us."

"I knew what you meant," Tim said laughing and he laughed again before saying, "So what? She heard you talking to your imaginary friend. When do I get to meet this Frank? You know you're crazy, right?"

"I'm not crazy," Jake said. "But she really did hear him and repeated a part of our conversation."

Jake leeched on Tim's nicotine intake as he puffed a menthol and gave some consideration to Tammy hearing Frank, when Tim said, "So what are you going to do about this girl?"

"I'm not sure. I walked her to her apartment after a dessert and had a few glasses of wine," Jake paused.

"And?"

"She asked me about college and persisted," Jake said. "Just like Michelle used to do. So, I left and bought a bottle."

"You left? Was she ready to go?"

"I don't know. If she was, she'll call me," Jake said. "However, she did change my life, though, I think."

"Dude, what are you talking about now?," Tim said before putting the cigarette into his mouth.

Jake's face showed the political swings of his mental debate before he sighed and said because of her advice that he had found his little ghost.

Tim said, "Did she really help you finally find that crying little girl?"

Instead of answering him directly, Jake asked if he had ever known him to be late. Tim said he hadn't. Jake recalled his morning for Tim and told him that this was the reason he was late. Tim listened as he finished his cigarette. He flipped the butt away into the schoolyard and turned back to Jake. With a piercing gaze, Tim asked if he was sure it wasn't another dream.

Jake told him he wasn't sure, but he had slept late. He said, "I haven't slept late in ten years and I have to assume to this was not a dream."

"So you are thinking this Tammy girl is really psychic?"

"Not any more than you think you are, but I think she might be more willing to embrace it. Ghosts and all."

Tim looked away and then back at Jake with smirking pride, "Man, it isn't that I don't want to be psychic. I just don't want to be like you. Jake, you might be rich, but you're a fuckin' mess."

Jake sighed, "I might be a mess, but I am still not smoking." He tapped a finger to his head. "There is something in here that you can learn from. You are my only true student and I know there's much I can teach you, if you'd only let me do my job."

Tim shrugged, "I just want to paint, man."

"I know," Jake said. "Follow your dreams, Tim. You know you can count on me for keeping those dreams alive. Just ask if you need anything."

Tim patted at his pocket and said, "I know that, man, I do. I really do.

But, if we are going to stand out here in the cold I need another cigarette. You want one?"

Jake did want one and very much so. He swallowed hard ignoring Tim's offer and said, "I have this fundraiser with the Urban League next week and I would like you to come with me."

Tim lit his second smoke and looked at Jake with contempt. "In other words, you need your token black man to go with you?"

"Hell no, man. If I needed you for that, I wouldn't be going to the Urban League. I want you to come and meet your community leaders. This is an important local group and I want you to meet them in a positive light. I am going to donate ten thousand dollars for their community arts program. You can be my gift, too. You are a great black man who will be famous some day and I want you to get to know these people, so you never forget that you also have a responsibility to your neighborhood."

Tim looked down with racial fury and didn't like a white man talking to him about his responsibilities as a black man.

Jake knew his thoughts and said, "Look, Tim, this isn't a race issue, this is about people forgetting their roots. If you were white, I would say the same thing and ask you to come to show you how responsible citizens give back to their neighbors and community."

"Come on, man," Tim said. "Save it for the fans cuz you can't fool the players. You wouldn't use black people to show some cracker how to be a member of his society?"

"There aren't many crackers doing something of community value to use as an example for anyone. I would have no choice, Tim.

"Think about coming with me. I feel it will be important for you."

Tim nodded, "I'll think about it."

"I hope you will and think about this, too," said Jake. "If you ever offer me another cigarette, Tim, I will pull your funding."

Jake turned and walked away to prepare for his next class.

Walking toward the school doors with his back to Tim, Jake said, "While you are thinking about staying or leaving, remember this… I've never judged you as a black person, I judge you as a man and my friend. But, I will not let you be less than a man on my dollar. I've seen too many ghosts to let you become just another one. I'd rather you hate me and create your own successful future than for you to think that I'm paying you to be my smoking buddy. No one gets a lucky break in this world, but you did. It's time to step up or walk away."

Jake opened the door and went inside.

Tim watched Jake disappear and looked at his cigarette. He said one word, "Motherfucker."

AFTER HIS SECOND CLASS, which was a nice success but not like the first one of the day, Jake took care of some business in his office. It was the trivial business of over-due bills, bull stocks, and flask drinking.

Jake decided he needed to leave to take care of his book order surge. He had short-term issues and wondered if he should hire a staff. Could he depend on temp services to fulfill his book orders any more than he could count on himself to get them out the door? If Jake could find two trustworthy people and a warehouse, he would get the book orders done in a month and could focus on marketing the bookstore to build a bigger customer base.

Before leaving the school, he went back to the first classroom where Tim was working on a large painting.

Entering with his heart on his sleeve and face, Jake said, "Tim. I want to apologize. I wouldn't care if you were a crack-head, I'll never pull your support as long as you are painting. I know that sounds like more racial bullshit, but you aren't my first prospective student and that crack shit isn't just a problem for my brothers. I have seen better than both of us fall to the temptations of this world. All you have to do is keep showing up and I'll keep sponsoring you."

"Ease up, Jake. You're going to start cryin'," Tim said. "I know all that and I'm sorry, man, for asking if you wanted a cigarette. I wasn't thinking. But, I have been thinking," Tim started to move across the room. "I've been thinking that you were right. I don't care if you pull my scholarship. When I stop being a man, I will walk away."

Jake started to interrupt.

Tim raised his hand and said, "Let a nigga finish. You might be a rich fuckin' white boy, but you don't get the last word on this. I am a man and I will not take your charity. Me and the lady were talking about this last night. She said that we don't need your money anymore since she got this job at the State. I told her that you are my boy and I was earning your money. Jake, you have something I need and want, so I'm going to keep earning this scholarship!

"When we have this gallery opening next week, you'll make back every cent you've ever given me and I know that, but I ain't going to get a chance to show my shit without you. I've tried other galleries and they don't work with blacks cuz I've seen that cracker shit they have on their walls.

"You are my friend and I know this. We are in this together. But, shit. You hurt my feelings today and I sure as hell ain't going to offer you another cigarette, you are on your own if you want one. I ain't even gonna smoke with you, you fuckin' mind-leech.

"Bottom line, I busted my ass these last six months and have done my best work. You don't like it, tell me to walk. If not, keep your fuckin' threats to your goddamned crazy self."

Jake took it all in for few seconds and stewed over all the arguing he felt like interjecting. He finally said, "Earlier today, you asked me what I did before I got rich. It seems funny that I haven't told you after bringing you into all my other nonsense. I mean you even know about Betty."

"Who's Betty?," Tim said.

"Betty is my little crying ghost. Tammy told me to name her. That's how I found her."

"Right-right," Tim said.

"Right," Jake said. "You asked what I did before getting rich and I'm trying to tell you."

Tim waved his hand and looked like he could care less.

"You asked and damn it, now I want to tell you. It will make sense if you don't get mad and shut me out."

Tim waved his hand and shrugged, "Spit it."

"You don't know what I did because I hated it. I am a college dropout and got a job based on my portfolio. I knew computers and took a migrant wage at an art agency as an intern."

Tim turned his head and showed he was interested in Jake's story with a snide smirk.

Jake continued and laid out for Tim his work history. In his former profession as a commercial artist, he excelled and got two promotions in a year. In his third year, he helped the sales team seal deal after deal and the company had a record year.

At the end of that year, Jake got a bad review and flipped out saying that he was the key to the best sales year in the company's history and ranted at his boss demanding a raise and a better review.

His boss chuckled and told him, "You know I am a no-shit kind of guy and I'd love to help you, but your work dropped off this year while you were focused on sales, and trust me, you're no salesman. Your job is to design and draw, not sell.

"'So what?,' you are thinking. You did great on the big deals, but what about your daily work that wasn't being done. Our business was built on our local customers who give us an annual retainer and they need fliers or spot ads for the weekly inserts. You didn't get three of those regular customer jobs done by the deadlines. Am I supposed to overlook that?"

When Jake started to defend himself, he was interrupted again.

"Right-right. You did a great job supporting the sales team. Those people in sales make a lot of money and they don't need help on the sales side—they need you to do your job to keep selling."

Before Jake could defend his role in their record year, his boss interrupted.

"Whoa, wait. Maybe you are thinking about sales, don't. I can't put you in front of a client, you're a jabbering retard. Stick to your fonts, photos, and drawings, and let the sales department do their job."

Jake told Tim that this review was the biggest insult of his life. He was giving the sales people a psychic's insider angle to perfecting their pitches.

He finished the story with a confession and said, "I told the guy to stick it up his ass and I walked. I didn't know what else to do, so I started playing the stock market after being penalized for cashing out my 401-K. It was just like I know you've heard, your first million is the hardest one to make.

"In six months, I had turned my meager five-thousand dollar 401-K plan into three million in assets. By month nine, I'd bought the ad agency just to shut them down.

"Those bastards had it coming, so meanwhile I opened a new agency and hired the entire staff away. The clients followed the staff and I was turning a profit again.

"I needed a write-off two years later, so I sold the agency for a loss to a friend. They are still doing great. Damn, I have to stop in at the non-profit later. We are launching a campaign to get people to install solar panels on their—

"Never mind. Even after that, I hounded this fucker who told me I was a retard and started three rival businesses to the companies that he took jobs with just to make him fail.

"I finally gave up on destroying this guy two years ago, but then heard the guy hanged himself in his office last year. I didn't like it, so I did some research and founded a trust fund in his kids' name, two of the three of them are in college now.

"You know Cindy in Life Drawing?"

Tim nodded.

"That is or was the dick's youngest daughter and I will support her as long as I'm alive. I didn't mean for the guy to kill himself, but he did and I still feel responsible. That taught me a valuable lesson about my powers."

"Got a lesson for me," Tim asked.

"That's why I am telling you this," said Jake. "I came to apologize for being like that dick. I always fall back into that role, since this enemy of mine and his insults were what I needed to hear to step up and do what

I've done. He changed my life when he told me directly that I was a retard. I needed to hear that."

"You callin' me a retard?," Tim said.

"I am saying we are all retards, but we don't have to be."

"I got you," said Tim. "Sorry I got so pissed off, but I couldn't let you hold my scholarship over me."

Jake smiled and said, "If I was going to hold it over you, Tim, I'd be telling you to help me with my book orders."

Tim laughed, "You and your books. Why do you waste your time?! You keep losing money on that bullshit."

"Maybe," Jake said shrugging and stuck out his hand, "Are you still my friend?"

Tim laughed as he took Jake's hand and said, "You white people trip me out. I wasn't mad like that, I was just telling ya that I don't need your goddamn money and that you don't own me."

"You might not need my money, but I do. And you, m'man, are my money and own me. So, finish another fuckin' painting, bitch!"

Laughing, Tim threw Jake's hand away and said, "You are a retard. And, I *will* get another painting finished, if you get the fuck outta here. And, please take your ghosts with you." Tim turned back toward his easel. "Especially that old hag you have working in the front office."

Chuckling, Jake said as he turned to leave, "I only keep her around to remind me of my working life."

They both laughed and parted. The weather was threatening evening snow as Jake jogged eighteen blocks to his non-profit ad agency to review the mock-ups for his *Plugging into the Sun* campaign.

7

The overcast sky darkened the cityscape. Arctic winds growled down from the northwest attacking the trapped humidity from the Pacific Ocean that was pulled up on the jet stream through the Baja. The atmospheric convergence hit critical mass above Denver and fired off the evening's first razor-sharp flakes of the coming spring ice-storm.

In spite of the great work his team had done on the solar campaign, Jake St. Johns pulled his hands tighter into his pockets feeling guilty about leaving his dad angry with him and for threatening his only real friend.

Jake stuck out his chin into the storm to punish himself with a dense blast of driven snow that hit him in the face. The blowing ice bit harshly against his flesh.

He lifted his head to expose his neck in defiance of the driving winds.

Something from inside him pushed back at nature, the flakes were repelled into a mist by a radiation that emanated from Jake's face and body.

He didn't mean to push magic into his shoes, but since he had… Jake began running toward the edges of puddles in the street, just to splash water without getting his shoes wet.

Levitating about an inch above the street, Jake propelled himself along the ground at the speed of a sprinter toward home to get out of the growing intensity of the storm…and he was having fun.

Jake reached out into his mindscape and turned off his thoughts. Not touching the ground and projecting two rainbow-like wings of energy behind him, Jake looked like an ethereal hawk in a dive.

No one was walking on these cold and bitter streets nor would anyone in the houses notice but a glimpse of him as he shot past like a hockey player.

The snowflakes thickened and became a low cloud covering the neighborhood. Jake cut foot-over-foot boldly around a corner stomping the air and grinding against the pavement with telekinetically-edged blades of psychic energy, he darted into a dark and weather-obscured street ahead.

When Jake's mental focus drifted into his feet to feel the imaginary ice skates, his concentration collapsed within him and the skates disappeared. Realizing what had happened, he tried to run out his speed like a skateboarder launched forward from their board, but fell as his feet slid across the wet, slick snow and out from under him.

He laughed as he pushed himself up from the ground.

Jake stood tall and began to walk off the pang in his side and butt before he noticed a dozen dark, hooded figures with bright red eyes sliding out from behind the trees ahead.

Like viscous ink dropped into a cup of water, the specters moved through the long shadows and left swirling trails of darkness as the sinister spirits flowed toward Jake.

Terrified, Jake jumped with a start and picked up his pace to a sprint, while digging into his pocket for the gate keys.

He hurried through the gate and up the snow-powdered stairs into his yard through a gale of snow.

Jake looked back over his shoulder behind him as several of the red-eyed specters flowed through the open gate and followed him upstairs into the yard. He stepped a little faster forward.

When he had turned to look in front of him again, several raggedy ghosts had gathered on the lawn and sidewalk in front of him.

Seeing that he was trapped, Jake teetered on the precipice of panic when he realized himself and re-focused his psychic energies. His hands flared with fantastic flames that shot out toward the ghosts blocking his way.

The ghosts all stopped advancing and were quick to move as Jake began a haughty march toward his doorstep. He fingered slowly through the ring and found his key.

When Jake turned back to glare at them, nearly twenty spooks of various-shapes had gathered in his yard as an audience. The glowering specters continued to move toward him.

He shouted while fitting his key into the door, "Go somewhere else. Nothing to see here!"

Not knowing what else he might need to dispel the specters, he opened the door and turned on the spotlight that pointed to the massive crucifix inside. Jake turned back to the foot of his porch; his body glowed bright as the snow blew passed him through the open doorway into the house. Like the marshal who had just entered the saloon, Jake stood there for a moment looking over the ghosts in his yard and sized them all up.

Jake squinted with malice, "If any of you come any closer, I promise to eat you up."

With spite for the red-eyed specters—who failed to heed his warning and continued their approach—Jake swelled up with colorful energy as his aura bloomed into something only seen in comic books. He projected a diffused energy into the night at the crowd of undead in the yard and pulled it back to his extended hands, he seized six of the glowing-eyed specters in closed fists of light. Jake took a step toward the ghosts, his visible energy intensified and his gripping appendages of light tightened as Jake began to draw the specters toward him.

The nightshades fought in an effort to free themselves, but they were trapped within the superhuman brilliance of Jake's focused will. Their spirit bodies dropped to the ground and dug at the winter-burnt grass with bony fingers to stop the traction that Jake was applying.

The captive specters began to dissolve into the taut, thick ropes of bioelectricity that were tethered to Jake's raised fists and began to taint the pureness of the luminance with creeping veins of darkness that had started to flow back up the beam toward his body. Pulling harder, Jake strained his will to pull more of the fiends into the light and then let go of the malicious spirits before their dark essences could enter him.

Once the drained specters were released, they and the other red-eyed ink spots darted away like bolts of darkness into the night aiming for the longest shadows of the street and abandoned the other defenseless spooks.

Jake had never tried to manifest anything like that before and was eager to do it again. He shouted into the night, "Don't test me again, I am King of the Wild Things!"

He turned away to enter his house and slammed the front door behind him.

JAKE ENTERED HIS FRONT room and turned on the lights. He kicked off his shoes thinking about how to safeguard his house against the ghouls he had found waiting for him. He had no desire to wake up and find any of God's forsaken zombies milling around in his house.

This was a problem bigger than burning a simple smudge stick of Native sage.

After a few seconds of stewing on the front yard's undead assault, Jake had to chuckle to himself when his mind began to turn through a mental encyclopedia of occult remedies and landed on a spell for concealment.

Jake flipped on all the lights and turned his face to the Jesus hanging on his wall. He said, "I hope you'll approve of my burning some myrrh in honor of the Virgin Queen."

He removed his coat and moved into his kitchen to retrieve the ingredients for his incantation. From the fridge, Jake took out an incense stick of myrrh and frankincense for the Altar and a vial of Abramelin Oil to dab on the door handles, first-floor windows and in the mouths of the lions guarding the stairs. His refrigerator held nothing but jars of dried and oiled herb essences, and a pitcher of purple Kool-Aid.

After lighting his incense sticks, Jake moved about the house dabbing oil and chanted in Hebrew and Enochian. He also randomly shouted English phrases into the house like, "Betty-Betty oxen-free!" or "Your soul is not welcome here."

There was no answer from Betty. Nor was there an answer from any other spirits for that matter.

Jake, in thought, took care of his priestly duties while calling into the house for Betty like a haggard spinster calling for her cat or long dead children.

He called into the house, "Hey Betty...! Come on out, Betty!"

Where is she?, was written on his face as he finished lighting a second round of incense under Our Lord in Death. Don't they call it *The Ecstasy*?

He said, "Every other ghost in the neighborhood is gathering on my lawn, but can I find ours?" Jake sighed out, "It's back to the books, Jesus."'s

JAKE WALKED INTO HIS super-hero office with half of a glass of Kool-Aid and ice. He sat into his leather chair and grabbed a bottle of vodka from the desk-fridge. He tapped his computer to life and poured booze into his cup. With a couple of swirls, Jake drank as he waited for connection.

When the computer displayed a Web site and announced, 'Welcome to The Anarchist Bookstore dot-com.' Jake discovered there were even more orders than expected as he scrolled down the program window.

Jake said, "Damn, I'm running out..." He groaned knowing that he would be spending tomorrow shopping for books instead of working on orders. He manually started printing the new orders.

He projected his voice and said, "HEY! Print a list of back-ordered books. HEY! Get inventory, post in table 'results' and sort descending greatest 'order amount' against least 'available quantity.' HEY! Print pages one through three of inventory 'results' table."

It was going to be a long night, so instead of starting work he listened to his printer hum and scrolled down the order list comparing it in his head to the books he had on hand.

When he envisioned a list of book shortages, he decided to procrastinate... again.

Setting his cup on the desk, Jake picked up the receiver of his phone. He took up a pad of paper with handwritten notes on it and dialed Tammy's number.

TAMMY WAS AT WORK on her computer with file folders piled around her, when the phone on her desk rang. "This is Tammy," she said, putting the phone under her chin and continued typing.

Jake's nerves were on edge as he switched ears and sat forward in his chair saying, "Ooh baby, you will not believe what's happened since I've seen you last."

Tammy stopped working to lean back in her chair and said, "Mark?"

Jake said, "No. This is Jake. Who's Mark?"

Tammy sat upright in her chair and appeared to be surprised at herself before she became sincerely excited to hear from Jake. She said, "Hey, Jake. I was just thinking about you."

"Really? Who's Mark?"

Tammy said, "Mark's my brother in Alaska. So, what're you doing tomorrow?"

"Oh. That's cool," said Jake with a shrug. "I have a problem with the phone. Uhh. Tomorrow, I have to go to a bunch of bookstores and get more books. Want to hang out?"

Tammy got real sexy and said, "Well, I might be able to hang out. Do you know a place between us to meet?"

Jake smiled thinking she wanted to go shopping with him and relaxed into his chair as he said, "My dad owns a diner at about halfway. Well, it's a little closer to me. Have you ever been to Tom's on 15th?"

Tammy nodded her head like a fisherman with a hooked trout on the line. She wanted to meet him tonight and danced in her chair. She said, "Yeah. I know Tom's. I've been there. Most of the time before bed after dancing though...I love hip-hop and there's a place right by there where dancing's free. Do you like to dance?"

He wasn't ready for that question and whined a bit as he said, "I love dancing, but I can't go out in places like that. Too much psychic feedback for me. So we are meeting at Tom's in the morning for breakfast?"

Tammy face showed disappointment as she switched ears and said, "We could now."

Jake smiled assumingly, "Great. Let's meet at 7:30?"

"I meant we could meet now," Tammy said with a saucy tone to her voice. She was trying to reel in her catch and purred, "How about in forty-five minutes?"

Completely unaware of her suggestive tone, Jake laughed and said, "Tonight doesn't work for me, I told you I have to work on these book orders. Holy crap, you wouldn't guess what happened today."

Tammy blinked her eyes a few times at their miscommunication and shook her head in disbelief. Knowing this was her last chance to make it clear that she wanted to see him tonight, she said, "Jake, I'm really glad you called and I want to talk to you tonight, but I'm still at work and need to finish something real quick. I can punch out in minutes. Do you want to—"

Jake was surprised for a moment that she had given him her work number and not home. However, he didn't want to intrude and interrupted, "Yeah-yeah, sure, we'll talk tomorrow and I'll let you go since you're busy. Meet you at 7:30."

His obtuseness and rejection of her suggestion of meeting tonight were almost personal disappointments for Tammy, but she decided that it wasn't her fault that Jake was a blockhead. "Okay, you can tell me about your day tomorrow," she said.

"See you tomorrow," Jake declared. "And, I'll tell you about Betty." CLICK!

In keeping with the metaphor, Tammy had been so sure she would be reeling him that an obsession flared when he got loose and she saw the prize fish as it flipped out of the water. With a growing urge to know more about Betty, Tammy fought to not call him back.

Jake hung up the phone with a smile for a beat and then groaned with internal grief at realizing he had just brought Tammy into his life. He looked blankly at his computer screen. Jake talked to himself and whined that maybe he should leave to try to meet with Tammy. He shook his head at the thought of calling her back.

Books, books, books… I need to hire a crew, he decided. *Tomorrow books, Wednesday get a warehouse.*

He gulped down booze-juice, shivered, and tilted back his head to shout into the house, "Betty…!"

At that moment, there was a loud rustling noise outside his window.

Jake wondered if his banishment spells had finally set his Betty free. She had never been affected before in his mystic efforts to get rid of her, but now that he had found her, maybe she had gone.

Maybe she was a mourning spirit, he thought. Jake laughed at a duplicitous thought, *Morning ghost more like.*

There was another bump and rustling at the window, he got up and pulled up the window blinds with a *THWIP!*

The window was filled with six zombie-like ghosts pressed up against the glass!

"Gahhhh," Jake shrieked with surprise. "You're in the backyard now, too. Go away or I'll scream… Again!"

Jake snapped his raised hands out at the ghosts to startle them without any affect. He dropped the blinds with a *SHHWIP!*

8

In their sedan, the Special Agents had been following Jake from corner-to-corner, when Charlie saw Jake run under a streetlight.

Beaming out a radiant aura, Jake created a halo mist of atomized snow around him as he turned the next corner in a burst of speed.

Charlie had caught a flash of it as Jake exited the beam of a harsh sodium-yellow streetlight.

Under the sharp yellow light of the next streetlamp, Jake had manifested a clearly visible mental force field. His bio-energy projection actually displayed his energy against the waves of moisture like a magnet on a piece of paper with iron filings. If anyone had watched Jake skating up the street, they would have witnessed the visual evidence that one would need to believe in the metaphysical.

Clueless of his pursuers, Jake skated down the middle of the street and then tightened his stride to the right curb of a two-lane road as he neared his street corner. Skating on his imaginary ice skates, Jake cut around the corner like an Olympic speed skater.

Joe was driving and didn't see what Charlie only caught a glimpse of—Jake had pulled his hands behind him as he took the turn and stepped foot-over-foot carving the corner.

Joe said, "This kid is really on the move. It makes me wish I were young and on the run, again."

"Joe, he isn't running. He's skating."

"Skating on what?," Joe said. "I don't even see him."

"Isn't it funny that he has been ahead of us at each turn since the snow started? I'd swear he was skating."

Joe looked at Charlie and said, "Are you kidding me, Chuckles? Good. He had purpose in evading us and is now trying to escape from known government agents. That makes it second degree."

Charlie looked at Joe with a cynical frown, "How is this a good thing? He is evading agents on skates that he didn't stop long enough to put on and is skating on ice that isn't there."

Joe parked with a quick jerk up the street from Jake's house and said, "Why aren't you taking pictures, then?"

Charlie grunted and had the camera up as quickly as Jake had entered his yard.

Click-click-click, Jake paused in what appeared to be a drunken stagger and had just fought back his panic of finding an army of ghosts in his yard.

A moment after Jake had opened his front door, he turned back to shout at the night standing on the front step of his house. He was shaking his fists and draining the invisible specters he had captured with his golden radiance. The specters retreated into the shadows when Jake released them.

Click-click-click went the camera until Jake slammed his front door and turned on his slow-responding condensed florescent lights in his front room.

Joe spoke first, "Is he just shouting at his neighbors and the world or did it look like he was talking to someone nearby? Who's he talking to…? Did you set the aperture right?"

"It's set right," Charlie said.

"It better be cuz this guy is crazy or someone was there," said Joe. "If we want a warrant, the photos need to show him talking to himself, acting in a questionable manner after evading agents and requiring intervention. Or—"

"Or, they need to show someone unseen in the yard," Charlie said as he hit a button.

The camera whirred rewinding the film. Charlie lowered the camera and said, "If we wanted to nail him, we should have stayed with him yesterday. That Natalie chick wasn't even there."

Joe said, "Hey, could you at least look at the digitals to see if it was set to the right aperture?"

Charlie didn't look at the settings or viewfinder display. Dryly, he replied, "I guess we'll know soon enough."

Joe started the car.

Charlie said, "Where are we going now?"

Joe pressed the gas pedal and said, "This weather is friggin' cold and we've got to look at the pictures before calling it a night. This guy isn't going anywhere."

He told Charlie without sarcasm that he was getting as irritating as the Denver weather and needed to drizzle out already.

The sedan pulled into the street, did a u-turn, and disappeared into the snowstorm.

TUESDAY

1

The bright warm day was made brighter by scattered and fast moving puffy white clouds. The west wind was cold and the warmth of the day shifted bitterly when the clouds passed over the sun.

Jake stood at the edge of a field and could see the front range of the Rocky Mountains.

He was smoking a cigarette.

When Jake exhaled, he created a fluffy white cloud that was heavy and sank low to the ground. The wind picked up again and the smoke stole past Jake on the breeze into a valley beyond. Smoking and looking over the fields at the clouds, Jake stood scanning the sky. The sun erupted into brilliance and warmth again as a cloud jetted out from under it.

The roar of airplanes sounded in the distance, Jake looked off to see a formation of jets moving into focus. As they approached, their roar increased. The closer they came, the more he could see that the black wings were flapping.

Suddenly, an air-raid siren echoed from an unseen tower. Jake turned and found his eyes on the cigarette he was smoking. He remembered himself and jerked to flick the cigarette butt away, but couldn't. Jake flicked several times at the cigarette stuck to his fingertips.

JAKE JERKED AWAKE FROM the dream snapping his hand into the air over his bed. He sat upright in his bed at the chirping of his alarm clock. Surprised at the sound, he hit the snooze bar. He groaned lying back onto his cold, sweat-drenched pillow.

When he turned to get away from the damp and cold side of the mattress, Betty was sitting on the bed next to him. He looked at her and for a split-second she was a faceless bloody child from his dreams.

Jake shouted, "Whoa!" He sat back up with a start and crawled without much effect to the corner of his bed. Normal again, Betty began weeping quietly and lowered her head.

Scooting back to the center of the bed, he said, "Don't be sad. You just scared me, that's all. What's wrong, Betty?" Jake reached to comfort her, she hugged him in return and began to sob.

"Ahh, it's okay. Don't cry. You don't have to cry anymore," Jake said.

Betty cried, "It is not okay. It is terrible."

Jake lied them back onto the bed, smiling with her in his arms. Betty thought for moment before resting her head on Jake's chest, he rocked her back and forth over his rounded shoulders.

Jake broke the silence, "It isn't all terrible. I found you. And, Tammy might be everything I've been looking for in a student. If she's psychic, too, maybe we can find some ghost kids for you to play with."

Betty pushed away and looked at Jake through drying tears. She shook her head and gave him a stern look, "Do you think this is a story about a single father and his daughter needing a wife and mother, Jake? It is already coming and you will have to fight. Tammy was a missing link and she has set off a chain of events that you cannot stop. Can you not see what is coming?"

"Nope, and I don't want to know either," Jake said. "Let 'em all come. I'm ready for a challenge, but let's try to rest up, Betty."

Betty set her head back down onto Jake's shoulder with a long heavy sigh. "You are not ready and your mind should be looking forward and preparing. You need to embrace life to find hope. Heroes cannot overcome death by force alone they must win because their world embodies something divine which cannot be lost. Do you not see?"

Ignoring her warning without comment, Jake began rocking her again. He tried to snooze, but his mind had taken Betty's warning as a directive, he peered into the future looking for a clown and bloody children and snoozed until his alarm sounded again. Betty was gone when Jake awoke.

ON THE BENCH IN front of Tom's Diner, Jake sat reading a paperback novel out in the cold. He was sitting on a folded newspaper that was still warm from being inside the diner. Though the bench had been swept clear of the snow, the icy hard stuff would have to melt off.

The front walk was shoveled, graveled and well-traveled this morning. He turned the page of his book and read on without looking away to the world around him.

Tammy walked out from the alley beside the diner. Seeing Jake, she moved quietly next to him. He didn't look up from his book until Tammy shouted, "Hey!"

Jake jolted back to reality and blinked himself to consciousness. He repressed his annoyance at her shouting in his face, but nicely replied, "Hey."

He knew she would hit his shoulder next. Why do some people think that a coat is padding for their playful aggression?

Tammy hit his shoulder and said a little too loudly, "So, how do you surprise a psychic?"

"1-800-flowers?," replied Jake with a big smile and tone of overexcited sarcasm. He stood up closing his book and said, "Unique up on him, of course. I was reading."

"It's still funny. What are you reading?" Tammy said as she considered cuffing Jake's arm again.

"It's a Heinlein book about a hero's journey. I'm priming my mind for some subconscious manifestation of trined planets in my dental charts or something. Shit happens, but you don't have to stomp in it and make it happen to you."

Tammy didn't understand and her voice said more than asked, "Come again?"

"Old Bob could turn out a desirable and wacky cosmic adventure, the weirdness gets more interesting instead of just life-threatening," said Jake as he found the two fifty dollar bills he put in his coat pocket after Sunday morning's breakfast at the diner and stuck them into the book to mark his place. "*Job* was too much like what could happen, so I thought *Glory Road* was appropriate as a metaphor that would help me visualize a fun adventure."

"So, you are talking about a book," Tammy said.

"Sure. Maybe, that's what makes a great author," said Jake. "However, other times, I find myself writing the books as I read them. That might seem a bit delusional, but it happens." He shoved the book into his coat pocket while using it as body-language punctuation and said, "As I drove over, I kept seeing things in shadows of the corner of my eye that turned out to be mailboxes and fence gaps."

Tammy smirked and said, "You were reading while you drove over here?"

"No-o-o. It was a bad idea to come here. This is a sad and evil place full of shady things. It was a bad omen, I never, or rather, I always see stuff that isn't there, but it doesn't change into clothesline posts. My imagination is running with scissors toward scary dark things that aren't there today."

Tammy frowned, "Maybe you are getting well, the first step is admission. Come on, cuckoo, how can a place be sad and evil? My psychic powers tell me that everything will be fine. This place is great and... warm."

"Suit yourself," Jake said. "If your powers tell you that I drink a lot, it's because I need a girlfriend and a new hobby." He moved toward the door and didn't wait for Tammy's inevitable tart reply to his statement...

She didn't disappoint and paused acting like a thoughtful contrarian as she said, "You don't have a girlfriend? Let's see, your hobbies are drinking too much, spontaneous employment, the paranormal, and storming off in huffs...you're the bad investment that little girls dream about."

Without looking back to acknowledge her mockery, he said, "Don't forget, you can also use, 'reads minds without asking, cheats on his taxes, sells devil books, smoker, and still reads comic books,' if you really wanted to hurt me."

Tammy replied, "I thought you quit smoking."

Jake made a sour face before taking the handle of the door and opening it for her. He said, "I do, however, open the door for a lady. After you, Ms. Investment-Choices."

She smiled entering the open door. "Some crazy snow last night, huh?," said Tammy walking up the main aisle. "Why didn't you wait inside? It's too cold to be reading out there."

Jake said he liked the cold air because it reminded him of smoking, but reading was actually a better reason to sit outside doing nothing. She asked if he was still not smoking and he answered that he wasn't doing as well as he had hoped, but was not smoking.

Jake and Tammy walked to a booth and sat across from each other.

Tammy said, "You know I was just teasing you back there. You are cute and toss around money for a lady. And, for someone who sees ghosts, you are very..."

Jake interjected, "Sane on the surface?"

"Actually, I was looking for a smart word to say, well read," Tammy corrected. "Pedantic?"

"Try 'quite erudite,' it's sing-songy and still implies literary knowledge. Didactic is a fitting word for me, too. Pedantic is too closely tied to unimaginative ilk."

She smiled coyly over the table and said, "Well, I certainly wouldn't want to imply that. For someone who sees ghosts, Jake, you are very sane on the surface. Nerd."

A pretty and feminine waitress in her twenties with long dishwater hair pulled up in a ponytail, stepped up to take their order. Her name-tag said, *Shayla*.

"Hi Jake," she said in a friendly high-voice. "What can I get you two to drink?"

They said coffee together.

"Jinx. Someone owes the other a Coke," Shayla said jotting with her pen. "Cream and sugar?"

Jake winked at her and said, "Nope. Just the regular cold and bitter stuff for me, Shayla."

Shayla and Tammy rolled their eyes.

Tammy said, "Do you have skim?"

"Yes, we do. Sugar?"

"Maybe some honey...?"

She said with a bright grin, "I can do that. Anything else?"

Shayla smiled at Jake, her visage quickly flickered with her rapid-fire thoughts as Jake unintentionally overheard them, *High-maint— Like her. Cute-sugar-honey-sweet.* "I'll have to try honey in my coffee sometime," Shayla said. Her smile told him, *I still miss you, Jake.*

He smiled back with an unwarranted sweetness, "Thanks, Shay. How are you doing?"

Shayla smiled with warmth and said, "I'm still here." She shrugged and nodded away to her feet, which followed her eyes. Jake watched her go.

"She likes you," Tammy said. "And, she's cute. Maybe a nice new hobby."

"I'm not ashamed to say that I know Shayla likes me," Jake frowned. "She's just too nice and has been the hardest girl to just let be. We dated a little, but she wouldn't have understood the truth about me. Not the psychic, not the magician, especially not the drunk. She could only see the tortured artist and would have taken the rest of my shortcomings personally. She deserves a nice normal guy to be happy with."

"Don't we all," Tammy said, "So what did you do to ruin it?"

"How 'bout 'dat, your psychic powers do work, eh," mocked Jake. "I ruined it on my birthday when I walked her to my front door after playing pool and watching one of my favorite movies that she'd bought for me. She stepped in to make the first move and tiptoed to kiss me good night with puckered lips. It was the sweetest thing I'd ever seen and I felt dirty in her presence, she was broadcasting the most divine songs of true love. I pulled up from her kiss and could only hug her. She was so innocent and untainted."

Uninterrupted, Jake shook out of a brief coma and continued, "She is beautiful inside and out, which also attracted me for the two weeks of our romance. It was unreal... Being with her was like being strung out on nice pills." He laughed at his joke and said, "She still likes me, and maybe, she fell in love with her version of me, but I liked her more because I could never hurt her."

Tammy interjected, "That was very ignoble of you not to break her heart and decide for her. Why not let her love you? Love lost was once found."

"And, noble would be better to have loved and there is nothing worth having...? Blah-blah-blah, more twelve-step bullshit, you must have majored in criminal behavior. Look, I don't have some starry-eyed personal version of her, either. I cheated and peeped in her head. I would have hurt her bad. There was stuff in there that only I could do to betray her. She can't even think 'bad' of someone like you. Shayla is a very nice person and I would've been her greatest sorrow as I whittled her down with my cynicism of God and man. She is a reason to save the world and I should die to save a world so good. I've learned everything I knew from women who wanted a hero. I am Paris declaring Venus the fairest because I had thought the petty gods were vying for me. Trust me, I'll never pick Helen, again, and will thus find my petty goddess."

"Ever thought of writing poetry or acting Shakespeare?"

Jake recovered his mind from the tide of his Shayla memories and said, "I wrote poetry until I found out that I could also draw an equally beautiful series of lines that broke the language barrier."

"Drawing is the language of love?"

Missing the joke, Jake said, "I guess so. Certainly of passion." He grabbed a menu from the wire condiment rank on the table. "This is on me and I'll accept no argument."

Tammy took the menu and smiled as she thought to herself, *He sure is a pushy nerd... Is this the face of the modern criminal?*

Goodbye, 'Forgettaboutit, babe. Order whatever, it's on me,' she thought. *Hello, 'I will accept no argument, female unit.'*

AFTER THEIR ORDERS WERE prepared, Shayla returned to Jake and Tammy's booth and set two plates of breakfast sandwiches in front of them. Jake finished his coffee and asked Shayla for another. It only took a moment, so he waited for her to fill his cup and leave before he started speaking again.

"So, I told you about the Satanists, right?"

Tammy picked up her breakfast sandwich and said, "Yeah. Are the orders still rolling in?"

"Yeah. Too many," said Jake. "Like I was saying outside. Something has happened, I have tapped some cosmic vein...or something. Now, my world is overflowing with weirdness. Last night, there were ghosts waiting for me when I got home."

Chewing, Tammy grunted out through close teeth and pinched lips, "More than one ghost, now? How's your other little ghost?"

"I have too many ghosts now. Your 'name her' thing worked, too, and Betty came to me yesterday morning. I actually went back to sleep and was late for work. She was there again this morning."

"You found your ghost," Tammy asked. Then tilted her head and said, "Wait. I thought you said you didn't have a job."

"Sure, I work, life is work. I have a gallery and an art school. It's more like a salon. I credit my students a fair monthly allowance to their company expense account and lecture them twice a week. My school also provides them a workspace and premium space at the local arts show I hold once a month. They only have to pay taxes on the work they sell at the shows."

Tammy said, "They can't do that unless their sales exceed their expenses."

"They do. And I roll my gallery profits into an environmental non-profit," Jake said. "I'd rather talk about something else, but we also provide educational scholarship grants for higher learning and require that our students give back twenty hours a week to their communities. I don't think of it as a job, though. Just work."

"Sounds like a cult, you don't play guitar, do you," Tammy asked snidely. "Hey, work is work and you were late. What happened?"

"Finally! This is why I called last night. I'm never late in the morning. I named her and she came. I fell back asleep and woke up late. I couldn't say it wasn't a dream until this morning, but Betty was back, crying. I'd swear she was all bloody for a second. Then she was normal again and told me that 'they're coming and I'll have to fight.'"

"So, POOF, you find your ghost just like that and it isn't a dream? This sounds like one of your anarchist pick-up lines," she said. In a flash of disbelief, Tammy paused and said before taking a bite, "That is weird. Who do you think is coming... The government?"

Shrugging with clashing emotions, Jake exhaled through his nose before he calmly said, "I don't care if you believe me. I'm just being honest and thought you'd like to know that your idea worked. As to her saying someone is coming—If they're coming, they're coming. Maybe she was talking about all the spooks in my life...I don't know."

With a touch of concern in her voice, Tammy said, "Are you planning for a fight? Is that why you were reading that book?"

Jake shrugged in silence and took a bite. "If you are really asking me that," he said chewing. "Yes, I am always ready to kill whitey. Do you have a first strike plan for us?"

Tammy just looked at him.

They both chewed their breakfast sandwiches for an uncomfortable moment of silence.

"If you like this breakfast sandwich, you should try the lunch wraps," Jake said.

As if in response to his statement, there was the uproar of laughter behind him at the counter. Jake looked back and said something about the guy at the counter getting lively. Tammy didn't see anyone at the place at the counter he had indicated.

"No one is at the bar?," he said to her.

Then it dawned on him. Jake looked back and shouted, "Jerry, no! I didn't know you passed."

Jerry shrugged, "It was a stroke and you know my family. The landlord found me."

"How'd you get back here," Jake asked.

Jerry acted ashamed and said, "I followed your dad back from the funeral."

"No shame in that," Jake said with his internal voice. "I'm glad you did. You boys just keep it down over there."

He nodded at Jerry with a smile before turning back to Tammy and said, "You couldn't hear that buzzing?"

Tammy shook her head while she chewed.

"Nothing?," said Jake.

Tammy smiled and shook her head again, swallowing.

READING THE NEWSPAPER, Frank had been sitting at the end of the counter and exhaled smoke as he turned his chin over his shoulder to watch Jake and Tammy.

They were eating together at the booth and engaged in casual conversation about their meals.

Jake nodded up at Tammy and said, "So, what're you doing this morning?"

"I ditched work. You said something about a bookstore, didn't you?"

Pleased, Jake smiled, "Bookstores. Do you want to come along?"

Tammy chewed, not able to reply like a lady, but her head wagged wishy-washy.

Before she could answer, Jake and Tammy were interrupted by Frank, who exhaled smoke into the air between them with a grunt.

Frank said, "So are you going to introduce me?"

Jake acted inconvenienced and said, "Tammy, this is Frank. Frank, Tammy. Dude, when are you going to get that I can't introduce you to anyone. You're a ghost."

"I'm a ghost?," said Frank overacting his response like a sarcastic ass. "But she can't see you talking to me...? Are you a ghost, too?"

"I'm here with a girl, Frank," said Jake rolling his eyes. "Beat it."

Frank made a sour face, "Maybe, she's the ghost. Or worse. Didn't Betty tell you, yet? They're coming."

"Frank. I'm with a girl. Bye!," Jake said.

Jake looked across to Tammy, "You really don't hear that annoying buzzing?"

Tammy said she didn't nor did she seem to hear Frank or tune in from the clues he had dropped.

She can't hear Frank after all, Jake thought. *How did she know he said my fly was down? Was it down? Was she possessed by Frank when I met her?*

Jake said to Tammy, "If you come along, I can show you my haunts and tell you about my mission at the art school and for my bookstore. You can tell me about your tarot cards. Want to stop by my favorite occult store for some new tarot cards?"

"That sounds fun," Tammy said. Her tone flattened as she said, "But, only if you don't ditch me at some mall like you left me at my apartment."

Jake was made uncomfortable by the barb and tried to explain, "About that. You touched a nerve about college, I was an alcohole because I had book orders. It was time to work. Sorry if I was abrupt."

She looked at him, her face was giving just enough encouragement for any man to hang himself in the rope she was tangling.

He smiled, "You caught me off guard. My last girlfriend had a fixation with my going back to college. I flipped out on you cuz it felt like too much, too fast. You were crashing on me like an ocean. Did you start reading Alice?"

After a few chews and a big gulp, she replied, "Not yet. I did look at all the pictures, though. Amazing."

Frank leaned into Tammy's face as she turned her wrist to look at her cute little watch. He snapped his fingers and she froze in mid-motion looking at her wrist.

Frank said to the frozen Tammy, "He already has girls following him. Stalking him, in fact. There's this one girl—"

"Leave her alone," Jake interrupted with authority.

Frank looked at him, "I thought she couldn't hear me, dipshit."

"I can hear you, ya' twat," Jake said raising his hand with a backward peace sign. "Now, undo your spell and beat it, Frank."

"You can't just fuckin' dismiss me," he shouted back at Jake. "You will not ignore me. Should I tear out her entrails, right now? Will that get your attention?"

Tammy wasn't moving and sat frozen looking at her watch. The world was frozen.

Jake sighed in defeat, "What do you want, Frank?"

"We still need to talk about 'the favor.' I need a ride across town and Tammy has other things to do. Don't you, Tammy?," said Frank as he snapped his fingers again and disappeared into a cloud of smoke.

Tammy focused on her watch. She blinked her eyes several times and reacted with surprise at the time, "Hey, Jake, I gotta go. I didn't realize it was this late. Weird." She looked down at her half-eaten sandwich and said, "Didn't we just get here?"

She looked at her wristwatch again with disbelief and tried to recall events. "I need to meet a girlfriend in a half-hour and we're shopping for her interview shoes."

Jake said, "For shoes? You can't really be serious. Get shoes tomorrow." He was trying to force Tammy to break Frank's magical suggestion. "Let's get some new tarot cards for you."

She scooted to the edge of the booth and pulled on her coat as she decided to say, "I can meet you after lunch, if you are still book shopping. I'll call you." Tammy was in a strange panic and took a big bite of her sandwich before standing. Not revealing her teeth, she grinned at Jake like a chipmunk with one pouch filled and said, "Walk me to the door?"

She stood and chewed her last bite as she moved up the aisle with a soft click-clack of nice shoes that Jake had overlooked. They were power shoes.

Setting his sandwich down, he stood in response and quickly followed her to the door. "Maybe I should call you at one o'clock. I don't have a cell phone."

Tammy shook her head with disbelief and paused for a moment as she said, "What, really? Okay, call mine. The cashier will have a pen."

The entire place watched the handsome couple move up the aisle together.

They stopped at the register and Doris gave her a pen, Tammy took Jake's hand to write on it. She penned a little heart below her number and said, "Call me at one sharp." She almost turned to leave, but then swung back with open arms, "Hugs?"

Jake hugged her stiffly for a second. He could feel that she was going to hit him, again.

"You need to work on your hugs, mister," Tammy said with a grin as she smacked his shoulder. "See you later, I hope."

She left the diner with a sassy wave, Jake turned back to the booth with a smile.

The undead lunch-counter diners were very interested upon his return and had turned toward the aisle to face him.

Jake went to the booth and tossed a hundred-dollar bill on the table. He moved to the counter with his plate in hand and sat onto an empty stool beside an old woman in a floral-patterned dress, who was eating a huge meal while reading the paper.

Jake called over into the prep area to the cook and said, "Where's Tom, Juan?"

Juan looked back and shook his head in reply, "Tu papi se fue la casa. Malo, no bueno."

From over Jake's shoulder, Frank's voice whispered in his ear, "He said, Tom went home cuz he wasn't feeling well."

Frank was right there in Jake's face when he turned to the voice. "Tom's having a heart attack," Frank reported.

In utter dismay, Jake shouted, "What's your goddamn problem today!?"

Everyone in the diner looked at Jake, who was sitting beside the old lady and shouting out loud at her. The woman acted overly surprised and shocked at his outburst.

Jake could only shake his head in defeat and whispered to the old lady, "Sorry, Irma." He said over his shoulder, "Look what you did, Frank. They all heard me!"

"What did I do? You're the idiot who shouted for everyone to hear, ass. Hey, Irma and I are outta here in seconds. Give me a ride to the bingo hall and I'll show you something to make up for my rudeness this morning," Frank said with a wink and several long slow nods to egg Jake on.

Jake stepped up tall from his stool and stood face-to-face with Frank.

With anger in his eyes, Jake glanced back at his unfinished food and finally said pushing past Frank, "Fine. Let's go. Maybe you'll get lost."

Most of the staff and patrons in the diner watched Jake walk up the aisle and out of the diner with Frank trailing behind him.

Before exiting, Frank turned to look around the room holding up his middle finger, "If you don't like it here in the ugly world, go someplace with a family section and crayons."

Everyone watching looked away uncomfortably as Frank followed Jake out the front door.

2

It was a busy morning in front of Greenwood Academy, an upper-class private school. Cars pulled up and children got out at the curb.

Mike, wearing a beanie-cap and black turtleneck under his big army surplus jacket that made him look like an undercover cop, sat in his green truck up the street with a clear view of the school. He watched as shouting parents pulled up, dropped off their spoiled produce, and drove away smiling.

Gary, the weekend's birthday boy, climbed from a Mercedes and stepped out onto the walk with a backpack in hand. He slammed the door and the sedan moved up the street.

When the Mercedes pulled away from the curb, Mike the Cop's truck followed it into the neighborhood.

IN A MALL PARKING lot after a cross-town drive, Mike pulled his truck into a spot near the parked Mercedes.

Mike stepped out and paced as he inspected the luxury sedan for a second.

Within a subtle and casual movement, Mike bent to look at the rear wheel of the Mercedes and had removed from his coat pocket a thin, short blade that looked like an ice pick for tires. He tapped the tire tool under the wheel well with a quick jab and snap off the blade in the tire putting a puncture into it that would look like a nail had done the damage.

Mike listened and it sounded like a light hiss that wouldn't flatten the tire for a few hours. He stood hoping it wouldn't be much more than six hours and considered making a second hole before replacing the tire tool in his coat pocket.

He backed away looking at the car like a fan with admiration for this classic Mercedes and walked back to his truck.

When his cell phone rang, Mike had just closed himself into the truck cab. After belting up and turning the ignition, he answered the phone before dropping the pick-up into gear.

It was his chief officer asking him to report in a few minutes early. The Chief made a brief apology and said that Mike had been requested from upstairs for a short-term assignment.

It sounded too coincidental. Were they looking to set me up now?, thought Mike. *Did a rat take the bait and squeal me out this morning?*

Either way, Mike embraced the news replying that he was interested in any referral from upstairs and looking forward to hearing about it. They made farewells. He clicked the flip-top phone closed.

The truck exited the parking lot and Mike began to laugh. His plan was coming together like a miracle. It was time to attack and raise the bets. This was fate—or a setup—Mike didn't believe in fate, so he would drive forward with a keen eye watching for any setup.

Mike had made sure that Patterson couldn't let anyone scratch too deep into the bodies that were left behind last night, but Patterson might still try to dig a hole for him next to Sarconi. Mike decided it didn't matter, Patterson's shelf life was now a week—at best. Mike had made sure of it.

Either way, the power goes out tonight. This is about taking down the pieces and putting the king in check, Mike thought as he turned his truck onto the boulevard. *Lights, camera, action... Come get me!*

MIKE'S TRUCK DROVE PAST his police precinct and turned into the lot beside it.

In the locker room, he had changed into his uniform and reported for duty.

His boss briefed him on his temporary assignment to help out a couple of IRS Special Agents from Missouri.

Mike was quite pleased by the information and almost laughed. It confirmed his hopes and fit very well into his plans. A special assignment with non-locals would give him all the freedom he needed to go all in.

It was fate, he thought. *This isn't a setup at all.*

Five uniformed officers, all male and of various ages, were gathered in a break room when Mike entered and moved to the fridge. He removed an old, thick Tupperware bowl from the top shelf of the lunch-packed fridge and stepped over to the microwave, which had something cooking in it.

Behind Mike, a younger officer asked, "So what was Internal Affairs snooping around for on Sarconi, Patterson? I thought it was a clear case of self-defense."

A neurotic tic pulled across his face as Mike set his bowl down and listened to the chatting officers as the central officer, Don Patterson, began retelling his story to the other four.

Patterson said, "Listen, you guys don't know him like I do. I had to talk straight to Internal Affairs about him. He's always been a fuckin' loose cannon. Come on, he was off-duty and shot two rich guys…they might be mob, but one's dead. I hated to do it, but—"

The microwave beeped.

Mike opened the door, removed the food container and placed his Tupperware into the oven.

"Hey, is that—," Patterson started to say. "Uh, hey, Mike. That's mine. Did it feel warm?"

Mike punched a few buttons to start the microwave and said, "Yeah, your Lean Cuisine should be fine. Most of the rats I know don't care if their food is a little cold." He picked up the container that he had removed from the microwave and tossed it on the table in front the surprised officers.

Mike continued, "Sarconi is a good man and my first choice as a partner."

Patterson acted offended and looked at the officers around him for support. Not finding it, he offered it to them, "I meant, no one but you can handle him, Mike. Come on guys, who else could keep Sarconi in line. Mike's an animal." Not forthcoming, Patterson continued, "I mean no one else can do it, Mike."

Mike chortled and said, "Why don't you take your bullshit and dog food back to your desk before I tell these guys about the time Sarconi saved your ass cuz you couldn't pull the trigger."

Shocked at the response, Patterson picked up his lunch from the table and put on a serious cop face that told his thoughts long before he said them to make his point clear, "Don't fuck with me, Mike."

Mike was indifferent to the threat and crossed his arms leaning back against the counter. "Scurry off, rat, before you piss your pants again."

Patterson exited and the others followed him seeing that Mike was not in a social mood.

The last officer paused in the doorway turning back toward Mike and said, "Sorry about Sarconi, Mike. I told IA that he was one of our finest."

Mike nodded and said, "Thanks, Danse. You watch, Patterson is going to eat those words when I dig up the dirt on him."

"What's wrong with you, man. Patterson is untouchable until they vote the Judge out," said Danse. He nodded to Mike and said, "Don't push it too far, Straka. I'd hate to be telling IA about you being a good cop, or worse. Sarconi is lucky to be alive, the guys he shot weren't just some punks. It's just getting hotter for him inside and out."

"The Judge and Patterson set Sarconi up to kill those guys. And I'm going find out why they were shot."

They looked at each other in a mental rapport that only cops know.

The officer broke eye contact when the microwave beeped and laughed.

Danse said, "Did Patterson really piss himself?"

Mike smiled, "He did. Too bad the bullet didn't cut through his vest."

3

In the parking lot of Tom's Café, Jake held up a step to let Frank catch up to him. With a cigarette in his mouth, Frank paused parallel with Jake as he lifted a lighter in his left hand to light the cigarette. Exhaling a cloud of smoke, Frank turned his left hand up and had made the lighter disappear into thin air with a sleight of hand flair.

Jake watched Frank who turned his left hand down and quickly snap it up again with an open pack of cigarettes that magically appeared in his fingertips.

"Wow," Frank said. "That was some magic. Want a cigarette?"

Jake looked at the offered pack in temptation, but said, "I'm not a smoker, Frank."

"Sure you don't want to see that trick, again, though? It was pretty slick." Frank turned his hand and now held a lighter with the pack.

"I don't want a cigarette," Jake said before swallowing his lie.

Frank shrugged and said after a long, snide pull from the cigarette dangling from his lips, "I guess not, junkie."

The pack and lighter were both gone when Frank plucked the burning cigarette from his mouth with his magical left hand.

He said through a smoke-filled throat, "Let's go already. Where we going?"

"Where do you need to go," Jake replied.

"I asked you first. Where are we going?"

Jake sighed, "I'm buying books across town."

"Hey, why not leave your car here and ride the bus with me instead? It'll be pulling up out front in a few minutes and I've got a fever that only the bus can cure."

Jake began walking and said into the air ahead of him, "Nope, the bus won't work for me today. There are too many places to go and too many books to haul around. I need a lot of books, Frank." Digging out his car keys, he paused and continued, "If my orders don't slow down, I'll be selling new books for a loss next week."

Exhaling smoke, Frank said, "Used books are a diminishing resource, buddy. I mean recycling the paper was a better idea than encouraging people to burn them. You'd be surprised how many people would freeze to death rather than burn a book, but tell them to recycle and bye-bye books. So, if you get enough book orders, will my Satanists put you out of the book business?"

"Nope, I am on a mission and have already thought about hiring a staff," Jake said jingling his keys to prompt Frank to make a decision. He said, "If you are going to bingo, this bus is leaving."

Frank looked right to left and then back to face Jake as if he was weighing the options of causing trouble on the bus or focusing it just on Jake.

Jake had unlocked the door of a snow-free, newer model, Japanese pick-up truck and decided to be clever when he said across the roof to Frank, "I'll let you smoke in the car, if you can tell me what you know about the ghosts in my yard."

"Not my business, so you are on your own there, jackass," said Frank, snarling smoke from his mouth. Frank made it a point to hold up his hand in the air above his head when he flipped his cigarette butt across the parking lot. "Let's talk about Michelle and your new friend Tammy, instead. Please try not to get pulled over cuz the only things worse than you monkeys are your shitbird overlords."

In the distance, several crows cawed in laughter as if responding to Frank's joke.

Frank pointed it out and said, "Hear that? They love me in Crowurbia." He raised his voice and shouted, "Thanks, guys. I'll be here all week and please tip the excellent wait staff."

"Dummy," Jake said. "The crows can't hear you either. One of them just shit on the driver's side of a windshield or found a quarter."

Frank's eyes lit up and he said, "Oh, evolution jokes are my favorite. Poop jokes and money were key to your re-evolution, freak." Frank climbed into the car and said, "Proceed, please."

Jake had just snapped his safety belt and lifted his keys to the ignition slot, when Frank paraphrased himself saying, "I said, let's roll." With a snap of his fingers, Jake's car started. Jake was caught off-guard.

Frank acted urgent, "We need to go now." He grabbed the console's drive control stick and shifted into reverse.

The car jerked out of the parking spot. Frank shifted into drive and off they went into motion.

"Frank! Stop it," Jake grabbed the wheel and jammed the brake. Frank smiled as the car darted from the lot into the street and said, "Sit back and enjoy the ride, honey. I can't have the crows telling anyone that I let a monkey use a stick and wheel to drive me about according to his will. I'm the driver, mule."

Jake offered the keys to Frank, who waved them off and said, "I'm glad you learned something today, now move your other hand. I want to feel the wheels drag against some pavement."

Jake put his hands into his coat pockets and leaned back into his seat. Frank jerked the truck around the corner into traffic with the sweet sound of crunching sand.

THE G-MEN, JOE AND CHARLIE, sat in their sedan watching Jake from across the street. Joe held a camera to his eye and said, "Can't get a good one of the other person. It looks like an old lady. Here—" Joe handed the camera to Charlie and asked him, "See if you can get one of both of them together."

Charlie took the camera and had just lifted it to his eye, when BAM a white tropical bird with long head-feathers and bright yellow on its chest and tail slammed onto the hood of the car.

Both men jerked with surprise at the thud of a parrot hitting face down on the hood; its wings still out and flapping in a dazed reflex.

As suddenly as it had hit, three big black crows followed its fall and attacked. They made an uneven jackhammer noise as their beaks struck metal and parrot flesh, adding to the abrupt suspense of the scene. Neither of the men moved, both in shock for the moment.

As quickly as the crows had landed and pecked the parrot to death, the lead crow flew off with the white bird in its claws.

Looking at the men through the windshield, the other two crows pecked menacingly at the hood a few times before winging into the air.

The violence had only left a few bloodied white feathers on the hood of the car as evidence to the murder.

Joe shouted, "What the hell was that?"

Charlie pointed across Joe toward the parking lot and shouted, "Go, go! St. Johns is on the move!"

Jake's truck jerked right leaving the opposite side of the parking lot.

Joe fired the ignition, dropped the sedan into gear and stomped the gas. "Damn it all! You did see the birds, right?," he shouted.

The sedan jerked hard across the street and into the parking lot, it sped across the lot to the opposite side.

When they reached the street across the lot, Frank had just jerked Jake's car around the corner and grinded against the gravel and sand. Joe punched the gas and they raced toward the corner as the light turned yellow.

Tires squealed across the pavement and ice as the sedan cornered into the second lane of a four-lane street.

Joe said, "You saw those goddamned birds, right?!"

Charlie scanned the area looking for Jake's truck and said, "Yeah, I saw the birds. Now pay attention, it's icy. There he is!"

The sedan followed Jake's truck around the next street corner and into morning traffic.

AFTER A BRIEF DRIVE, Jake's truck pointed down a street with too much daytime traffic. Frank took his hand from the wheel and pulled an imaginary cord overhead between them as he said, "Ding-ding! This is my stop, Jakey, so you may now drive me to bingo."

"I thought you were going to show me something," Jake said taking the wheel.

"As if I didn't, I showed you how to drive. Now drive and show me what you've learned," said Frank as he narrowed his eyes. He laughed while shaking his head with a smirk, "Whatever. So I didn't show you anything. It's my prerogative and I lied to spend some quality time with you alone, Jake."

As Jake pulled into a mini-mart storefront and rolled slowly up the main lane of the lot, Frank grabbed him in a headlock and gave him a quick jostle.

"Hey, I'm driving," Jake shouted as he braked to avoid colliding with a parked car.

Frank broke his hold and said, "You know, you should stop standing on the shoulders of others and be the giant by writing your own stories. Do a graphic novel, chicken."

Jake turned back with his patience peaked and said, "Yeah, what story do I have to tell, Frank? I'm psychic and get to watch a demon's stupid old lady magic tricks." With hostility in his eyes, Jake motioned for Frank to get out.

Frank opened the door, sat forward and climbed out without answering. From the pavement, he said into the truck cab, "What story do you have to tell? Try the one that started when Betty found you. You can use this ride as a nice turning point."

Frank had become the old woman that Jake had sat next to at the diner – Irma, who had worn a floral dress with her hair tied back in a bun, leaned her head back through the door.

With Frank's voice, Irma said, "Thanks for the ride, Jakey. Me and Irma are going to whip some bingo ass!"

"Irma and I am," Jake corrected. "I hope you meet a nice priest, Irma."

"Where's the fun in that?," she cackled in her own voice as she slammed the car door.

When the door closed, the car died.

Taking out the keys from his coat pocket, Jake exhaled a sigh of bittersweetness as he shook his head starting the truck again. He shifted it into drive and darted back into traffic.

Jake crested a hill and snow-covered mountain peaks loomed behind the Denver skyline like a backdrop painting. The vista captured the attention of Jake's artistic eye and the government sedan followed behind him undetected as he drove toward the city.

4

Jake had parked at a mall and removed his safety belt. Leaning over the center console, he reached under the passenger seat and removed a half-filled canvas book bag from beneath it.

He walked across a parking lot toward the main entrance and carried in both hands the retrieved book bag as if it were fragile.

In this same yellow-lined mall parking lot, the agents were parked under a lamppost several rows away and waited until Jake got out. When he had committed to the mall's entrance, they got out to follow him at a slow pace. Charlie and Joe weren't being very careful to keep Jake from learning that he was being followed—they wanted him to know it.

The agents were silent for the moment and reflected on the events leading them here.

How about not being able to take a photo of an old lady in the diner lot?, Joe thought before breaking the silence. "Fuckin' crows," Joe said shaking his head. "Did you see them tap their beaks at us?"

"Yeah, I saw it," Charlie said with a grunt.

"You didn't think it was weird?," Joe insisted.

"Yes, it was weird. And we almost missed St. Johns because of it."

"That's all I wanted to hear, Charlie. I thought the same thing. It was like a distraction. What if this guy is a magician?"

"A magician?" said Charlie. "Like some magic spell made it happen?"

Joe laughed, "No. Like, maybe, he's going to the joke shop next."

Charlie didn't laugh and groaned picking up his pace toward the doors that Jake had entered; Joe chuckled dogging his heels.

WITHIN THE WARM COMFORTS of the mall and under the mock sunlight from overhead fluorescents, Jake thought about the mall's designer trying to make every entrance point feel like a return to the safety of the womb. He turned from the main thoroughfare into an open-front mall store.

He didn't scan the titles of the books stacked on the wall racks or the postcards in spinning racks, nor did he look up at the comic books in bags suspended on hooks from the ceiling tile struts.

Jake stepped directly to the counter.

The storekeeper, Todd, was in his late-thirties and wearing an unbuttoned short-sleeved button-down over a superhero t-shirt. He sat behind the counter reading a big Harry Potter hardback book.

When he saw Jake, Todd quickly marked his place and set down the book. As Jake approached, Todd called out to him, "Hey! Whatcha got in the bag, Jake? Got some books for trade?"

"Nice try, Todd. No, I'm on a mission and bringing bribes," said Jake. He pulled out a stack of bagged and boarded comic books from his canvas bag and set them on the counter-top. "I need some novels and this is your advance."

Todd picked up the comic books from the countertop, his face showing interest as he flipped through them like a kid in a comic store. He said, "Whoa! This is more like extortion. It's a slow month and I can't afford any of these, Jake."

"I was thinking incentive bonus. Those books are worth twenty-five hundred dollars easily, and hell, once I finish my book rush, I'll come buy them back for the usual marked-up retail price," Jake said as he slapped down a sheet of paper on the counter. "Can you get me these books?"

Todd fought to set Jake's comics aside and had a hard time focusing back on the business at hand as he look over Jake's order sheet. "These are yard-sale novels."

"I don't care what you think of them, Todd." Jake said, "Can you get them?"

"Count on it," said Todd. Without taking his eyes from the paper, he said, "What is wrong with you that you would get rid of these classics for a bunch of cra—"

As Todd spoke, Jake looked at a halved apple and a flawless ripe banana Todd had on the counter. Suddenly, Jake seemed to have an otherworldly internal insight and snapped out with a prophecy. "Can I use your phone real quick," Jake asked.

"Easy, man," said Todd, perturbed by the unusual interruption. He turned the phone out toward Jake and replied, "Sure. No long-distance calls, though. Are you really giving me these?" Todd looked dazed as picked up Jake's comics again.

"Yes," Jake said punching in a number. "They're yours."

"Really," Todd whined with disbelief. "Superheroes are hot again. These might be reaching closer to ten grand."

Jake waited for a beat with the phone to his ear in silence, while Todd leered at each book through its Mylar protection bag to find its flaws.

"Yes, it is a good day," Jake responded to the other person on the line. "Hello, Martin, this is Jake St. Johns. Hi. I need you to leverage half of my Microsoft holdings and buy equal shares of Apple."

He paused listening and responded, "It's bananas, in fact. I got a feeling they're going to take a big shift this week. When Apple hits $180, dump them until you cover the margin and then hold again. Thanks, Martin, gotta go."

Martin tells him to consider it done, but continued saying, "Jake, your account history has been requested by the IRS and we should meet as soon as possible to discuss any details."

"Please comply and give them what they are requesting," replied Jake. "The IRS is the least of my worries. But, we should meet if you get a call from the SEC. I do have to run, though, I'll call you back next week. Bye."

Jake hung up and slid the phone back to Todd, who was focused again on the book list.

Todd said with a tone of uncertainty, "Jake, I can get these books, but now I am looking at your quantities... Like I said, I'm a little tight on cash and I can only get half of these on credit. It'll take a month to fulfill this with my regular orders."

"So, you need some cash upfront?," said Jake.

"Whoa, dude...," said Todd, insulted. "I ain't beggin', I'm just telling you it will take at least a month through my distributor."

"You're killing me, man," he responded. Jake pulled out a money clip and peeled off several hundred-dollar bills. "I don't have a month. Get me that list by Thursday and give me a receipt with your retail values." He tossed a handful of bills onto the counter. "Call me if you need more cash to make it happen."

Todd picked up the cash and shook his head with a smirk; Jake exited toward the mall.

Todd shouted after Jake, "So, are these comics really mine?"

Jake called back without looking, "They're a bribe, Todd. That's how they work. If you call me tomorrow with good news, I'll pay you another fifty-percent over your numbers."

"Consider it done," Todd shouted back.

Todd looked at the list for a moment. Then, he thought for a brief second about the call Jake had made and looked online to find that Apple stock was trading at one hundred and fifteen a share.

If Jake was right about the amount of potential gains and he was certain enough to leverage Microsoft...

Smiling, he picked up the phone and pressed redial. As the phone rang in Todd's ear, Charlie and Joe entered the store and moved toward the register. He was looking at the list when the call was answered. "Uh, hi, I was recommended by a friend's father to call you. Martin, right? Cool. I would like to open an investment account. Can I do it all online?"

Todd held up a forefinger of pause to the G-men, who were now at his counter.

"Okay. Cool. I just got a hot tip and—," Todd said, counting again the cash as he listened with the handset under his chin. "Uh. I have... a few thousand dollars in cash that I'd like to invest." Todd paused to listen to Martin on the other line. "Really? Cool. I'm in the Eastlake Mall at a store called, The Book Attic. 'Addict' is misspelled like an attic." He paused again. "You know it? Great. See you this afternoon."

Todd hung up the phone and called after Charlie and Joe, who had left the counter and were walking toward the mall's interior artery.

"Hey, can I help you guys?," he said.

They didn't look back when Joe called out and said, "You just did. Thanks. Don't leave town."

"Thanks. Come again," said Todd to no one shrugging his shoulders. "Weirdos."

He took a big bite of his apple, chewing it in thought for a beat before picking up the phone again to call his book distributor.

ON THE WAY OUT, Jake passed a bank of payphones and called Tammy, even though it wasn't quite one o'clock. She didn't answer, so he left a voicemail saying that his next stop would be at The Neighborhood Bookstore on Third and Cherry and if she was going to meet him, he would be there until at least two-thirty.

After making several other visits to places with used books, Jake parked his truck in front of The Neighborhood Bookstore.

He entered and diligently pushed closed the weather-beaten door behind him.

Owner said, "Hi there. Nice day out, huh?"

"It's perfect for the season. It was starting to feel like summer and we can't have that yet. Can we?," Jake said.

"It won't be long. It might be chilly, but the snow from last night has already melted," Owner said looking out the front window.

Jake looked out the window and wondered if his books in the truck bed would be safe. He was about to blow off the thought, but said, "Hey, would you mind keeping an eye on my truck?"

Owner nodded with a smile, Jake smiled back and moved into the store walking directly into the back room. He turned the corner disappearing into the basement.

Jake was looking through a shelf of books when he jerked up his head to stand tall as if he had heard a dog-whistle. He turned side-to-side as if he was listening for something.

Meanwhile, upstairs at the front desk, the owner was frustrated by what he found when he looked out the window and noticed several boxes of books in the truck bed. This reminded him of the call from the IRS that he received on Sunday.

Was this guy the other bookseller they had talked to Natalie about?

He found the folder with the information that the agents had left with Natalie.

When the owner looked at a photo of Jake St. Johns, he turned to his card catalog and removed a card. "St. Johns, not Charles or George," he said with bitterness. "Damn it and I gave him those books on credit. Well not today, mister."

Down a flight of stairs in the basement of the building, Jake was still listening for something when a very feminine hand stroked the hair on the back of Jake's neck. The hand belonged to a ghost wearing nothing more than airy lingerie. He turned around, giving her a look of disapproval, and said, "Please stop it, you're distracting me." He shook his head and continued looking through the shelves in front of him, forgetting about the danger that had pinged for his attention.

After a solid hour of browsing, Jake moved to the counter with a tall, single stack of hard-backed books escorted by the three women wearing turn-of-the-century lingerie.

"Don't I know you," Owner asked as Jake approached. "You were just in here a couple of days ago?"

"I don't think you know me," Jake replied, his aura making his visage hazy. "I've been here before. You have a lot of great books."

The owner looked at him with a hard glare and struggled to focus on Jake's blurred face.

Jake used the silence to change the subject and said, "It's been a while since I traded in any books, but I might still have some credits."

Owner said, "That's right, you had credits. It's all coming back to me. What's the name again? George? John. John St. James?"

Taken aback, Jake disliked that the owner remembered him. He began to consciously press his psychic will into the owner because he was pissed off that he had to use his real name again and replied, "Jake St. Johns."

A strange smile of victory registered on the owner's face before moving away to check the card catalog. Jake noticed the owner's aura had changed since earlier and it was now broadcasting fear and tension. He knew several things had changed and an altercation was coming. Jake could read only parts of Owner's racing memories knowing he had seen the books in his truck, someone had talked to Natalie, and there was a photo of him. Now the thoughts were so obscured by adrenalin that Jake couldn't make sense of any of them.

Why would they have a photo of me, Jake wondered.

After shuffling for a beat or two, the owner found an index card and paused. The owner said, "Jake?"

"Yep," said Jake. He knew that the altercation was cresting.

The owner returned to the desk and pulled Jake's books back toward himself. He said, "It says you don't have any more credits."

Jake was surprised at his statement, "What? I should have plenty of trade credits."

The little man behind the counter said, "Sorry, I've put a note on your member's card that says your account has been permanently closed."

This was not acceptable and Jake swelled with rage.

Siding with Jake, the ghostly women looked harshly at the owner for suggesting that he be banned.

"You can't do that. I have a lot of credits," said Jake.

"I'm sorry, not anymore," replied Owner. He continued, "Some men were here asking about you and they told me you are reselling my books. Reselling my books is a violation of our member's agreement."

In an effort to recover and quell his rage, Jake redirected. "Look, I'll pay cash then," he said reaching for his money clip as he pushed his will into the owner with a touch more intensity.

The owner's resolution was holding against Jake's aggressive will and stammered, "I'm sorry. Your membership's revoked and I'd like you to leave."

Losing all temperance, Jake swelled with a dirty gold aura. The women reacted in fear and began to vaporize into the walls with an urgency to leave as Jake glowed with an impressive visual manifestation of unrestrained psychic abilities and filled the front room. The radiant energy from his body shoved into the owner.

The owner stood bolt upright under Jake's mental control. His arm lifted against his will and violently knocked the stack of books from the desk across the room.

"Keep your books," Jake snarled and directed the owner to strike himself across the face—the impact of the slap rang through the store like a folded belt being snapped together.

The owner was shocked at his involuntary physical actions and looked at Jake with terror. His own hand struck him again.

Furious, Jake shouted, "You're lucky I don't need the credits! I'd destroy you... Eric."

With that Jake released the owner, who shuddered trying to stand strong and not cry. Jake stood up even taller and leaned across the desk. He chomped his jaws together at the owner and said with a low growling voice, "Don't act tough, Owner, because... I. Know. You. Eric Thomas, 725 South Broadway, Apartment-A."

Jake walked away, but turned back with a look to kill. The owner was about to go mad from the emotional trauma of being totally violated, it was a tearing at his guts and he felt like he had been raped.

Jake slammed the door as he left and knocked the bell to the floor with a clang.

The owner was frozen for what felt like hours. After he watched Jake drive away, he picked up the phone from his desk and punched a series of numbers with trembling hands. The phone rang on the other end.

The automated voice of a phone operator said, "Please leave a message at the tone."

The owner shouted, "It's two-twenty on Tuesday and Jake St. Johns just left and he is—"

He paused turning to look out the window and tried to calmly say, "He's driving north on Cherry." The owner gripped the phone and pleaded into the receiver, "Please call me back. He knows where I live. This is Eric Thomas at The Neighborhood Bookstore."

He hung up the phone and looked ill.

There was a sudden and violent thump on the roof above – it was followed by the unnerving wail of a screaming woman whose cry was a bellowing, 'No!'

5

Mike was in police uniform and carrying a report log when he entered the bookstore. The owner was behind the desk and he looked up from his paperwork turning in his chair to greet the visitor. When he recognized Mike as an officer, he stood up with uncertainty and out of respect.

Eric Thomas said, "May I help you, officer?"

Mike smiled warmly to break the tension and said, "Hi. I am following-up for the IRS agents that you are cooperating with regarding Jacob St. Johns."

Relief spread across the owner's face and through his body, he relaxed and said, "Yes. I called them less than an hour ago. I had hoped to hear from them in person. They said they'd come..."

Mike spoke in calming tones, "Relax, there is no rush. Let me ask you a few questions to get us started. Do you have a place for us to sit down?"

Eric grew flustered, looking around at the door and toward the back of the store. He finally said, "You can have my chair...?"

Mike smiled again and said, "Please, sit down. I have been sitting all day, so I don't mind standing. May I come around, so we can speak more comfortably?"

Eric sat back down and waved for him to come around. Mike moved around and leaned back against the desktop. He spoke as he walked, "There's no pressure. I just have to ask you a couple of questions, so I can file a report and request the restraining order."

Thoughtful for a beat, Eric weighed the many options for the right words before he said, "Is that enough? What if he comes back? You don't know this guy."

"That's why I'm asking you questions about him," Mike said. "If I can determine that there was an assault, I'll go pick him up to make the point that he is no longer welcome here."

Eric liked the idea of this big guy scaring Jake St. Johns and raced through the details in his mind to distort them for an assault charge as Mike opened his report log.

Mike asked, "So tell me about him."

"This man's dangerous. Not in a typical way either. He's...evil," Eric said with a hushed voice and dramatic gleam in his eyes.

Mike confirmed the statement and said, "Evil. Okay. I think I understand. This is just for background." He paused with concern, "So, how long were you two in a relationship?"

The owner was shocked at Mike's assumption, looking side to side before saying, "We weren't. He was a customer... uh... don't you know the details of this case?"

Mike smiled in response to Eric's tone and said, "I only know that there was an altercation between you and St. Johns, and now you feel that you require protection from him at home. Evil is a word I often hear couples say, so I assumed your relationship was domestic. My apologies. Tell me what happened."

There was no way that Eric would tell the officer that Jake was psychic and had put his mind into his body, making him do things against his will. The question of gay love had made Eric's psychological violation even more vile and thwarted his innocence. He became defensive and said, "I wouldn't sell him books because the agents told me that he was making profits from reselling books that he wasn't claiming as income. He slapped me twice in the face, which you might still see evidence of, and threw those books across the room." He pointed to the books on the floor and concluded, "I had never met him until a couple of days ago."

Mike looked uncertain of what to write next and said, "I don't know how to start this report. Evil is an unusual word and I don't understand how you can judge him evil because he is profiting from used books. You'd say 'liar,' 'cheat,' 'bastard,' or something like that. You'd say evil about Hitler or a fart. You said it somber like someone talking about Hitler. My second hold up, I understand that he knows where you live and has threatened you at your home."

Eric dodged the evil reference and replied to the second part, "He did threaten me and told me my address to emphasize his point. Maybe he knows the IRS is following him and he found me listed in the phonebook to be prepared for this?" His only thoughts were to press a simple assault charge and get a restraining order. Eric finally said, "He just makes me... very uncomfortable. I feel threatened at home and work from a person I believe to have the capacity to commit greater violence."

"That helps," Mike responded as he wrote into his report log.

Eric looked away with a blink from Mike's gaze as he recalled the truth.

Mike finished writing and looked at his watch. Seeing the time, he stood from the desk snapping his logbook closed and said, "It feels like you are leaving something out, but that's enough for me. Getting slapped might make someone say the slapper was evil. Sorry to press you about it. The IRS wants an assault charge for a restraining order on St. Johns, so I will get that drafted up, too. Anything else?"

Eric's mind was churning to criminalize St. Johns and said, "He is reselling my books, which is a violation of his membership agreement. He might be guilty of defrauding me."

Mike smiled, "I'll look into it."

"What if he comes back?," said Eric.

Moving around to the front of the desk, Mike said, "If he comes back, be honest and stern with him about your working with law enforcement and any additional contact will not be good for his situation. Be cordial when telling him he is no longer welcome here. Give him some books if you have to, but don't be confrontational or emotionally reactive. If he tries to argue, you tell him that the matter is out of your hands now."

Standing in front of the desk, Mike fished out a business card and said, "When he leaves, give me a call on my cell and I'll take it up with him for risking a first-degree charge of assault and harassment." He leaned over the desk and snapped down a business card. He then nodded with a professional, but false, smile and exited the store.

The door had hardly closed before Mike decided that he hated the tasks of this special assignment. *Trumping up charges on some guy by using his hostile boyfriend?*, Mike thought. The IRS's dirty tricks just rubbed him the wrong way. He'd see to it that this case would be filed under bullshit and walked away from it as he stepped to his car.

His report would tell everything that led up to what just happened, let them try to file for a restraining order. If they won, maybe he would fix them, too. But, Mike knew that first thing was first... And the first thing to do was to take down the Judge.

6

The final bell had rung. School was released for the day and talking kids filed out of the building. A tan unmarked police squad car was parked near the end of the schoolyard.

After leaving Eric at the bookstore, Mike had driven back to the school where he had been that morning before work. He was sitting in the car and reading a pulp fiction novel when he'd heard the school bell ring. Mike read another page before he set the book aside to watch the exiting students.

After a few minutes, the other standing vehicles had collected their passengers and drove away. Gary stood at the curb alone where the buses had been.

Mike pulled his undercover police car up to the curb in front of the kid and rolled down the passenger-side electric window. "Hey, kid, is your name Gary?"

Not sure of the situation, Gary said, "Yeah…"

"Climb in," said Mike in an embracing tone of inclusion. "The Judge told me to stop by and give you a lift home."

Gary peered through the windows into the car and said, "Where's the Mercedes?"

"It had a flat. Triple-A couldn't get there soon enough to pick you up, so the Judge called me."

Gary acted reluctant for a moment.

"Come on, kid," Mike said as he leaned across the center console to look at Gary. "You haven't done anything wrong, have you?" Mike centered himself behind the wheel and answered for him, "Of course not. Jump in the back."

Gary opened the backdoor and climbed into the cop's car. "Cool," he said. "I always wondered what it was like to ride in a cop car." Gary slammed the door and slid over to look through the divider window. He said, "I didn't know you guys had computers."

"We got it all. I even picked up a couple of corndogs and a pop," said

Mike reaching through the window and handing Gary a paper bag. "Eat up, it's the perfect after-school snack, eh?"

Gary took the paper bag and dug into it, Mike put the car in drive and rolled out.

Gary shouted upon his discovery, "You only got me a small drink. Smalls are for babies." He removed the cup and shoved a straw into it as he said, "Watch. I'm going to be done with this in like five seconds. So, why did Dad send you?"

Mike looked back in the rear-view mirror, Gary took a couple of good pulls from the cup before he answered, "He knows I patrol over here and I owe him one."

Gary sucked at the straw with urgency to make a childish point. He rolled his eyes and said, "Well, this small drink ain't going to win you any points. It's almost gone."

Mike smirked into the rearview and said, "I'll remember to tell him after I talk to your mom. Thanks for telling me he was your father. He'll take some work, but I already have a plan for her."

Mike looked back from the front-seat to observe Gary's response of confusion that interrupted his drinking harder at the soda cup.

"What," Gary asked with sarcasm. "I never told you about my dad." He paused in a sudden swoon and said, "Whoa... Hey, I don't feel so good."

Something was wrong and Gary knew it. He pulled at the door handle beside him—the door was child-locked.

Mike laughed at Gary's urgent struggle and called back to him, "Don't worry, Gary. How about a joke to take your mind off it? So, there was this superhero, who worked kid-parties. Stop me if you've heard this one?"

Right then, it dawned on Gary and he slurred out, "You're the guy from my party... Look... I'm sorry."

Mike said in reply, "No, I'm sorry..." He closed the divider window between the front and back seat. Gary began to cry as he pulled weakly at the door handle, again. Panic was written on Gary's face with tears and reflected his tension.

Mike shouted, "Let me finish my joke. There was this super-hero who was really a cop and he was tired of a-holes like your dad putting rich kids, like you, back on the street while he strapped a heavy legal boot onto people just doing their jobs and trying to survive. It just so happens that this super-hero worked those parties to profile future criminals." He paused smiling into the rear-view mirror and said, "You fit my profile, Gary."

Gary's whimpers lost steam as he fought to hold his head up.

Mike said over his shoulder, "I bought you a small drink on purpose.

It was drugged, Gary. I told you to cut me a break, but you didn't. I knew you would drink a small to spite me. It was your final test." Mike turned back and shouted with sudden rage, "Only sociopaths talk to their mothers like you do!"

He gunned the engine and accelerated the unmarked car into traffic.

Gary slumped over into the backseat from the inertia of Mike swerving the car around the street corner.

7

After leaving the bookstore, Jake returned home and received a message from Tammy saying she was sorry about not meeting him earlier, she had been called into the office. However, she would be available for drinks and an early dinner. If he was up for it, he should call her cell phone and plan on meeting her at some trendy restaurant across town around four o'clock.

Jake hated places like the one she had suggested and was about to just call the whole thing off. Instead, he quieted his thoughts and turned inward to analyze the options. Jake concluded that if he was going to find out if Tammy was psychic, he had to at least try once more. After all, she'd heard Frank and suggested the winning approach to finding Betty.

He called Tammy and got her voice mail, this further irritated him. His message was brief because his nerves still tingled from the altercation at the bookstore and if he vocalized a complaint it would become a rant of negativity. His voice had a tone of inconvenience when he confirmed that he would meet her at four o'clock, but warned that he wouldn't stay past four-thirty if she wasn't there. He was a busy man and had an appointment to keep that evening.

The message he left for Tammy played in a persistent mental loop along with the urges and problems that had recently consumed Jake's thoughts as he changed his clothes.

For a brief second, Jake was paused by a wave of panic. *What if that Eric Thomas called the police and lied*, he thought. *Or worse, if he told them the truth.*

He focused on his breathing as he prepared himself and had successfully silenced his thoughts by the time he rubbed an electric razor over his face and neck. The vibrations of the shaver added to the Zen of the moment that Jake focused into existence, his mind was as peaceful as a slow flowing river.

THE CROSS-TOWN TRAFFIC was thick, but at six-after-four, Jake entered the restaurant carrying a single white lily. He was very well dressed in a sharply tailored suit and looked like a model posing as he stood erect to scan the clientele; his entire being projected that he was extremely rich and had a proven self-confidence.

Spotting his target in the bustling early dinner crowd, Jake walked with super-human grace into the restaurant's dining room to the booth where Tammy sat. With the soft smile of a prince, he offered Tammy the flower.

She blinked a couple of times as she looked over the new and improved Jake before she looked into his eyes and said, "Wow. You look really... good." She took the flower with a smile and said, "Thank you. I love lilies."

Tammy smelled into the flower as Jake sat into the booth across from her. He said, "Do you have plans tonight? I'd love if you'd come with me—" Jake interrupted himself and said, "Wait, you are not going to believe my day. I am being followed by G-men and they're sabotaging my bookstore connections."

"Whoa! Stop. You are ruining the moment," she said.

Jake twisted his lips and started to speak.

Waving her hands, Tammy said, "Wait. My turn first."

She paused long enough to make solid eye contact before saying, "Right now, I am interested in finding out how psychic you are."

"Seriously," asked Jake. "You're kidding, right? Can I tell you about my day, first? I'll be brief."

"No," replied Tammy. Confident that she had nicely stacked the deck against Jake this afternoon, she said, "You have been rude and it's my turn to test your social grace."

Defensive, Jake said remembering her disappearance to buy shoes, "Rude? How was I rude to you today?"

"Your tone on my message and you were late."

Jake held up his hands in surrender.

"Okay, that's better," Tammy said. "So, I have been a practicing Wiccan since high school and I am pretty rounded in the craft, but—"

"But, you want me to teach you how to be a better witch," Jake interrupted with optimism.

Tammy laughed and said, "No, I want to teach you how to be a better psychic."

In frustration, Jake shifted in the seat reacting, "You need to stop. What do you know about being a real psychic?"

"Plenty," Tammy answered with a smile as she rubbed her hands together. "Come on, it'd be rude not to play along. First, an illusion. Give me a five-dollar bill."

Digging a hand into his pocket for his money clip, Jake groaned and said, "Smallest bill I have is a twenty."

"We got a rich one here tonight everybody," she mocked to an imaginary audience. "It will do, yuppie. Give it."

Jake peeled a twenty from his nice grip of cash. He held a bill out to her and said, "I would have given you a hundred for a good trick. Is this for a hand job? Cuz I am pretty good at that myself."

Tammy took it with a snide grin and put it into her shirt pocket, she said, "It's for nothing, psychic. First, I have to teach you to use your powers in the present moment." She emphasized the word 'powers' with single finger quote marks beside her face. "If you do well, I'll give you your money back."

Jake rolled her little trick over his mental tongue to taste for the humor in it and his face broke into a smirk. "Okay, I should've seen that coming," he admitted. "However, you should plan on that twenty paying for drinks when we're done with your little game." He said with a coy wink, "In fact, count on it. If this game isn't better than Wall Street, I already have you trumped."

Tammy looked at Jake sideways with a snide grin, she sniffed at the flower again.

From the aisle, a hostess interrupted them at the edge of the booth and said, "What can I start you off with today?"

Jake wanted to have several drinks, several strong drinks. His face twisted a bit reflecting his internal struggle and he said, "Water."

"Sangria for me," Tammy said with glee.

The hostess nodded with approval and left to place the order.

Jake yearned to have a cigarette and a drink. The desire burned and it felt urgent like he had to piss. Jake, gritting his teeth to turn off the emotional tension, looked at her and said, "So are we done with all this joking around? Can I tell you about my day now? I need to vocalize some things to sate my rage against the world." He fought to re-center himself and thought, *I am a peaceful river.*

"Not yet," she said. "I have one more little game for us." Tammy shuffled through her purse and removed a worn deck of tarot cards. She removed a black and red band from around them and said while shuffling the deck on the table, "It'll be fun. Unless, you aren't really psychic."

Her hands shuffled the cards again and she turned her focus on Jake. "When we met, you asked about my tarot work. This is my deck."

Tammy prompted a response from him with a look of expectation and set the cards on the table between them with a snap.

Jake said, "I'm not really in the mood to read your fortune with your cards. I've evolved beyond your magic and its ritual channels of prophecy."

"We are not fortunetelling, Jake," said Tammy. "We're reading minds. I'll look at a card and you'll tell me what it is. You're psychic, remember? We can start with suits. That'll be easier for you."

Jake groaned, "I really don't want to read your mind."

"Come on," she chided. "I thought you'd be more into this."

"I'm into you enough already," Jake responded. "I am just a little surprised."

Tammy quipped, "I'm full of surprises. You should know that. What suit is this?" She took up a card from the top of the deck and held it up with its back to Jake. She looked at it and asked him to predict it with a wanton glance.

Jake said, "Six of hearts."

"I thought we were starting with the suits of the tarot. Nice try, though, it was the six of cups." Tammy turned the card over in front of Jake.

"It's your deck. Call it like you see it."

She said, "You are going to have to listen to the precise thoughts that you hear."

Jake shrugged in blasé disagreement and replied, "Hearing thoughts isn't exactly the way it works, ears hear. Besides, I called the card. Hearts are cups."

Tammy ignored Jake's response and turned up another card. She looked at it before she turned her eyes to Jake, who was expectant and met her eyes deeply. She closed her eyes and looked away from his glare.

Jake said, "The Fool?"

Tammy laughed turning over the inverted Emperor card. She said, "Nope, it's the Emperor. Are you really trying?"

Jake grew frustrated and said, "You are misreading the cards. An inverted Emperor card is the Fool and indicates leaving what you rule."

"I did read the card that way, didn't I," Tammy replied as she giggled. "That was rotten, I know. You are reading my mind, but can you see what I see?" She reached for Jake's hand and said, "Go deeper. If you want to prove to me that you are more than a grifter, you need to become a wine taster using all your taste bud regions. Think about it as tasting me with a—"

Not missing the sexual overtones, Jake interrupted, "Tasting you with a cleared palate. I get it. You tricked me, again." He pretended to spit wine into the aisle.

When Jake turned to face her, he began to emanate a white glow from his hands and eyes as he reached across the table to take the cards from Tammy. "Please give me the cards," asked Jake.

She gave him the cards with a touch of hesitation.

"Thank you," he said. Jake smiled cutting the deck and said, "Please understand, I'm on a short schedule now and I want to talk about other things. This trick will give you a demonstration of the true craft."

Tammy watched Jake as he took the top five cards off the top of the deck and fanned them. Without showing or looking at the cards, he said, "Here are your suits. Two rods, a sword, a cup and the Hierophant."

Jake turned them over and spread the cards. The cards were as he declared they would be.

Tammy waved the cards back to her and said, "Try a little harder and tell me the numbers, too."

Jake looked at her with impatient eyes and said, "Our drinks are here."

Tammy leaned her head into the aisle to look behind Jake. With a drink in each hand, the hostess was returning. She arrived at the table to place a water glass in front of Jake and a tall glass of sangria before Tammy.

Hostess said, "Are you ready to order?"

Detached and tense, Jake did not even offer a look of courtesy to the hostess before he pushed a beam of his bioelectric energy into her. It entered her head and projected outward like a halo. He gave her a stern rebuke for her interruption, "Leave us to our drinks, I will summon you when I want you. Go."

Tammy was surprised at his lack of manners and looked at him with shock, but did not see the hostess's eyes glaze over when Jake took control of her unconscious mind.

"Why were you just so rude to her," she asked quietly.

Jake smiled and said, "You're testing me, again? To place an auto-suggestion in other's mind, one must be stern and direct. Please continue your game." Jake set the cards in front of Tammy.

With a tone of remaining annoyance, she said, "Let's try this again with three cards."

Tammy took up the deck and shuffled.

"Let's cut to the chase. I'll show you my best card trick to prove to you that you are being silly with your teacher. Shuffle those cards up real good."

Hesitating for a beat relishing in Jake's insult, Tammy began shuffling again.

Jake prompted her onward and twirled his forefinger at her from across the table. "Shuffle them good," he said. He drank what remained of his water as she shuffled the deck a couple of times.

He set his ice-filled glass aside and said, "Now, set them down and cut the deck."

She set the deck down and cut it.

Jake was enjoying the tone of his voice and projected it at Tammy again as he pointed at the uncovered half of the deck saying, "Now, re-stack and flip up that top card, so I can teach you the big picture lesson."

Tammy re-stacked the split deck. Looking at him with expectation, she pulled up the top card.

When she turned her eyes to the card, her surprise at the card affected her face. Tammy darted her glance from it to Jake, who met her eyes intensely.

Tammy said, "Well...?"

"Well... it means our little game is over and we are again at the end of it." He narrowed his eyes and said. "Throw down your Death card."

She flipped it onto the table between Jake and her.

There lay the Death card. Tammy looked over at Jake with concern.

Jake said, "Don't look at me all crazy. This day didn't go as I planned, either. Prophecy can be as harsh as one-ply toilet paper." He shook his head and pointed at the flower, "I even knew what flower to bring to this funeral. Enjoy the lily, Tammy. I wish you luck in finding new students."

He stood with disgust and dropped another twenty-dollar bill on the table. He said, "Please excuse me, I have to prepare for a gallery opening. Before that though, I want you to learn that seeing is not perceiving. Look at the card, now."

He pointed at the Death card—It was now the Empress instead of the Death card that had been laid on the table.

Jake said, "I could have made you a goddess to the people that you want to help." He nodded to her with a bow, "G'night."

The shock of Jake's abrupt departure left Tammy stupefied, her confused eyes followed him as he walked away. She turned her focus back to the Death/Empress card—

Neither card was lying on the table!

Was there ever a card?, she thought.

Tammy picked up the deck and flipped through the cards. She quickly found and removed both of the cards that she had seen on the table from within her deck of tarot.

Examining the deck in her hand, Tammy tried to rationalize what she had just witnessed. Maybe Jake was serious and not just putting on some David Koresh psychic act.

She should have been mad at Jake for his arrogance, but instead she was really turned on by Jake's psychic demonstration.

Looking at the cards again, she tried to figure out how he had tricked her eyes in a weak effort to smother the spark that he had struck onto the tinder of her heart.

Tammy struggled to organize the memories of Jake's anarchist talk and his call to rebellion against the system; she began to perceive it was all a cleverly worded invitation to other psychics to join him.

The emotional spark lit the tinder and her heart blazed with romantic interest. She didn't want to talk to Jake again—she needed to talk to him again. In an effort to prove he wasn't psychic, Tammy knew she had done the opposite and needed a way to rebuild the bridge.

She stood and threw the twenty-dollar bill from her shirt pocket that she had taken from Jake on the table. Before walking away, she inspected the booth and table in a final effort to find any evidence of Jake performing a slight of hand. Not finding it, her attraction to Jake was further fueled by lust and curiosity.

Who are you, Jake St. Johns?, she thought leaving the restaurant in an unforeseen swoon of rejection and undeniable attraction.

8

Jake moved about in the spacious showroom of a tasteful art gallery. There were small crowds of various couples and individuals who were dressed in semi-casual attire with glasses of wine, bottles of micro-brew, and bottled water. The crowd milled around from painting to painting as a waitstaff offered them hors d'oeuvres from silver trays.

The soft murmur of hushed voices mixed nicely with the occasional non-verbal responses, bursts of laughter, and gasps of pain-joy-rapture that echoed within the gallery. For Jake, the experience was best compared to the stimuli of an improv jazz club with live music playing; he heard the hushed voices of an audience, but also felt their enjoyment and the live music was their mind songs that sang in harmonious appreciation with an expectation of miracles. He also watched a colorful bio-electromagnetic luminance radiating in waves from the bodies of his guests.

To a mental parasite like Jake, this was the finest of dining. He danced in step with a god complex and was pleased to accept their worship for his gifts of love, hope and charity. From God to Adam, the first gift to humanity was, of course, beauty.

I am a very kind God, Jake thought in self-affirmation.

Jake nodded to patrons and made small talk as he walked through the showroom. He snatched a caviar cracker with a wink to the pretty hostess, she winked back before moving on. The look on his face was pure bliss.

Here! In this crowd…I find my home, he thought.

He stopped at a main bar with two female bartenders ready to serve and asked if either had seen Tim, yet. They hadn't. While Jake nodded to thank them, his face broadcasted his frustration at not finding his featured artist. He moved to the side of the table and scanned the room.

He tried to look for Tim, but his focus drifted as he watched the flowing auras of the people in the crowd; their individual lights would rise and fall in dancing exchanges of energy. Jake saw a brilliant display of human magnetism that dimmed the Northern Lights.

The world is my private collection and its true beauty is mine alone to offer, thought Jake.

His eyes came to rest on the posterior of a dominant figure dressed in all black and was unique in that he bore no sign of having an internal radiance. With his hands locked behind his back, the man stood in front of a large painting of a menacing clown.

The clown of the painting had leapt into a bright and broad light source from the matte-black darkness of the canvas's background. Around the clown were soft transparent ghost-like children painted with a glaze of glossy layers that caught and reflected beams from the overhead spotlights. The children appeared to stand at different depths within the mid-ground of this framed space to create an infinite depth in the matte-black backdrop, this added mass to the illusion of the central clown figure. The overhead lighting made the children appear to float under a personal light source.

Driven by an uncontrollable urge to find out why this guy didn't have an aura, Jake approached the dark man and spoke a few steps behind him, "This is an amazing piece of art that I commissioned a couple of months back. It was as if the artist had seen it through my mind's eye."

The man did not respond to Jake and continued to stare forward at the painting.

Jake recognized that the man was a priest as he moved beside him. "Timothy could do the same for you, Father." He offered an extended hand in greeting and said, "Jake St. Johns, welcome to my gallery."

Jerking his head in response like a surprised predator, the man was indeed a priest, but was wearing horrible clown make-up. The nightmare priest lifted his hands to attack Jake's throat and shouted, "Blasphemer!"

Faceless, bloody children climbed from the frame of the painting into the gallery and gathered around the struggling men chanting, "Kill him! Kill him! Kill him!"

Jake fought to get the priest off of him without success and the hands of the priest tightened around his neck. His pain reception and panic grew to a climax — Jake's world went black.

WEDNESDAY

1

Jake jerked awake gasping for a breath and exclaimed, "Gahhhh!!" He was confused for a moment and slow to connect with the dark world around him. When lightning lit the early morning sky through his bay window, he finally grasped that he was home in his own bed.

Jake was surprised to find Betty beside him sitting on his bed. She patted Jake's hair and said, "Shhh...I'm here. It's okay. Go back to sleep."

Remembering that he had just died in panic during the nightmare of the art gallery...and the priest, the children. *Betty,* Jake shocked himself by thinking she might have been causing the nightmares.

He said, "What is happening to me, Betty!? I'm losing myself."

Petting his head, she pulled Jake to rest it on her shoulder. Betty said, "Shhh...it is the quickening. And it is almost over, Jake. To overcome fear, one must face it. There is no greater fear than death. You have faced yours and you must face it again. Rest now, find your peace and strength."

Before Jake could speak, she laid him back onto his pillow and said, "May I tell you about my father?"

Jake settled back and replied that she could.

"My father's an angry man," she confessed. "When he returned home drunk and tired from his work, we would put on music, feed him, and get him another drink to put him to sleep. Sometimes I would have nightmares. One night, I woke him and he came to stop my crying. And, here we are."

She reached up her hand and touched Jake's forehead – He fell asleep and Betty was gone.

2

Drizzling rain fell against the roof of Mike's house with a soft and even pattering. The only illumination in the neighborhood was a sodium-yellow streetlight and under an unseasonal flash of the lightning overhead.

An alarm clock beeped out its alert.

Upon waking, Mike turned off the alarm and arose from his bed.

The streetlight cast its yellow beam through the window on to the wall and lit the room enough for Mike to negotiate his way. He dressed into a t-shirt and sweatpants that were retrieved from the floor at the foot of his bed.

Mike entered the garage of his home holding a flashlight in one hand and a tray in the other that carried a canteen and a bag of fast food. He set the tray on a worktable near the door and placed his flashlight next to it.

Turning the beam of the flashlight, he pointed it on Gary who was taped upright to a chair and sleeping with an unfolded TV tray beside him. There was a collar with a small, pager-like, black box locked around Gary's neck.

From the worktable and near the flashlight, Mike picked up the remote control to a dog's shock-collar. He pointed the controller at Gary and woke him with a couple of quick shocks from the collar prods that were set against the skin near his throat.

Gary jolted awake!

He looked around and for a moment did not recognize the garage he was in. And, then Gary remembered everything and it shook him from the inside out.

Gary looked at Mike and fought back the tears of his panic by yanking against the tape around his wrists that held him to the chair. He stammered as he said, "What-do-you-want? Call-my-dad. He'll give you whatever you want."

Mike began pacing him and said, "I know, he's raising you to be his heir. But, I don't want anything."

"If you don't want anything, why am I here," Gary asked pleading, not understanding.

"Why?," Mike replied with a question before answering bluntly. "Because your mom hired me to remind you of when life was fun and simple. Now, I have to show you how hard life is. You shouldn't pick a fight with a superhero, if you don't want their measure of justice."

Mike picked up the bag from the tray and removed two corndogs from inside. After flattening the bag onto the TV tray and setting the corndogs on it, he said, "You didn't eat your corndogs yesterday."

Gary showed little fight left in pulling against the restraints and blubbered with insolence as he said, "I don't want them, they're old."

"They're old," asked Mike with disbelief. He picked up one of the corndogs and took a big bite. "It tastes fine to me. Aren't preservatives great? Eat up," he said through a mouthful of food.

Mike tossed the corndog back down onto the bag and took a lock-blade knife from the tray. He unfolded it with a sharp snap of his wrist and cut one of Gary's hands free from the tape.

Fearing for his life at his captor's blade, Gary had closed his eyes and couldn't move. Mike pressed the remote control again, jolting him. He jerked alive in surprise.

Mike said, "If I wanted you dead, Gary, I wouldn't use a pocketknife. Eat." Slowly, he crossed his arms to hide the controller under the muscle and bone of his massive arm, Mike stood with proud authority over Gary.

Gary reached out his hand and selected the corndog that Mike hadn't taken a bite from.

"Good boy," Mike said. "It's raining and likely to storm all day, so finish those corndogs and get comfy. I'll feed you something warm around noon, if I don't have to leave. Either way, the sun will come out soon enough and you'll start digging or you will sit in here and shock yourself trying to scream through your nose after I tape your mouth shut. Sorry to say it, but there's really nothing happy to look forward to, Gary."

Gary was not listening and couldn't hear over the roaring panic in his ears. He chewed and forced down another bite as he swallowed back his tears.

Mike basked in the moment with a smile knowing that Gary was going to finally play by the rules and that he had already broken the boy. He looked like he enjoyed winning and relished in watching Gary indulge in a final meal...the boy had hope and was embracing life.

3

It had been a dreary morning, but Betty had not returned after his nightmare and Jake slept until ten o'clock. He didn't have class this morning and had kicked himself a couple of times for wasting valuable hours sleeping that would have been better spent fulfilling orders.

Wearing cheap black-rimmed bifocals, Jake stood at the plywood worktable in his home office and had just finished taping a box.

He kissed and hugged the box. "Oh, sweet Emily of Cleveland. Your library is so beautiful. You aren't like these Satanists..."

Jazz music was playing into the converted bedroom from a good sound system and Jake set the package down on top of a stack of other shipping boxes in time with the end of the song that was playing.

After his outburst at Tammy in the restaurant and finishing up the preparations at the gallery with Tim for his show that would open on Friday, Jake returned home last night to find there were no specters waiting in the neighborhood for him. However, there were more ghosts gathered in his yard. The moaning coming through the windows was a distraction and Jake could only force himself to do about two dozen single book orders that he had cherry-picked out of the multi-book orders.

When he started working that morning, Jake had to take the shipping boxes to the curb level outside the gates for pick up. There were too many ghosts lingering around in the yard to make the fat UPS jerk climb the stairs.

Most of the time, Jake made the driver come to the door for pick-ups because the guy had consistently left packages with expensive artwork at the gates. Even though he had carried the boxes down, Jake expected the UPS guy would still shove the next package an arm's length through the wrought iron bars. That was no way to treat the Bernie Wrightson original artwork from the limited edition of Clive Barker's *The Illusionist* that he had bought, but still Jake couldn't have him huffing and puffing wind through his yard full of ghosts.

Occasionally throughout the morning, Jake looked out the window to speculate a count. There were much less in the daytime, but the spirits who remained, paced around his backyard in idle contemplation.

It had never been like this and the gathering of so many ghosts bothered Jake. He had grown quite used to seeing ghosts, but this was a different beast. He wondered if there was anyone else who knew the ghosts were gathered in their yards, trying to find a home.

What did these spirits want? They couldn't expect him to absorb them all into himself and carry them around like well-used and travel-stickered luggage.

After doing a quick review of the math and an analysis of the sheer number of people that died every day compared to the number of ghost that he would see on any given day, the numbers didn't add up.

What happened to everyone else? Was this a proof of there being a divine grace?

Some stay, others go on...where do the others go? Is there a Heaven that angels swoop down from to take up the dead or are the people left behind those blessed with eternal life? Is that all there is, or did the ghosts unaccounted for follow an angel of mercy that led them to a door down the hall and find themselves being slapped and crying as they were born again. Or even worse, given the quantum mechanics and special relativity of life and death, finding themselves to be birthed back into their lives and having to live again and again in an alternate universe with only the subtle guide of déjà vu to refine them for a higher dimension.

What was the duality of a man who could see both sides of the divine relationship? Was I the only one that looked into the sky at night seeing the vast depth of the universe knowing that it was all relative and gifted with a divine understanding of a creation that is as big as it was small...or was I the fool who teetered on the edge of a cliff at the great divide projecting meaning into personal abstractions.

Last night as he and Tim hung a dozen large paintings, Tammy had quickly become the new Michelle in Jake's mindless chattering and he wondered aloud if she would ever talk to him again. Tim could only remind Jake of his warnings about chasing a new girl when he wasn't ready. Even if she was only supposed to be a student—Tammy was still a woman and he was longing for her attention.

In an effort to stop thinking, Jake squinted his eyes at a corkboard mounted to the wall above the desk. He scanned the board for the next order and fought to not think of Tammy as a woman, it didn't work.

In the end, Jake just wished for a magic cigarette to appear and make his hunger for comfort disappear.

He turned around to examine his workstation monitor for a moment to look over the remaining orders – there were only another nine hundred and eighty-three. Jake groaned returning to the corkboard on the opposite wall. He tilted his chin up to look through his readers at several printouts tacked up. He looked down on five open boxes in front of him.

The next song playing ended and a sweet-voiced female radio station deejay started to talk about non-profit sponsorship and launched into a typical fundraiser analogy saying, "If you are still listening, I know you are a dedicated listener because only a dedicated listener would still be listening to a fundraiser. Now is the time to put a price on your dedication and make a financial commitment. Our jazz station needs your support."

Jake closed his eyes and winced as the plea for money continued. Having heard enough, he went to the phone and dialed the number that the woman had said to invite renewing members and new listeners to call the station with a pledge.

When the line answered, Jake responded and said, "What is the balance for this drive?"

There was a long pause as Jake waited for a reply. The voice came back and said that the drive's total goal was one hundred and fifty thousand dollars.

Jake asked, "If I covered that amount, is there a way that we can just get back to the jazz?"

The voice said to hold on.

There was a long pause and a new person got on the phone. The response was, "Did you want to make a challenge?"

Jake laughed and said, "No. I want to underwrite the entire drive. What do you need from me to end the interruptions, so you just go back to playing the music?"

The man was slow to speak, "Uh, sir, the balance for the rest of this drive is one-hundred and twenty-seven thousand."

"Can you just send a trustworthy person to my door," asked Jake.

"What are you saying?," replied the voice.

"I am asking if you can take one hundred and twenty-seven thousand in cash, so we can have some music today without a bunch of embarrassing pleas for money?"

The voice chuckled and said to hold on. The line was silent for a long moment.

A third person picked up the line and asked if Jake was serious about underwriting the rest of the fund-raiser drive with cash. Jake said 'yes' and asked if there was someone that could come to him or would he have to bring it to them. "Where are you at," asked Jake. "I'll take a cab to renew my membership. I know it's only noon, but it's been a long day and I've been drinking."

The man on the other end laughed and said they could send someone for the cash if he was already drinking. The voice of the man continued saying that if this wasn't a joke that he would shortly be joining him in a drink.

Jake gave the man his address and made him promise that cash would be okay. With a laugh, the man promised.

Jake left his office and marched into the hallway. Moving across the front room past the staircase, Jake patted both of the lions guarding his staircase on the head. He moved to a door and entered the basement.

His entire house was equipped with the speakers of a sound system because Jake turned a dial at the foot of the stairs and James Brown and the JBs's *Soul Power* blared.

Jake took up a box of matches bobbing his head to the music. It had to be matches with a sulfur-tipped flame because a flint-sparked flame didn't hold the magic ingredient he needed to perform this spell. Flames had memory and the match would remember the sulfur and vibrations of his incantation when he struck the match with his thumbnail to light the largest of three candles on the wall.

When he had lit the other two candles that were arranged to each side of the burning candle, a regular-sized door adored with brush-drawn runes and symbols of light appeared in the wall around it as if the central candle hung as the knocker. Jake opened the door and went in.

Inside the invisible door and concealed room was a vault filled with racks of artwork, comic book boxes, and an enormous amount of cash.

NOT LONG AFTER JAKE had taken a hundred and thirty thousand dollars cash from his basement vault, two young but very large men had driven across town from the historical Five-Points neighborhood to take his donation.

The two men were real clean-cut men with ham-sized fists and a gentle demeanor. They had made good time and arrived within twenty minutes of his call.

Still in his sweats and t-shirt, Jake smiled as he invited them in.

He stuck out his hand and said, "Jake." They all shook hands. Closing the door, he said, "How you doing, guys?"

"I'm glad it finally stopped raining. Snow and now rain. The world's gone crazy," said the dominant male. "My name's Marty and this is Victor."

Victor waved and said, "We spoke on the phone."

Marty continued and said, "We're here to deliver your donation for you. I heard you have cash and that you can't drive."

"Yep. You want that drink now, Victor," asked Jake as he bent to lift a canvas handbag from the floor. He pulled open the bag to expose hundred-dollar bills in paper bands. "Ready? Let's count a few stacks of money to see if they all weigh the same."

Marty smirked and said, "That will be fun."

Victor smiled back when they looked at each other with a coy nod.

"It is always fun at first. After counting a hundred per stack, it becomes work. We can count one each, rotate it to get a second count, and then weigh the others," Jake said with a wink and pointed to the pool table. An electronic scale was sitting by the corner pocket and a place had been cleared of books for them to count the money.

Marty smiled a big warm grin and said, "Let's count and weigh some money. This is like some crazy gangster movie."

Victor looked around the strange room and said, "So you like books?"

Marty laughed and said, "Damn! Just collecting your favorites in here?"

They all laughed, but Marty laughed harder as he took up several books of the same title. He thought it was hilarious and said he had never seen so many books in one place, let alone of the same book. Jake sharing in the humor said that it was easier to rotate the stock and kept the spiders away.

They all settled down when Marty asked who the hell Jake was and Jake said absent mindedly that he was just some stupid old rich cracker and not a drug dealer or anything like that – it was as if he had been with them when they had been joking about him on their way over. Their faces showed a quick response of second guessing themselves. Jake picked up on it and dumped the money on the pool table as he said, "You never get used to the sight of money in a pile."

Jake passed out a stack to each man and it was back to business, they counted their stacks in silence.

"So do you guys know about Muddy Waters and Leadbelly?," Jake said.

Interrupting their counting, they looked at him with an uncomfortable and quizzical glance.

"Do you know about the real blues?"

They looked away without answering and started their counting over again. Jake chuckled and said, "Okay-okay. I get it. You guys count and I'll refresh my drink."

Victor looked up and said, "Please stay. I'll need you to sign this receipt."

"You have a fine voice, Victor," said Jake walking away. "You guys aren't going anywhere for a few minutes, so I'll get my drink and be right back."

JAKE HAD RESUMED HIS routine of fulfilling book orders with jazz music playing in the background and took up a piece of paper from one of the two book-order boxes remaining on the work table to check its contents against the order sheet.

He bobbed his head to the music playing and taped a box closed in time with the beat. He moved it to the pile of shipping boxes and set the box down to punctuate the end of the song before taking up a new order sheet.

When the deejay came on after the music ended, he said, "This next session goes out to Jake St. Johns and the *St. John's Art Foundation*, who has just donated the full amount, and a little more, to our spring drive. He said that everyone should continue pledging to help grow the station, but he wanted to listen to some 70's action soul jazz mixed with album cuts from a list of the greats today, so I am playing a full set of it with only station breaks."

The voice chuckled and said, "The phones have been ringing off the hook, so pleas-s-e call back if our volunteers can't answer right away. Thanks, Jake. This is listener-sponsored radio, Jazz 88 Denver. The sound of our city."

Jake paused when he heard the announcement and held up his fist in the air.

I rule, Jake thought. The nightmare nagged him for a breath and he turned it off, thinking.

Nope. I didn't learn a thing.

He smiled when Miles Davis's *Kinda Blue* began to play its melancholy jazz perfection. Jake considered the cost of buying every song he had ever loved and figured that it would be cheaper than buying his jazz station for the afternoon. But then, no one else would be listening with him. He considered for a second that maybe he should just buy the station.

Yuck! Stress meant cigarettes, Jake thought. *He had had enough of stress and would enjoy the end of these book labors. Throw money at the problem and make it go away.*

He had just started to work through the last box on the table when the phone on his computer desk rang.

Jake replaced the sheet of paper into its box and moved to the phone behind him. He smiled in expectation of a friend calling him to say that they had just heard his name on the radio.

He lifted the phone to his ear and hoped it would be a call from Michelle. They used to listen together.

Jake said through a hopeful smile, "Hello?"

The diner was busy during the rush hour with cars driving by and customers filing in.

Sid's voice was clear over the phone from the backroom office of the diner. "Hey, brother," he said.

Jake was surprised to hear his brother's voice on the other line. Calling from the diner was breaking the rules they had set to make sure Tom wouldn't find out about forgotten relationships. Doris must have told him to call after all.

Jake said, "Sid?"

"Got another brother, Jake?," Sid mocked. "Listen, before you say something stupid. I need to tell you…Dad died this morning."

In the diner, Sid sat at a big messy desk with the phone jammed to his ear and chin by his shoulder. It was little more than a closet office in the back of an oblong squared diner. The cooking staff could see him through the doors in the office/kitchen/pantry, if they dared to look through the windows in the doors and give him a pained look of sympathy.

Sid didn't look so good and appeared to have been crying. "Jake. We—I could really use your help."

In shock from the severity of the moment, Jake sat down in his computer chair thinking of his dad dying and his son being nothing more than a mobster.

It took a second, but Jake finally said, "Sure. Anything. How's Mom?"

Sid, setting down a stack of papers in his hand, said, "She isn't good, man. So, I told her I'd handle everything. It's all a bit rushed, but we talked this afternoon for a while, and, uh, we covered everything and thought you'd agree. We don't want some idiot up there talking about Dad. I keep thinking I can do somethin'—But, I can't do it, Bro."

Jake's eyes filled with concern and empathy as he picked up a pen and scratched down some notes. "I can do it, Sid. Let me write something, okay? What else do you need?"

Sid sniffled, exhaling hard to suppress his emotion, then he looked at the paperwork and began to ramble, "I gotta figure out what the hell Pops was doing to keep this place afloat and fast. He didn't tell me shit. You know how crazy he's been."

The brothers had a moment of silence together. Jake was just about to speak and tell his brother that he would take care of the daily expenses until he figured it out, when Sid spoke over him, "Listen, don't get cute with some speech, Jake. Just keep it simple." Sid looked away and started digging back into his bills and invoices.

"Not a problem. What else can I do," asked Jake.

Through the receiver, Sid's voice carried into the room. "Would you pick out some music, too? Goddamn Marilyn Manson made me cry on the way over this morning."

Jake laughed and said, "I can mix up a CD of Dad's favorites."

Sid was quick to say, "This isn't funny." He sniffled, holding up a bank statement to refocus on something outside of himself and chuckled back in reflection. "Okay, it is a little funny. But, let me be clear, if you mess this up, I will—"

Jake interrupted and said, "You'll kick my sorry ass...I know. Don't worry about it, I have it covered."

"Too busy to worry. You got two or three days tops and Mom wants to see it all beforehand," Sid said. "So she can add a personal touch."

Jake leaned back in his chair and said, "No surprises, I promise. Talk to you tomorrow. Maybe we can all listen to the CD beforehand and have a good cry."

Jake paused listening to the silence on the other end of the line and replied, "I'm sorry, Sid."

"You don't have to say you're sorry to me. He was your dad too," said Sid. "Look, I got to jam. Call me the day after tomorrow about the CD. Hey, I love you, brother."

Jake paused thinking about how to say, *I love you, too, brother.* He couldn't, so Jake said, "Me, too, man," and hung up the phone.

He looked up at his office's ceiling and shed two big tears before pulling himself together with a couple of long exhaled breaths and picked up the phone.

Jake dialed a number and held the phone to his ear.

"Mom? It's Jake," he replied to her greeting. "Yeah, it has been awhile. Mom, I was just talking to Sid and he told me about everything. How are you doing?"

4

After getting off the phone with his mom, Jake called Tim at home to ask if he would teach his classes tomorrow. Tim had already had a few beers and asked Jake to repeat the question. Jake rephrased and told Tim that he needed him to take over the classes tomorrow. Tim was still being deliberately slow to understand, so Jake told him what had happened to his dad and how Frank had told him Papa Tom was having a heart attack.

"I knew yesterday," said Jake with a pause. "But, I didn't do anything. I don't know if there was something I could have done, but it doesn't change that I didn't do anything. Now I have to write the eulogy." Jake knew Tim would need the whole story to urge him along in stepping up to handle the classes and managing the gallery opening in his absence. He added, "I'll need you to open the gallery, too."

Upon hearing the situation, Tim accepted the responsibility at once, but immediately doubted his ability to pull it off.

Knowing this would happen, Jake said to comfort him, "Let it all happen naturally, man. The classes will be a snap. And, I've been planting the process in your head each time we've opened the gallery together for the past two years. You know everything that you need to, Tim, and you will have a great opening. And, it's very appropriate that you lead your first show solo."

"But, I can't—," Tim tried to say.

"Look, Tim, everyone at the gallery has been trained in the same way regarding their roles and overlapping responsibilities," said Jake. "You only need to be on time, dressed for success, and believing in you as much as I do."

"But I'm not—," Tim tried again.

"Goddamit, Tim," Jake said losing his patience. "The gallery was never mine! It's yours and there is no better time to start running it than on the night of your first feature show! The showing doesn't mean anything to anyone compared to what it means to you. Embrace it, man!"

Tim was silent.

"But...watch out for Helen," Jake said. "She will work to tear you down. It is the reason that I hired her."

Tim was still taking it all in, silent.

"Tim," Jake asked. "I can't read your mind over the phone. Are you ready to step up and be the man I know you are?"

Tim's voice wavered with optimism, "You know I am Jake, but—"

"No more buts, Tim. I am also calling Helen to tell her that you will be taking over my overpaid position at the school. It's done," Jake said hanging up the phone.

Jake smiled to himself knowing Tim would be furious that he hung up on him.

Tim would need to be prideful, angry, and single-minded, if he was going to pull off his new job.

Wait until he finds out about the trust fund I setup for the school and gallery, Jake thought. *It's all on you now to succeed, Tim.*

He then called Helen to tell her about Tim taking over the school and asked her to prepare the paperwork, secure a witness, and have her notary stamp ready in the morning when he arrived. He didn't mention anything about his family matters. It wasn't her business and curiosity would keep her on her best behavior toward Tim, hoping for some gossip about Jake's abrupt departure.

After the orders he had pulled were done, Jake drank himself out of his book-order fulfillment mode and the ability to walk. He just sat listening to 1960's jazz from Al Mingus in deep reflection, while leaning back against his chair and holding a half-glass of purple Kool-Aid; there was a large half-full bottle of vodka on the desk.

The radio announcer came on at the end of the song and said thanks to Jake once more; Jake waved a raised hand. He said the drive was over, but members should step up as this jazz lover did and become a listener member. "Let's get back to the music. How about some blues for this late afternoon set? This is classic huckle-buck and a re-mastered version of Leadbelly's *Good Morning Blues.*"

Jake shook his head as if to say, 'I just can't win today.' He sat forward with a dizzy groan and picked up the phone to dial.

He switched ears as the other line rang and held the receiver too close to his mouth.

Through the receiver into Jake's ear, a woman's voice said, "Hi. This is Tammy. Please leave a message."

Jake slurred at the tone with the phone under his chin, "Thishh ishh Jake... Sorry again about my second outburst. I wanna explain why I lost my temper. Please give me a call cuz my dad died today. I just need—I just need to talk to someone… real."

***

TAMMY, CARRYING A FILE FOLDER, entered an office area walking on short dark pumps and in an official-looking skirt suit; her crisp skirt played friction music against the back of her off-white nylons as she marched through a cubicle farm. The dark suit contrasted Tammy's Granola-Girl look as much as the sharp military-style heel turn that took her around the right corner. She disappeared around a wall into the exterior hallway.

She moved into her window cubical and slammed the file folder down on a stack of folders that cluttered her wrap-around desktop. She sat into an economy ergonomic chair and turned to face a monitor. The desk was covered with piles of other file folders.

Beside the monitor was a framed photo of a handsome man who didn't resemble her brother. He was a happy beefy man who had his arms around her neck and was dressed like a professional bull rider.

Tammy's eyes caught a glimpse of the picture. Her lips pursed and she laid the photo face down on her desk, "Not today, Mark."

Her hand woke the computer with the mouse and then pressed a button on her phone.

The speakerphone said, "You have two new messages. First new message."

Jake's voice said, "Thishh ishh Jake… Sorry again about—"

Her hand snatched the receiver from its base cutting off the speakerphone.

As she listened, her face said that she had taken in Jake's message with some soft feelings after looking at her watch. She thought, *Only a chronic drunk or someone hurting is wasted at four o'clock.* She pressed two keys.

"Message saved. Next message," the phone said into her ear.

The unmistakable voice of Joe said through the phone, "Good morning, Ms. Jensen. This is Special Agent Joe Gaines of the IRS Criminal Division. Would there be a time today that I could ask you a few questions about a Mr. Jacob St. Johns? Please give me a call by—"

Tammy hung up the phone and clicked off the message. She looked into her monitor.

From behind her, the same voice from the message arose into the air again, and said, "You're a tough one to catch at your desk, Mrs. Jensen."

Tammy turned her chair around, finding the doorway filled by Joe and Charlie, and said, "Look, uh, fellahs, I'm kinda busy this afternoon. How about we schedule something for tomorrow?"

Disregarding her offer, Joe motioned himself to sit into the guest chair and said with a quiet voice that was choked by his constrained chest as he bent into sitting position, "Whoa! I don't think this is starting off so good. Just tell us what you know about Jake St. Johns and we'll go."

Tammy crossed her arms like a hostile witness, "I can't pin a crime on him yet, but I toyed with him about being psychic and found out he's a little psychotic."

Charlie started to write on a pad and restated, "A little psycho? He was just calling and you saw him yesterday. What's his relationship with you and can you help us?"

Tammy's dislike for Charlie's implication was evident, so instead she said to Joe, "I met with him yesterday undercover and he flipped out for a second time."

"So you've seen him more than once," asked Charlie.

"Yesterday and on Sunday, he was hustling books both times."

When she said, *Sunday*. Charlie and Joe exchanged a quick look; Charlie's look was bitter toward Joe, who smiled at his partner's disgusted grimace and turned back to face Tammy with a grin.

It even surprised Charlie when Joe said out of the blue, "We think maybe you like him. How close have you two been? Did you plan to call him back as only a friend?"

Tammy was nonplussed and said in a raging, but whispering cubicle-voice, "What the hell are you guys playing at here? I am a professional and I don't—"

Joe interrupted with a less than considerate cubicle-voice and said, "Look, Tammy, it's your job to bust the psychos before they hurt people. Right? How close can you get to St. Johns for us?"

Tammy stopped using a lowered voice and reacted, "What?! This is my case, so back off."

Joe stood up and his knees popped, "Well then, you're off the case. I pulled his file and am having the evidence delivered to my office."

Tammy stood up to meet his eyes and said, "That's bullshit! St. Johns is my perp and I didn't plan this takedown for some accountant from the Midwest to come in here and ding him for not claiming capital gains on some forgotten IRA account. He owes me an apology and I'm getting the dirt on him for conspiracy against the State."

Joe stepped up to meet her and was about to lay in, but he caught himself and took a breath before stepping back again. He smiled holding up his hand and looked her up and down before saying, "Just stop, Miss Jensen. We know this much, your Anarchist Bookstore angle won't stand up against an entrapment defense.

"However," he continued. "We've been watching him and his contacts are investing cash for insider gains to manipulate the market. He's sheltering gains in 'collectable merchandise' losses. We're already looking into his gallery profits."

Charlie took over and said, "And all the while, you're having drinks with him. Your last report said that he displayed 'psychic abilities?'"

Tammy looked at Joe with disbelief and said, "I was saying he's a convincing con-man. He pulled some advanced sleight of hand on me yester—"

Interrupting, Joe said, "Look, Tammy, I like magic too, but this is a federal case now. I've never been an accountant and we have some serious criminal allegations to make on St. Johns from the Motel 8. You have nothing to show, but some drinks for a taxpayer-furnished and funded fifteen-hundred dollar a month apartment...Oh, and he owes an apology?"

"I lost you. You guys are all over the place," said Tammy. "St. Johns is calling me drunk and I can meet with him right now."

Joe paused and responded by looking at Charlie first. Charlie said, "So you are offering to bait him in? How close can you get to him for us? If you can get real close and personal with him, we can really turn up the heat."

"Sorry," she said. "I want the collar, but I won't whore myself for you Feds."

Joe said, "No? Well, I'm sorry, Jensen. You're a liability to your position and our investigation. You will make no further contact with St. Johns until notified by myself or Agent Stillford. I will be talking to your chief about your posturing toward us before I leave town for my favorite calculator."

Tammy stood her ground, knowing she had been trumped and held a losing hand.

Joe slapped down their business cards on a stack of file folders and said, "Don't mess with the IRS. You should feel free to call if you change your mind about helping us."

The agents nodded to her and then to one another before they turned to leave.

Tammy hesitated until they had stepped into the hallway and then forced herself to say, "Okay, it's true. You need to know that I think he's really psychic. He pulled some freaky stuff yesterday and has told me that a ghost told him we were coming for him."

Joe and Charlie stopped mid-step and looked back at her through the cubicle's entrance. Both burst into laughter when they looked at each other. Charlie said, "Did this ghost tell him that we're taking him down?" Laughing, they exited her doorway into the walkway disregarding her.

Tammy folded her arms with an uncertainty on her face, her mind replaying the most ridiculous sequential ninety-six hours of failure in her twenty-eight years.

There was nothing left to say, so Tammy could only force out the word, "Bureaucrunts." She slumped back into her chair.

SLOWLY, JAKE DIALED THE last few numbers on his phone with the receiver under his chin and one eye closed. The phone rang on the other end of the line.

Tammy's voice message answered, "Hi. This is Tammy. Please leave a message."

In a drunken slur, Jake said, "Look, Tammy, I know you're there, so come on, pick up. I'm sorry, I washed my hands and lost your cell phone number. Call... please." He hung up and rolled his eyes knowing that his message would sound embarrassing to him when he sobered.

TAMMY HELD THE RECEIVER with both hands, listening to Jake's message. Her mind drifted to thinking about Mark, her estranged husband, and then back to Jake, who was really a psychic.

Jake's dad had just died and he was reaching out for help, thought Tammy. She interrupted herself with a question, *Have I become a liability to the case or could I have busted Jake's piñata?*

There was no second-guessing now, she pressed a few buttons on the phone.

The phone said in her ear, "Message forwarded." Tammy looked disappointed with herself.

5

Gary stood in a hole that was waist-deep and about three feet wide. Heavy boots entered his eye-line beside the hole and a couple of bags of topsoil were dropped from a man's shoulder into a heap beside it.

Gary continued digging.

A canteen was tossed down on the pile of loose soil that Gary had dumped beside the hole.

A voice said to Gary, "Drink."

Wearing clown make-up, Mike carried a heavy, healthy five-year old tree still in a nursery dirt-bag that was ready for planting. He set it beside the hole as Gary drank gulps from the canteen.

Mike hunkered down beside the hole and examined it. He said, "Looks good, I think we're done. I hope you learned your lesson. Want to say anything about your work?"

Gary whined out, "No. I just want to go home."

"Well, you can't take my collar with you. Come here and give me your shovel."

Gary leaned himself and the shovel toward Mike, who removed the shovel from the hole and set it out of reach beside his foot.

Mike took a pair of pliers from his hip pocket and nodded up for Gary to raise his chin. Gary leaned toward Mike raising his chin. Using care, Mike used the pliers to release a tension lock and pulled the collar belt free from its lock pin.

Mike tossed the collar toward the grounding stake in front of Gary and picked up the shovel as he stood. Gary looked at his captor's torture device with an equal amount of disgust and relief.

Mike replaced the pliers into his hip pocket and said again in a different way, "Nothing to say before you go?"

Gary said, "No. Is that it? I can go home now?"

Mike shook his head and said, "Sorry, kid, this is your home. Welcome to my orchard."

Dressed like a priest, Mike raised the shovel over his head—Gary's face filled with terror.

The sound of the impact echoed through the yard.

Mike narrowed his eyes looking into the grave and began to shovel dirt back into the hole.

Mike's neighbor came rushing out onto his back porch. Bob was wearing a t-shirt and jeans holding a beer. He leaned around a tree trunk and disappeared. His head reappeared as he looked over the fence, Bob said, "What the hell was that?"

Mike stood behind the hole and looked into it. The hole was just deep enough so that Bob couldn't see the body within it. Mike looked back up to him and smiled.

As he tossed a thumb behind him in the direction of the fence gate, Mike said, "I had a kid here for boot camp. The shovel was left head-up against the fence and it fell before I could grab it."

Mike lifted the shovel before he jabbed it into the dirt pile and tossed a load of soil into the hole.

Bob wasn't convinced and said, "I guess it sounded like something hitting concrete."

"I ain't talking bad about them, but kids today have all lost their common sense. The Bible says to blame the parents."

Bob chuckled, straining to tiptoe up and look over the top of the fence; he turned to peer over the orchard in Mike's backyard. Changing the subject, he said, "So, that's it, huh? The last tree."

Mike looked at the tree beside the hole and said, "Yep. This is the last one." He turned a shovel full of soil into the hole before saying, "I'll have to find a new project."

Bob laughed.

Mike lifted up an open bag of topsoil and emptied it into the hole.

Bob laughed again and barked to Mike over the fence, "I can't believe people pay you to punish their kids. So is there a discount if they plant the trees, too?"

Mike dropped the empty bag to the ground and looked at Bob, who was already showing fatigue at holding to the top of the fence, and said, "You know. I think it is more valuable for them not to participate in the good deeds they've done. It will sit with them forever that they never saw the fruits of their labor. I honestly believe this will save them from an eternity in Hell. You see the Lord, Bob, He has a plan for us."

Bob lost his interest and stepped off the fence to sip off his beer. He climbed back onto the fence and said to Mike, "Well, you already know that I'm not interested in your whole Jesus thing, Mike, so you can save it. I just heard a bang and thought I should take a look."

Mike said, "Thanks for checking, Bob."

Bob waved his hand once in the air over the fence and said, "So do you think you'll have any fruit this year?"

"I hope so," Mike said as he looked back into the yard. "If I get a good crop, I'll make sure to bring a bag over for you and the wife."

Bob walked away from the fence toward his backdoor and shouted back, "She's just my girlfriend, Mike. Good luck with the trees this year, though. See ya later."

Mike smiled and began to shovel dirt into the hole with a quick pace. After a couple of minutes, he looked down at the soil covering Gary and decided that was the right amount. Mike took up the tree from the ground and set it into the hole. It took him no time at all to finish the job once he'd secured the tree to the straps tied to the posts in the ground. He replaced the shovel into the shed and placed the garbage into a curbside trashcan inside the shed.

From within the inside of the shed, the door slammed cutting off the sunrays in an eerie finality.

THURSDAY

1

Waking from the darkness of a shed and into an early morning's darkness, Jake jerked up from his bed and said, "No... Not again!"

Half-dressed and looking ten-years older on his bed, Jake rubbed his pained head and smacked his stale mouth. This reminded him of one reason that he smoked, stale cigarette breath always smelled the same and better than stale toothpaste breath.

Cigarette.

Under a bitter hangover from his binge the night before, Jake nearly vomited at the intensity of his urges for a cigarette and in recalling the dream of a boy being buried by yet another clown; he cursed the world and its bad dreams.

At that moment, the loud sobbing cries of Betty echoed through the room and Jake uttered a groan. He dropped back onto his bed.

Jake said, "Betty! Come here!"

The crying continued and Betty didn't appear while Jake waited.

"Go on. Bawl your head off alone then!" Jake rolled over to his stomach and covered his head with a pillow.

Betty never came and Jake slept late without nightmares. He just dreamed the same dream over and over. He was in an office at a computer and designing a newspaper-insert ad layout over and over again; it just couldn't be finished correctly and it never looked or flowed right.

An unending thought string looped like a skipping disk, *Will I have enough time to take care of us all?*, and he thought about the 'right' investments, but he could not concentrate on the numbers. Over and over, his mind raced from fixing the advertisement to worrying about his investments and taking care of us all...

2

Mike's house faced toward the morning sunshine and it looked like it would be a beautiful day.

Inside, Mike was doing dishes in the sink under a window looking out into the shaded backyard. The yard was an orchard with nearly a dozen well-placed fruit trees of various ages and kinds that were budding flowers over its early seasonal leaves. The planks of the fence were painted dark green and mounted inside the yard to fence beams behind them. It looked like a trap to keep cats in rather than to keep them out.

Mike looked out from the kitchen window to watch Gary dig a hole near the house. The hole would complete the orchard and was clearly marked by four stakes with white marker tape wrapped taut around the heads of these posts.

The backyard was still shaded near the house, but the sun had broken the angle of the roof and was casting light onto Gary who stopped digging and rested the shovel against his neck and shoulder.

He looked down at the round hole that he had started at dawn, but had hardly made a dent. His eyes went then to the ground-anchoring stake that he was tied to via a cable attached to the dog-collar around his neck. He turned his squinted eyes toward the sun.

Watching, Mike shook his hands down a few times over the sink and took up a hand-towel to dry them; he glared out the window into the yard at Gary.

Gary took off one of the gloves to examine his aching palm. He jolted with surprise when Mike activated the shock collar from inside the house.

Mike shouted from the house, "It isn't break time yet. Dig!"

Gary heard the muted message just before he got another jolt from his neck collar and quickly returned to work without his glove.

A CORDLESS PHONE WAS ringing on the counter. Jen moved into the kitchen and answered, "Hello?"

Mike sat in the front room of his home at a clean and orderly desk holding a cheap cell phone to his ear. He replied without any emotion, "Hi, Jen. It's Mike."

Jen wasn't sure who the caller was and then remembered aloud, "Mike the superhero! Thank God. The caller-id said 'UNKNOWN' and I thought it might be..." Pausing, she closed her eyes with worry.

"The police station always comes up as an unknown caller," answered Mike responding to her concern. "Jen, I'm Mike the cop, today. I am getting off-duty at 3 o'clock and thought you might want to talk to someone. I heard that you and The Judge have reported Gary as missing."

Jen said, "We did, but even his dad has told me they can't do anything until 48-hours have past, unless there's a ransom demand. I really need to talk to someone on the inside, but not connected, you know? Gary wasn't at school today, but he has my cell phone number, if he needs me, so could you meet me somewhere? I mean what if someone comes here for me next."

"I can meet you, but if you are worried, I can get a squad car parked over there to keep a watch."

She said she didn't need that and was just being paranoid about Gary. He wasn't even supposed to come there this afternoon and should be at his dad's. She said, "He has a key, if he comes here to run away from his dad. It wouldn't be the first time—But, I keep thinking I hear the door opening and I need to eat something and talk."

"Do you have a regular place near you," he asked.

She said she didn't.

"No? Well, The Old Officer's Club on Golden Road is near you. It has good food and isn't a typical dive. I even know the owner."

She said that she drives passed it every day.

"Great. See you within the hour?," Mike said. He smiled, knowing his plan was coming together.

She kept talking in a nervous ramble that said nothing and ended by saying, "I just need to eat something."

"Okay. Wait—" he said interjecting. "I need to get changed if I am going to meet you in an hour. I don't want to go out in uniform. Hey, in good faith, the first round is on me, okay?"

There was a pause from Jen and in an effort to end the call, Mike said, "I can give you a ride home if you decide that you needed a few more drinks. Hey, it's only a ten-minute walk over from you, so you don't need to drive."

She liked the thought of walking over to clear her head and they said goodbye.

He assumed that she had been needy, but now she was completely vulnerable, as well. Now all he needed was to connect the dots to implicate The Judge.

He went into the backyard and beamed at Gary saying that his work was over for the day.

Looking into the hole, Mike said, "It's time to put you back in your kennel, dawg. Throw out the shovel."

Gary threw the shovel away from the hole. Mike removed pliers from his hip pocket and bent down to release Gary from the ground-stake leash.

3

After a brief visit to Todd's Book Addict in his mid-sized pick-up truck for the books he had ordered, Jake spent the rest of the morning loading, unloading and sorting the large order of books.

About a half-past three o'clock, he was getting pretty wasted again and wasn't having much luck ordering Chinese food, so he hung up the phone and laughed at the thought of trying to get an Asian call girl. He decided to order out for pizza instead, he knew they would be able to understand him and they had.

With a couple of pizzas on the way, he wished they could bring him a bottle and cigarettes, too. Jake was now sober enough to have a drunken purpose and started playing music from his computer in a random order to find songs his dad had liked.

Jake squinted one eye and swayed as he leaned close to look at his monitor, he fought to focus on Frank Sinatra. He clicked to play—

The snare tapped and Frank sang in on *Just One of Those Things*. Jake sat back and let the music play.

No cigarettes. No Michelle. No school. No friends. No dad. No vodka left. No Tammy left. He was alone with the ghosts, again.

He lifted the empty vodka bottle up to his mouth again and caught another few drops on his tongue listening to the music. Jake fell asleep and the three doorbells announcing his pizza delivery went unanswered.

FRIDAY

1

Jake was sleeping comfortably in his bed when his alarm went off. He was hung over and barely moved to press the snooze button before drifting back to sleep.

After a couple of snoozes, Jake was ready for the day ahead. No Betty and no nightmares.

Things must be turning around, he thought as he climbed out of bed and readied for the day ahead. Today would be an alcohol-free day until he finished his dad's eulogy and had a CD of music.

Jake worked for a couple of hours filling book orders in his office while listening to a music playlist that he created the night before. He would pause at his work from time to time to delete a song that didn't fit or add a newly inspired tune that reminded him of his dad. Jake looked over the remaining songs in the list and was impressed with his drunken choices from the previous day.

SHORTLY AFTER NOON, Jake had thought about it long enough and sat down at his desk to begin writing out the eulogy for Papa Tom's memorial on Sunday. Every so often, he would sit forward and take the computer's mouse in hand to move a song up or down in the playlist.

He worked all day and had finished for the most part. At least he felt really good about the music selections he had made. A CD popped out from the side of his computer; Jake took the disc, wrote 'For Dad' on its face with a magic marker, and placed it into a jewel-case on the desk. He then retrieved a printout of his retyped memorial for Tom.

After making a few edits from his proofreader marks on the printed pages, he felt he had a finished draft and e-mailed it to his mom.

He was about to call his mom to tell her the eulogy was finished and waiting for her, when something moved in his peripheral vision. Betty had appeared in his office doorway, Jake was surprised to see her and said so. He asked, "What brings you out of hiding today?"

"I have things to do," said Betty.

"You have things to do, eh? Do you have the time to listen to what I wrote for my dad," asked Jake, offering the paper to her.

Her disregard was obvious and she replied, "Your father is not of interest to me, Jake. We have something else to do now."

Jake immediately hit his boiling point and stood up from the desk looking down at his printouts. Turning to her, Jake said, "Dammit, Betty, I just had my best day since birth. Go hide somewhere and cry until tomorrow."

"The time to cry has passed," Betty said. "We must fulfill this stage of our destiny, St. Johns."

"Look, Betty," Jake said sitting back down. "I need to visit my mom. So, you go on with your destiny plans without me."

"You will be coming with me," Betty said with a rare smile.

Jake sat tall with a smirk and said, "I'd like to see you make me."

"I will make you if I have to," she said. "Now, get your coat and shoes, Jacob. It is time to go."

Jake shook his head and responded, "I'm going to my mom's, Elizabeth."

Betty walked to him smiling and he bent his waist to taunt her eye-to-eye from his chair.

Sweetly, she placed both her hands on the sides of Jake's face. "I told you they were coming. Now, you must lead them."

Betty slapped a severe right hand against his cheek and said, "Wake up, Jake! I need a favor from you."

Jake pushed her away, his eyes were cold when he said, "I'm pretty sure slapping me isn't the way to get it done."

Betty declared, "You must kill someone for me and it is time to go."

"I can't kill anyone, Betty. It's wrong," Jake said with an adult's disregard.

Betty stood tall and hissed like a howling cat. Her skin putrefied, the dress rotted, and Betty's eyes became black sockets. Her voice was hollow and dry when she spoke, "This is not a moral debate. It is a command. To measure out death on the unrighteous is your only virtue, Saint-Johns."

Betty became a skeleton clothed in flames and a fiery sundress. She floated into the air and darted out the door into the hallway.

When her feet touched the floor, the carpet caught fire beneath them. Betty said, "Drink deep and be somebody, Jake. You will obey me or I will burn your house down."

The paintings in his hallway began to smoke and catch on fire as Betty walked away from Jake.

Flames danced up the corners of Jake's office as she walked out of view leaving behind child-sized footprints of fire on the hard wood floor.

Responding quickly, Jake followed her flaming path down the hallway.

The fires were worse than he expected, so he reached back into the room and picked up a yellow Halon fire extinguisher.

He was careful to step around Betty's flaming footprints and shot quick bursts of the compressed gas to smother the flaming footsteps leading down the hallway.

Flames were spreading rapidly and had licked up in the corners of the house spreading to the edges of the pool table and bookshelves.

In a panic, Jake dropped the extinguisher and quickened his pace to follow Betty.

The front door was open and Jake could see that Betty was covered in flames and floating over the front yard. Jake shouted, "I'm coming, Betty... Please quit burning my house!"

He grabbed his coat and put shoes onto his bare feet before looking out again.

Smiling, Betty stood on the sidewalk and appeared to be the little girl in a nightgown again. She waved her hand for Jake to join her, a large number of ghosts had gathered around her on the lawn.

Jake looked back into the house and the fire was gone, but charred marks were left as a reminder.

He locked the door behind him and stepped into the yard looking pained as ghosts began to appear from every shadow cast by the afternoon sun across his yard.

Jake stepped to her and said, "Why are you doing this, Betty? You come to me crying with no message, no story, no instructions, and then this. It's all a little..."

His focus readjusted over her on the street and said, "Why is there a taxi here?"

Betty turned to look behind her and smiled seeing the taxi parked near the gates of Jake's home. She glanced over her shoulder back to Jake with that same smile and said, "Because we called for one. You said you wanted to find me and would help. Lead on, hero, your chariot awaits."

Jake straightened his posture with a deep breath to mentally align his energy chakras and draw in Chi from the earth's magnetic field. The bio-energy that he stole from the world was mentally distilled to fill the bottles in his soul.

As he walked down the sidewalk crossing over Betty to lead the way,

Jake found a novel when he had placed his hands into his coat pockets, remembering Tammy. Taking stock of the multiplying ghosts that now crowded the edges of the sidewalk to watch the man and child with intensity, he wished he had finished reading the book that he carried.

The driver turned a glance over his shoulder to see Jake exit the tunnel through his wrought iron gates and approach the rear passenger-side door.

2

Jake rode along in the backseat staring out the window at the world, the pedestrian and roadside worker's thoughts became a white noise of voices that filled his head and the scenery blurred passed at motion sickness speed in his fixed-focused point-of-view.

Sitting beside him, Betty held Jake's hand. She pulled his hand with a tug and said, "Tell the driver to turn left at the next street."

"Take a left up here, m'man," said Jake to the cab driver.

The cabbie, a black man wearing layered shirts and a ball cap, was visibly insulted at Jake's casual use of *m'man*.

Ignorant of the man's intense glare, Jake stared out the window and watched the world turn left.

Several minutes later, the taxi pulled beside a hearse at a streetlight. Jake looked in at an old woman riding on a slab in back; she turned her head and noticed him. She pulled herself from under a sheet and moved to the window.

Betty said, "Next right."

Her instruction didn't penetrate his deep concentration on watching the naked old woman, who filled the hearse's window and banged her fists against the glass. He could see the woman was mouthing the words, *Help me. Help me.*

The old woman looked up at the hearse driver in fear of him hearing her and turned back to Jake. Hopelessness and urgency was written on the old woman's face as the taxi pulled away from the hearse.

Betty nudged him hard. "Turn right here!"

Jake, snapping out of his morbid thoughts of having observed a ghost being born, sat forward and banged on the window. "Take the next right!"

Startled, the cabbie changed lanes and made a blind right turn as he twisted his angry face back toward Jake and shouted, "Why don't you just tell me where we're goin' and I'll take us there."

Jake said, "Sorry, I didn't mean to bang the glass. Look, I don't know where I'm going, yet."

The cabbie looked back and said, "Well, I know where I'm going in fifty-five minutes. And, if you ain't heading south, I'll be ending our tour of Denver." He laughed at himself, "Are ya hearing me? Cuz I got a date."

"I hear ya and I'll pay attention."

Driver said, "That's cool, but I hope *m'man* can pay better then attention."

The thought of money jolted Jake, who sat back realizing that he only brought his house keys and prayed he had something in the pocket of these jeans.

God loves children and drunks, Jake thought. *Damn this alcohol- free day!*

He stammered out, "I'll pay extra. But, I only know the way." Jake could remember setting his money clip and wallet on his dresser two days ago and hoped that the driver would look away, so he could check his pockets.

Jake pulled Betty closer to him.

***

THE BLACK SEDAN OF the IRS men followed the taxi. Joe drove with Charlie sitting beside him. Neither noticed the hearse, but both watched the quick right turn that the cab had made and they looked at each other.

Joe said, "That was an urgent turn. Is he on to us?"

"Like how he called Tammy twice and she forwarded each message to us the second after we had just said his name," Charlie said. "Or better yet, how about the night-vision photos that you said had ghosts in them. Now, he knows when he's being followed?"

Joe narrowed his eyes and said, "I keep thinking about those crows. That was really weird."

"Come on, Joe, snap out of it," Charlie said. "We saw some crows eat a parrot. It makes perfect sense in this world. Please tell me that Jensen's reports haven't made you fall in love with The Psychic Machiavelli."

Joe shrugged a 'maybe' while taking the turn and continued following the taxi. "I'm just saying that he might be psychic or magic, or, I don't know... But, I do know that you are our new Tammy and you are going to need to use all your charms to get real close to him for us," he said laughing.

"Just drive, Joe," Charlie pointed for Joe to change lanes.

BETTY PATTED JAKE'S CHEST and said, "This is it."

Jake looked over and Betty was gone. He leaned forward to look through the windshield.

Ahead of the taxi in the distance, Betty waved standing at the curb beside a field. Jake saw her hand in the air and said, "Excuse me. You can stop at this field. I'll walk from here."

The cab driver smiled looking back to Jake and said, "Now you got it. See, politeness is the key to a pleasant ride for everyone." He pulled over to the curb and said, "That will be $34.80."

Knowing that he didn't have any cash in his jean pockets, Jake got out of the taxi ready to run as he felt his pockets again. When he reached his hand inside his coat pocket, he found only the novel and started to panic as he readied himself to run away.

I have prepared for this moment for years, Jake thought. *Why am I nervous now? He can't catch me.*

As the word 'prepared' echoed in his mind, Jake smirked remembering the thin fold of bills he had used as a bookmark. He took out the book he'd meant to read preparing for this adventure.

Jake removed the two fifties he had originally intended to leave for a tip at the diner and later used as a bookmark. He almost laughed aloud considering how many books he had accidentally sent to customers that had cash bookmarks.

With a big goofy smile, Jake leaned in through the open passenger window and reached out his hand holding the only bills he had and said, "Thanks for the ride. I'd give you more, but I was caught low on cash."

The cab driver took the money with dollar signs in his eyes as Jake turned away to join Betty and called out from inside the cab. "Hold up, m'man."

Inside the cab, the driver dug a hand into his shirt-pocket and had fished out a business card when Jake returned to the window.

"The back side has a blank receipt, you call me if ya ever need a ride," the cabbie said as he leaned over the seat to offer Jake the card. "Just don't bang on the glass, ah'ight?"

Jake took the card and looked at it. He said smiling, "All right... Dante. I'll never bang a window again." Wondering what level of Hell he was entering and why his Beatrice was a child, Jake said, "Hey! Thanks, man. My name's Jake."

"Danny-T," projected the cabbie.

They shook hands through the open passenger window.

Dante called out a warning and said, "Be careful out there, money. This's a lousy neighborhood and we had a government-issue following us."

Jake nodded shamefully in agreement as he looked at the business card without looking back to Dante.

"Good luck, dog," said Dante as he gassed his taxi into the street leaving Jake standing at the curb. Jake turned to jog off after Betty, who was already walking down a path leading through the field.

The green shoots of spring growth were starting to show on the exposed soil and in the browned winter grasses; the single, dirt path that led through the field was dry and bare.

When Jake entered the field to catch up with Betty, meowing cats, snakes, and various rodents began gathering on the edge of the path following him across the field.

THE GOVERNMENT SEDAN WAITED up the street from the taxi as it had pulled up to the curb beside the field. Jake got out of the taxi and exchanged words with the driver.

Charlie lifted the camera and captured the moment through the shutter of a viewfinder.

Joe and Charlie sat in the sedan and watched Jake jog into the field.

Joe had a broader sense of perspective and said, "Where's this guy off to nowwwww—"

A crow landed on the hood interrupting him with surprise. Another crow alit onto the hood, followed by a third. The three crows commenced to pecking and scratching at the hood.

"What the—?," Joe stared at the crows and then looked at Charlie.

"Forget these crows! St. Johns is going in that direction," Charlie said pointing onward past the field. "Hurry, go around to the other side!"

Joe jerked the column-control arm into drive while saying, "Good call, Charlie. We'll pick him up on the other side of the field." He punched the gas and said, "Die, crow, die!"

The crows cawed with what could only be described as shrill laughter and flew up in different directions from the car when it shot into the street.

3

Holding hands, Jake and Betty walked down a neighborhood street and stepped toward the sidewalk in silence.

They had walked down the sidewalk past a house when Betty stopped at a driveway and gently led Jake to pause for a moment.

She said with the most sincere voice, "We have arrived, Jake. Do you hear them crying?"

"Sorry, Betty, I don't listen for them."

She showed her disappointment and said that he would need to start. She ducked her head and moved away from him up the driveway of the next house. She snuck into the yard, hiding behind a truck in the driveway and ran beside the budding hedges—Jake followed her in a stooping run.

THE GOVERNMENT SEDAN STOPPED at the top of this same street a moment too late and Jake was nowhere to be seen.

Charlie held binoculars to his eyes and was scanning the spaces between the houses. He said, "Do you see him?"

Joe exhaled a long sigh and slammed the sedan into park.

Charlie removed the field glasses from his eyes and looked around. "Well, he's on this street. The roads all dead end here against the highway and we would have seen him if he had gone east or west."

Joe said with a fresh spirit, "He didn't take the cab here. Wanna bet that he's buying drugs and we can turn this into a criminal case for the State and Feds?"

"I'll take that bet," said Charlie. "We can pass it all back to Jensen to do the paperwork."

They smiled at each other.

Joe said, "Watch the mirrors. I don't want that little creep to sneak past us. If you spot him, I'll buy beers." He turned on the radio and pressed the pre-sets until a sports announcer's voice came through the speakers saying, "...they're down four points as Smith comes to the line to shoot."

Joe leaned back and got comfortable while looking behind him in his side mirror.

BETTY STOPPED AT THE GATE and put her finger up to her lips for silence. She pointed at the gate and mimed opening it with care.

Jake moved to it and opened the gate as quietly as possible.

Betty stood behind him in the gateway, but then disappeared when Jake crossed over her to enter the backyard.

When Jake looked back and found Betty had gone, he looked more frustrated than surprised.

Nevertheless, he moved into the yard at the rear-exterior of the house. He looked around and saw an orchard of twelve trees. One was a newly planted five year-old that was tethered to four stakes.

Every tree, but the new one, had children of various sexes and races kneeling before it.

The ghost children of this blood orchard looked up at Jake and again lowered their heads weeping under the trees with random voices. "We're sorry..."

Their wailing voices overlapped and blurred into an eerie and discomforting cacophony that screeched like nails down a chalkboard.

Jake responded by pushing out a golden aura from his body and projected the bioenergy as needles and thread of light across the yard attaching his spirit to each tree. He shouted into the ether plane of the undead and said, "You can't pass over in fear. I need you all to come. Come to me and I'll take you home."

The spirit-children arose and began jolting into bursts of light that traveled the space between them along the energy tendrils that Jake had connected into the trees.

Suddenly, Mike opened the back door and exited the house—Jake was visibly shocked and shivered twice when his retracted magic snapped back into him and struck his mind like a bullwhip against his back.

Mike said, "Who the hell are you?"

"Hi. I'm Tom's kid. Uh...Mike, right? Did you know that you have a bunch of kids buried back h—"

Mike attacked Jake with highly-trained grace and speed. He knocked Jake out in three lightning-quick moves and caught Jake with his fourth move in an over-pronounced movement of concern for a friend.

He closed the gate holding Jake's full weight against his body and then threw his limp inside arm over his own neck to carry Jake shoulder-to-shoulder into the house.

Mike spoke in hushed tones as if Jake were a drunk family member being carried in from the street.

A GLASS OF WATER was thrown into Jake's face!

Inside Mike's house, Jake snapped awake to find he was duct-taped to a chair. Mike stood in front of him smoking a cigarette and flipping an empty thick plastic cup in his other hand.

Mike sucked his teeth and smiled, "Do you have a favorite meal, Jake?"

Jake looked at him with the confidence of a dreamer and said, "I'm not hungry."

Jake saw Mike biting a corn dog.

Mike took a step back and rested his weight against the top of a tidy metal desk in his front room. He stared at Jake trying to figure him out and took a long drag from his cigarette. "No? How about a cigarette? Want a smoke, instead, Jake?"

Mike was at a bar and pulled the handle of a cigarette machine.

Inhaling from his cigarette and exhaling smoke, Mike said, "Come on. I got these cigarettes for someone who only smokes at the bar. I've seen you smoking at the diner."

Mike and a woman were on the deck drinking and smoking, he waved to the waitress for two more drinks.

Mike took a drag off of his cigarette and said, "You smell like you could use a drink. Vodka?" He leaned in to pretend to smell Jake. "Did you want gin?"

Jake was silent, but his face churned as his blood raced and he fought to take control of the dream. He wanted a drink and a cigarette—

It is a dream…Smoke up! It's just a—

Jake denied the urge with an internal fury against it.

Breaking Jake's concentration, Mike slapped his upper thigh in thought and stood again.

"Suit yourself," Mike said. He picked up the pack of cigarettes and stuck them in Jake's shirt pocket saying, "You'll want them soon enough and wish you'd had a last one."

Silent, Mike started a slow pacing before Jake as he thought about how to fit Jake into his revenge plans against The Judge and Patterson and muttered aloud, "St. Johns, you are a most unexpected surprise."

Jake closed his eyes and gave out an intense mental cry for help. The visual effect was like the magnetic waves of an atomic bomb exploding. He said on a thought bandwidth, *I am going to die. Call the police. Blue house. 18-40 Adams. Green truck. Please help if you can hear me! I am going to die. Call police. Blue house. 18—*

He heard the rapid-fire thoughts of a woman calling out from the static of his mental tinnitus, *Oh God. Please. Truck. Garage. Help me. Mike. Cop. The Champion killed Gary.*

Jake became angry and pulled against his duct-tape restraints, the chair began to shake with telekinetic energy. He growled at Mike, "You have someone else here?!"

Mike laughed as Jake struggled and replied, "So what if I do, superhero? You can't do anything about it, so relax. Besides, the more you pull, the more it makes the tape tighten." He shoved the cigarette butt into an ashtray.

"I swear to God that I just heard you whispering, '18, 40, blue house, Adams, green truck. Was that a specific prayer to your personal God," Mike asked. He bent his taut midsection down to meet Jake's eyes and whispered, "Shout it. No one can hear you scream."

Jake squinted and shot his psychic energy at him; the beam of light stabbed like a knife into Mike's head. Jake began to weave a strange pattern into his mind and said, "Yes, they can. I didn't say that out loud and I didn't send the message to you. They are coming and you should get your service-issue."

Mike glared hard at Jake. "So, is this what your boyfriend at the bookstore was talking about? You acting like you are dangerous. You don't scare me, St. Johns." He stood menacingly close to Jake. "He told me that you tried to scare him with ghost stories. Is that why you said there were kids back there?" He punctuated the question by pointing to indicate the backyard.

"Maybe you should get your gun," Jake said.

Mike smiled and said, "Oh, I don't need my gun."

"Are you sure about that? God sent me to *judge* and kill you."

"Kill me?," Mike laughed. "You're taped to a chair."

Mike swelled his chest straightening up his shoulders and looked around at his house. "God cares about my sins as much as He cares about your whispered prayers. God doesn't care about me or you. Let me demonstrate." He hammered a fist into Jake's face and stunned him for a second.

Jake refused to back down and let this dream get the better of him, "God does care. Why else am I here like this? May I recount your sins, Michael?"

"Sure. This should be better than me telling you to pray that I not punch you again," said Mike turning to grab the chair from the desk. He pulled it in front of Jake and sat on it backward resting his arms on the back with a mocking look of anticipation. "Please. Do tell."

Jake closed his eyes and his body's aura glowed in a radiant golden light. The ray of light tethered between their minds hummed like a piano wire as it surged with energy.

Mike said, "I can almost feel you trying to power up. I told you that you can't muscle out of that—"

Jake snapped open angry eyes and ranted, "You are the portrait of a serial-killer hiding behind a mask. I've dreamed that you were a killer clown for years, but you are a vigilante cop trying to save the world from people just like you.

"The first thing you ever killed was your goldfish to get a hamster. You then killed your hamster for a dog. When Trixie became your dad's dog, you killed her, too." Mike's demeanor transitioned from mockery to anger as Jake continued. "You have cooked a cat and eaten it, but you haven't had sex since you were married ten years ago."

Jake inhaled, "The first person you killed was Kendra, your wife."

Mike stood and threw the chair across the room in a terror-fueled rampage. He shouted, "Who sent you, goddammit!? Patterson? The Judge?"

Mike's plans flashed out at Jake in a scattered timeline that assembled into a complete picture in his mind.

Jake said, "She was pregnant with a girl, Mike."

Mike hammered his fist into Jake's face, again, and said, "That's enough!"

Jake smiled a bloody checkmate grin and said, "Sorry, there's more."

4

Unbeknownst to the IRS Special Agents, the sedan was parked directly up the street from the house where Jake was taped to a chair at the hands of the Denver police officer that they were given for a special assignment.

A basketball game played on the radio as their eyes shifted from point to point with radar precision for the last ten minutes of the game. However, they grew restless and started fidgeting shortly after the game had ended while listening to the sportscasters talk about the Denver Nuggets post-season chances.

Three big crows landed in the trees across the street and had a good laugh. They dropped to the middle of the street beside the sedan. The crows strutted toward the sedan and cawed.

Charlie fiddled with his camera, while Joe stared at the radio for a second to set it to scan. He looked up and down the street, scanning for something as he listened. "It'd be nice to find a good blues station," he said.

The radio landed on Jazz 88 and the deejay said, "This one goes out to you, Jake. Muddy Waters and *Take a Walk with Me*." Classic acoustic blues came broadcasting out. Joe pressed the Scan button again and selected the station.

Looking around again, Joe locked in on the three birds.

When the crows had his attention, two of them bounced across the street. Joe continued to study them. The pair stopped and turned back to look at him from the corner of the street that the agents were stationed to surveil.

When the largest of the three crows bounced into the middle of the street, the sleek blackbird and Joe made eye contact—the crow didn't blink first.

Joe said without looking away, "Look at these friggin' crows, Charlie."

Muddy Waters's voice sang out the chorus.

"Look, I'm about sick of your *friggin' crows* already," Charlie said turning his eyes from his camera to Joe.

The crow shouted, "Attention!"

The men both jumped and stared to the middle of the street at the talking crow.

"Attention!," the crow said again. "Here and now, boys. Here and now."

Joe and Charlie exchanged involuntary smiles of disbelief and amazement.

The crows on the corner both cawed in a guffaw that blended into human laughter.

The central bird turned and flapped his wings twice to join his smaller buddies on the corner. He cawed, "Attention... Here and now, boys!"

The twin crows flew down the street toward Mike's house.

The big crow remained on the street corner and outstretched its wings whipping them in front of him.

Joe said, "He is saying to follow him or taunting us to a fight. You want to follow them?"

"I don't work with talking shitbirds," Charlie said looking back to his camera.

Joe said, "These crows are telling us to follow them. Hell, Muddy Waters is telling us to take a walk." He snatched the keys and said, "We're following them." Joe got out of the car walking after the crows.

Charlie set down the camera and followed Joe whispering under his breath, "Right behind you, Joe." He had to hustle to catch up with his partner.

They moved toward Mike's house following the crows. The crows bounced down the street looking back and waiting for them.

Charlie had second thoughts and said, "Hey, wait up, Joe. Don't do this. It's...Crazy."

"Crazy?!," Joe said. "Hell yeah, it's crazy. This is as good as it gets for an IRS agent, Chuckles. It's like an X-Files. Follow those crows and that's an order."

Charlie shook his head in compliance and picked up his pace to keep up with Joe.

The big crow took flight again and alit with several long hops to rejoin the twins. The crow trio bounced up the sidewalk into Mike's yard. They continued into the yard and up the sidewalk to the porch.

The agents looked at each other with utter disbelief.

Joe and Charlie turned back to look at the crows, who were looking back at the men in silence.

"They aren't making much noise now," Charlie whispered buying into the weirdness. "So, I suppose they want us to go quietly to the door."

Joe nodded in agreement and the G-men committed to the path leading through the yard to the front door. When they had entered the yard and moved up the sidewalk to the house, the crows flew up and disappeared overhead.

INSIDE THE HOUSE, Jake spit a mouthful of blood at Mike and fueled his mental attack with every free electron he could conjure to himself from the poorly insolated wall outlets.

The ghost children that had once wept in the orchard behind Mike's house now moved out from behind Jake and gathered around his chair. Jake activated several areas in Mike's mind and forced him to see the ghosts that were rescued from the backyard.

Mike turned around to grab his service-issue sidearm from within the desk. Jake glowed with a very tangible energy and forced his aura again into Mike's head when he turned quickly from the desk and trained the barrel on Jake.

Jake was calm and said in a Sunday-school teacher tone, "Shouldn't you say you are sorry to them, Mike?"

Preternatural energy filled into the room and Jake began to telekinetically shake the chair as his mental efforts grew more intense, his muscles were taut and he pulled against his restraints. The chair and Jake began to levitate from the floor as the orchard children began to fly around the room creating an empathic vortex of eternal anguish around Mike.

Mike fought to resist Jake's mind-control, but Jake had set his psychic hooks in deep. The struggle turned sharply against the weakening resolve of Mike when Jake directed his hand to turn the gun on himself and hold it up to the side his own head.

Mike slowly raised the gun to the side of his head and cocked the hammer.

There was the sudden ring of a doorbell that echoed through Mike's house!

The interruption surprised both of them and Jake lost the complete control he needed.

Mike snapped out of the trance and tightened his face before turning the gun back to Jake with a smile. "That was some really crazy stuff you just pulled. You might be evil after all."

A sharp knock at the door interrupted and prevented Mike from saying anything more.

"Well," Jake said bluntly. "It isn't me knocking. Don't you want to know who's here to save me? They'll be coming through that door any second."

Smiling broadly, Mike shoved the gun into the back of his pants and under his shirt. He grabbed one of the several mouth-sized strips of duct tape that he had thoughtfully placed on the side of the chair and slapped the strip over Jake's smiling mouth. Leaning close to his ear, Mike whispered, "Oh, I'll bite just to see that smile disappear when this mind trick backfires on you and there isn't anyone here to save you." Mike winked and moved to the front door.

Jake's eyes smiled above his taped mouth knowing that someone had come to rescue him. *Was it Tammy?* He had thought of her strongly when he broadcast his cry for help and hoped she had the sense to call the police instead of coming herself. *Tammy isn't coming or calling anyone.* His confidence faded and Jake wondered if Mike wasn't right, he couldn't assure himself that this wasn't a mutual mind fuck.

If I go with this panic and over-analyze something, I should be able to turn the dream and wake myself, Jake deduced. *Focus on the details!*

STANDING WITH JOE ON the porch of Mike's home, Charlie poised to rap a fist on the door again.

Mike opened the door. He knew they were cops on his first glance and said, "May I help you?"

Joe and Charlie flashed their badges and IDs to Mike. Joe said, "IRS. I'm Agent Gaines and this is Agent Stillford."

Mike knew them as his IRS agents, but looked closely at the badges.

Charlie held up a photo and said, "Have you seen this man?"

Mike leaned in for a close-up look at the photo of Jake before he said, "He looks familiar, but I can't place him. What'd he do?"

The G-men glanced at each other unsure of their answer.

Mike reached behind him—Joe and Charlie tensed up and moved their hands to draw firearms.

Mike removed a wallet in his fingertips and said, "It's ok, fellahs, I'm a local officer. Maybe I can help?"

Charlie looked at Joe with a smirk when they saw his badge.

The ghost children crowded the door around Mike and disturbed him. They were saying in broken rounds, "Tell them what you've done."

Charlie said, "May we come in?"

"How about I come out? It's a beautiful evening. Feels like springtime, finally."

He exited the house closing the door behind him. Mike nodded them toward the street into a beam of sunlight as he removed a couple of business cards from his wallet. "I have some solid connections with the local judges. Do you have a warrant on this guy, yet?"

Charlie and Joe took the generic cards in a polite gesture and moved with him toward the street. Mike was careful to keep his front facing them and did not chance revealing the gun tucked into his waistband behind him.

"We're working on a warrant, right now," said Charlie. He looked at Joe with a greedy smile that said, *Good job, but the crows were on our side, not St. Johns's.*

"Yeah? Well, give me a call this week and we can review the evidence to see how close you are to getting at least an arrest warrant," Mike said with a wink.

Joe looked at Mike and then to Charlie with skepticism.

The ghost children had left the house and began to appear around Mike nagging at him in a round of weeping. "Tell them. Tell them that you're sorry. Tell them about us."

Mike became edgy and said with finality, "Call me this week. I gotta get back to my dinner on the stove. Mama always said, 'An unwatched pot of pasta is boiling over.'" He offered a parting handshake to each man and backed up toward the house looking back at the agents with a final wave before climbing the two cement steps to his front door.

5

Tammy was focused on her work sitting in front of her computer when a luminous magnetic wave rippled through her cubicle and breezed through her hair—she sat straight up with goose bumps and raised hackles.

After shaking off the momentary shock of the revelation, Tammy picked up and dialed her phone.

JOE AND CHARLIE WALKED away from Mike's house moving back toward their sedan.

Scanning the trees for crows, Joe said, "Interesting, but weird, though."

"Nope. That, Joe, was our sign from your shitbirds and we're getting our warrant this week," Charlie said and held up a high-five when Joe's cell-phone rang.

No high-five, instead Joe pulled out the ringing phone and looked at the Caller-ID with contempt. He said to Charlie, "It's Tammy Jensen. Should I tell her you aren't here and went out for high-fives?" Joe lifted his hand to give Charlie a high-five.

Charlie was in no mood for Joe's jokes and glared at his raised hand.

Joe wagged his head in disappointment at Charlie and used his mockingly raised hand to answer the call.

TAMMY CRADLED THE PHONE and bounced in her chair with agitation as the other end rang in her ear.

Opening and placing his cell phone to his ear, Agent Gaines said, "Ready to work with us, Jenson?"

"Joe, Jake St. Johns is in trouble," said Tammy. "You need to find him."

Joe reacted with sarcasm looking at Charlie, "Hey. Jensen's psychic now, Charlie. Look, Tammy, we lost St. Johns after he ran from a cab, which means he isn't looking for help. But, we did find some of Dumbo's magic crow feathers."

Tammy switched ears and said, "Don't make me do this."

"What can you do?," Joe said. "We're IRS. Maybe, we should look into you and your estranged husband's tax forms from the last five years."

Tammy sat forward and blurted out, "Jake's on Adams Street and I saw 1840. It's a blue house and has a green truck parked in the driveway."

Joe looked at Charlie and then over his shoulder back to the house. "Forget it, Jensen. We were just there and the guy was all right. Local PD, in fact. Where you getting this—," Joe looked around and said, "Are you tailing us, Jensen?"

Tammy said, "It doesn't matter how I know. Just go back and ask to use the restroom. There's a bald man with a gun, so go armed. I'm coming down." She disconnected the line.

Challenged by Tammy's abrupt disconnection, Joe turned to face Charlie with an internal question. "Did you smell anything cooking? I didn't smell pasta and I would have...I'm starving, man."

"No, I didn't, but," Charlie groaned as Joe turned to walk back toward the house. A thought hit him like a gong and Charlie looked at the name on the card, *Michael Straka* was printed in a small font at the top left of the card.

Why would he try to trick us, he wondered.

He turned sharply on his heel to follow Joe, who had already drawn his weapon. Charlie reached for his holster, too.

In front of Jake, Mike was taunting him with slaps to punctuate his words, "I guess they weren't here to save you, after all. I told you God doesn't care. B'bye, rescuers."

Mike ripped off the tape covering Jake's mouth.

"I want to hear you beg, book-boy," Mike said removing the gun from the back of his pants. "I guess you weren't an angel of judgment after all. Well, not yet."

Suddenly, there's a sharp knock at the door! Once again, neither of the men moved.

Mike lost interest in Jake for a moment of introspection and Jake shot out a beam of aura in a weak unfocused spectrum from around his own head; he was spent and had no energy reserves left to mentally influence Mike.

"What now...? Mormons!? I've killed fifteen people and this does not happen in real life. No. No one can save you now. This bad dream's over." With a grin, Mike slowly trained the gun on Jake.

Charlie and Joe could hear Mike shouting inside. "What now...? Mormons!? I've killed fifteen people and—"

Joe had heard enough and said, "Let's go!"

Charlie made a grim face and then kicked the door.

THE SOUND OF THE KICK against the front door was deafening inside and it was accompanied by a crunch of wood.

Mike smiled thinking that Jake was trying to trick him again and cocked the gun in Jake's face. "I'm on to you, now. There's no one out there. There never was," Mike said. "Those were just the IRS agents from—"

The door was kicked open!

Charlie and Joe filled the opened front door with guns pointing in.

They saw Mike with his gun in hand as he turned it on them. The IRS agents opened fire without warning—Mike's flesh and blood were blown all over the wall behind him.

Joe entered the house, looking at the mess. He shot a hateful look at Jake and in frustration demanded an answer, "Who are you people?"

"Don't worry about me," said the swelling and bloodied Jake in gasps. "There's someone, a woman, in the garage."

Turning to Charlie, Joe said, "Search the house and I'll check the garage."

The G-men moved in different directions leaving Jake tied to the chair.

JOE HELD A LOCK-BLADE KNIFE in his hand under the beam of a penlight he had clenched in his teeth. He was intensely focused while cutting Jen's hands loose—she shouted in panicked breaths through her nose against the duct-tape over her mouth.

The first freed hand moved to and pulled against the second to make her bondage taut for Joe. When her arms had come free, Jen slowly pulled the tape from her mouth with both hands and gasped in the warm, stale air of the dark garage.

Joe took the light from his mouth and knelt onto one knee. He looked at her with concern and said, "Are you okay, Miss?"

With her hands in her hair, she started to cry and said, "Yes-yes. Thank you. He was going to kill me."

Touching her arm to comfort her, Joe said, "It's okay. You're safe now."

Jen threw her arms around Joe and began to sob, "He-killed-my-son! He has someone else—a man—inside, I heard him."

At the other end of the garage near the door, Gary awoke sharply and started grunting as he shook his chair against the ground. The tape on his mouth muffled his panicked cries for help.

The penlight beamed onto Gary, Jen expressed her surprise when she looked at him taped to a chair and shouted, "Oh god, it's my—Gary!"

She stood not realizing her legs were still taped to the chair and toppled to the floor. When Joe moved to help her up, she shouted, "No. Cut him free first!"

"Charlie! Get in here," Joe called out as he moved to Gary and commenced cutting him free from his restraints.

Jen fought against the toppled chair and pulled at the tape around her ankles.

Charlie rushed into the garage gun first and said, "Joe? What the...!?" He switched on the garage overhead light and rushed to Jen. He pulled out a pocketknife to cut her legs from the chair as Joe was finishing with Gary's bindings.

Cut free, mother and son were together again and they rushed to embrace one another.

JOE SHOUTED FROM THE GARAGE, "Charlie! Get in here!"

There was the loud thud of something heavy hitting a wood floor in an unseen area of the house. Charlie rushed from the back bedroom and passed Jake toward the garage.

From over his shoulder, Jake watched him exit. When he turned back to face forward, Betty was standing in front of him with the children of the orchard gathered around her over the body of Mike.

Betty said, "I have to go, Jake." The children before him all took each other's hand.

"I'll miss you, Betty," said Jake.

She smiled, "You'll see me again soon enough. Goodbye, Jake."

Jake watched with disbelief when Betty spread her unseen wings toward the sky. He blurted out, "Wait! If you are an angel, why were you crying?"

Betty gave Jake a sly grin and replied, "I just wanted to go home, Jake. Thank you." She smiled at Jake with all of her teeth and looked up. Leading the spirits of the children hand-in-hand, Betty flew up through the ceiling and they were gone.

Alone, Jake looked down at his wrists and feet to consider how to free himself. Upon careful examination, Jake didn't think he could free himself from his bonds and gratitude to the divine flooded through his chest when he realized that this was the reason the cops had come.

At that moment, Frank entered the room and lifted Mike's dead body over his shoulder in a fireman's carry. He paused long enough to taunt Jake. "Good job, Jakey. I couldn't stand Betty crying anymore. She broke my heart reminding me of home. Thanks for getting rid of her." Frank turned to leave, carrying Mike's body.

Pausing to nod up his chin at Jake over his empty shoulder. Frank said, "See you at the funeral."

"Frank! Help me," Jake shouted. "You owe me."

Frank stopped and turned back, his broad grin expressed that he had wanted to hear those very words. "Sorry, no can do. Piss doesn't work on duct tape. Besides, that would make us even. Don't waste my favor and just sit tight, hero. The G-men are here for a reason."

Frank lost his smile as he turned forward again. His visage changed as he and Mike's soul transformed into a flock of large, menacing crows that cackled as they flew like a viperous shade from the front door and into the evening sky.

6

When Charlie re-entered the front room of Mike's house, he had his knife in hand. He stopped in front of Jake pausing to look down at Mike's dead body before looking back at Jake.

He pointed his knife, gesticulating, "You were wrong. There was a mother and her son in the garage."

"Oops," Jake said. "I concede? Cut me free, man, I have to piss."

Charlie grinned thinking about it for a beat and said, "So are you really psychic?"

"Sure, I followed a ghost here to stop a killer," said Jake.

Charlie said, "Do you know why we are here?"

"I know you guys are IRS and you were following me around. Look, I am clean and my bookstore name is about buyers making the rules. They set their own prices."

"Here nor there," Charlie said. "I was just going to say if I was psychic, I wouldn't be taped to a chair."

Jake replied in defeat, "It doesn't work that way."

"Really," reacted Charlie. "How does it work?"

Before Jake could say something sarcastic, Joe rushed into the house crying out, "What the hell's taking so long? I told you to cut him loose and bring him—"

Charlie turned to look at Joe eye-to-eye before he interrupted, "Easy! I was asking him some questions."

"Did you ask him about the woman and Tammy hearing him," Joe asked.

Charlie shook his head.

"Did you ask him about those crows?"

Jake groaned with impatience and said, "Can one of you clowns just cut me loose? I'm injured." Jake coughed like he was in pain and choking on blood.

Snapping his knife closed, Charlie told Joe, "He said he has to piss."

Joe and Charlie looked at each other and then smiled with mischief in their eyes.

Charlie said, "So you needed me to bring the car around?"

"Better bring it around," Joe said smugly. "I already called the locals to tell them that we need an ambulance and the coroner." The G-men walked out of the house into the yard.

Jake, shaking the chair, shouted, "Hey! Cut me loose!"

"Just hold tight, hero," Joe called from the yard with a chuckle.

Jake grunted pulling against his restraints as a flock of crows laughed from the trees outside.

SATURDAY

1

Jake wrote with a pen on a laser copy of his eulogy. He put down the pen and lifted up the papers. Standing, Jake began to read aloud his mother-approved eulogy, "What can I say to begin to describe the man, Tom St. Johns. He was a good father and loved more than most can—"

The shrill alert of a phone ringing interrupted his monologue. Answering the phone, Jake said, "Hello?"

"Jake, this is Tammy. I'm sorry I couldn't call you sooner. But, it has been comp—"

"Look. Are you finished spying on me, Agent Love Interest?"

"Yep. I am officially forbidden to spy on you," Tammy admitted. "However, I can talk to you about anything unrelated to my case. I'm suspended."

She waited for an interruption that didn't come, so she said, "I decided to call you and let you know that after examining the tax evasion and conspiracy evidence, we didn't feel that pursuing a trial to prove the local hero was a psychic to be in our best interest. You are officially free and clear, but there is something you need to—"

"Great news, Agent Tammy X. Thanks for the heads-up, but I'm kinda in the middle of something. Also, I'm no longer taking on new students nor do I date cops. Good luck." Jake set the receiver onto the base and began reading his memorial again.

Immediately, the phone rang again. Jake answered with hostility, "I already told you, Tammy. I—"

"Tammy? Who's Tammy," asked the voice on the other end. "Jake. This is Michelle and I just saw you on the news."

Jake was paralyzed for a moment at hearing her beloved voice again and closed his eyes before he said, "Look, Michelle, when I showed you who I am, you left. Now you call me after—" Interrupting himself he sighed, "Chelle, I loved you, trusted you, but my dad died this week and I think I am doing A-OK without you. Please don't call—"

The phone line died.

Jake smiled knowing that he was finally over her and had found closure by getting in the last word. If only cigarettes were as easy to let go of wanting—he wanted one right now and thought back to his arriving home last night to find a pack of cigarettes in his shirt pocket. He was now very glad that he had crushed the pack into his garbage can, but found he had to fight hard against an impulse to go and make sure that every cigarette had been destroyed.

Let it go, he thought to himself.

Jake picked up the papers and started to read aloud, again. Then, he just set it back down to pick up the phone and quickly dialed a memorized number.

When the phone picked up, he said, "Mom, I am ready. Can I come over, so you can hear my memorial for Dad?"

When she tried to argue saying that he had been through enough and needed to rest. He politely interjected, "Mom, I already have the music, too."

SUNDAY

1

Standing alone at a podium to say a final farewell to his father in front of family, friends, and strangers, Jake turned from the podium to look at the corpse of Papa Tom in a coffin. Inhaling deeply to steel his nerves, Jake adjusted the shoulders of his suit jacket and began with strength, "What can I say to begin to describe the man, Tom St. Johns. He was a good father and loved more than most can—"

Sid started to cry and held their mom, they were both dressed in black. Jake paused. He had to stand strong against a tide of emotions crushing in and looked away from them when he started again, "He loved more than most can even understand. He wasn't just a father. He was a friend, a husband, and caregiver to thousands." He focused his mind on the strangers in attendance because their memories had little, if any, emotional value to Jake.

Jake now found it easier to pull back the reins on his emotions and renewed his resolve before saying, "In one way or another, big Tom was everyone here's Dad."

The crowd began to sob.

AFTER THE MEMORIAL, Jake's mom gave him a rib-breaking hug and said, "I always told my sister that you should have been a preacher." Her smile turned down with her chin and her concern was deep as she took his hands. "The last couple of years must have been so hard on you. If it helps, your dad hadn't talked about you more in years. Almost everyday, he had some story about Jakey Good-Tip...I'm so sorry, Jake."

"Me, too, Mom."

Carefully, Sid approached them as they hugged and kissed. After waiting longer than a thoughtful moment, Jake's brother said, "You ready to go, Mom?"

Seemingly concerned, she looked at Jake and said, "You're coming for dinner, right?"

Energy emanated from Jake into the air around him and floated like a billowed cloud to her, it laid over her like a shawl of comfort in mourning. He said, "I wouldn't miss it. I'm so sorry, Mom."

She kissed Jake a couple more times and said with weepy eyes, "Papa Tom would be so proud of you. That was...beautiful."

Intensely, she looked at Jake with a strange recognition of an otherworldly presence about him and almost said that he was glowing, instead she centered herself by wiping lipstick from his mouth and cheek with her thumb. She turned her eyes from Jake's to Sid and then back to Jake, "I am so proud of you two boys. I know your father was twice as proud."

Sid smiled to fight the tears and put his arm around her to lead her away as she started to cry again.

As Jake watched them walk away, Sid reached behind his back with a thumbs-up to Jake and shook his thumb side-to-side for emphasis. He snapped his fist to indicate clearly, 'Good job today, bro.' Jake heard his thoughts loud and clear without any confusion about the meaning of the hand signals.

They looked back and waved, Jake waved good-bye to them.

WHEN EVERYONE HAD DRIVEN off to their lives or the diner for Tom's wake, Jake looked around to see if anyone was watching before he whispered to the headstone and closed casket, "Pops? Hey, Pops! Where are you at, Tom?"

Wearing a fancy suit and a white apron around his waist, Papa Tom rolled out like he was standing from bed, he stood up from behind the suspended casket, and said, "Right here, son." He brushed his suit off moving around the grave to Jake before fixing his hair as if he had just been stirred from a church pew nap.

"Hey, what'd I miss," Tom asked. "I heard all that sing-song funeral crap. Who the hell were you talking about?"

Jake chuckled, laughing instead of crying, and told Papa Tom, "I was talking about you, ya ingrate."

Tom looked at himself in a suit. "What the hell is this? You guys buried me in a suit?"

"It was kinda funny to Sid and me, too. But Mom insisted on your Sunday best."

"These haven't been anyone's best for decades," Tom said waving a hand with dismissal and took off his suit jacket. He said, "Well, at least, you boys had sense to put on my apron."

"That was Mom's idea, too."

"You make it sound like she was planning it," Tom said, straightening his jacket over his arm and patting down his pants. Tom jolted and exclaimed, "Your mom isn't being suspected of murder, is she?"

Jake fought back the chuckle rising and said, "Of course not."

"Well, she should be investigated. She caused my stroke, you know."

Jake laughed out loud.

Tom was silent for several seconds before he draped the straightened jacket over the casket and said, "So, is this why you thought you were allowed to be a jerk all the time?"

Jake responded in defense and said, "I'm a jerk?"

"Yeah, you get to be a jerk cuz you see ghosts, right?"

Finding little comfort in being discovered, Jake replied, "I'll ask my analyst." He turned and began to walk away from the tarp-covered grave, coffin, headstone, and his father.

"That's the jerk I was talking about."

"Well, it's nice to have the old Tom back, again, too," said Jake still walking away from the grave.

Tom called, "Oh, come on. Quit acting like that, I'm just kidding."

"Well, ease up," Jake said, turning back with his hands outstretched. "My dad just died and I feel like a prick already. I need to take you home, so come on, let's go."

Tom hurried away from his grave to follow, Jake waited for him.

Tom said, "How's your mom doing?"

"She's alright, considering. Sid and Aunt Norma have been there for her and they even let me handle the big stuff so I would pay for it. Can you believe dying with pride costs at least twenty-thousand dollars?"

It was silent for a long moment as father and son walked together, Tom reflected on his life before he asked, "Was I really a good dad, Jake?"

Jake was stopped in his tracks and started to cry—he couldn't stop it as the good and bad memories flooded out from his eyes. He lifted his arms in defeat and could barely choke out, "I wouldn't trade you for anything, Dad."

Tom and Jake embraced for a long moment.

Tom said, "Thanks for calling me back, Jake." He was unsure of his responsibilities of comforting a crying man and only hugged Jake harder, "You were a great son, too."

They continued their embrace as Jake cried harder as years of pent up emotion drained from him.

Tom said patting his back, "It's all good. You've got me right here, Jake.

Get it out, son." Tom patted Jake's back and held him more tightly, rocking him; Jake released the pain of his torture in always being alone to the only person with whom he could now share the burden of his secret.

HANGING HIS HEAD AND CRYING, Jake stood alone in the graveyard.

MONDAY

1

Jake snapped awake and sat up looking around the room, listening to his alarm clock's alert. He shouted into the house, "Betty…?!"

When he turned off the alarm, the silence in the house was magnified by a couple of sounds related to an old house waking up and popping in the morning sunshine.

Rubbing his head, Jake said, "I guess that's really it."

From the silence came the sound of footsteps in the hallway.

Jake caught his breath for a second and called, "Betty?"

Frank stepped into the doorway with a touch of concern under his big smile. He said, "Sorry, buddy, it's just me now."

Jake lay back against his pillow with attitude and said, "Thanks for your concern, Frank. But, go away. I have school today."

"No, you don't. You signed over the school to Tim and cursed him with your gross mismanagement," Frank said as he entered the room. He scrutinized Jake's messy room and said, "This place is a mess. You should hire a cleaning crew."

"What do you want, Frank? I need to work on my books and I don't work well with others."

Frank sat down on the foot of the bed and said, "Forget about the books, dork." He continued after a dramatic pause with a sigh, "Sorry, hero, you're not done, yet. Now, there's a crying girl named Emily in Cleveland that needs to meet you."

Jake's surprise at hearing the name Emily of Cleveland was only outweighed by the frustration of Frank moving so freely in his bedroom and sitting on his bed. He said while kicking off his bedcovers at Frank, "Whatever, you need to get out. Before I smoke you out."

"I wouldn't assume you're allowed to talk to me like that," said Frank. "Now your little angel's gone home, hoss."

With total annoyance, Jake leveled a stern look at Frank and said, "No, really, Frank. What do you want?"

Frank hissed smoke at Jake through malicious teeth, "I want you to get your ass outta bed and get ready to go. You can call your mom from the airport."

Jake stomped his feet to the floor. "God damn you, Frank. I have things to do."

Frank stood from the bed and turned away from a confrontational Jake to exit the room. He said looking back at Jake, "Yes, you do. Don't bother to pack, the taxi is here and my meter is running. Hurry up or I will teach you a little something about Hell. Hmmph, what? You'll smoke me out with some effin' incense?"

Frank walked down the hallway from Jake's bedroom exhaling smoke into the air as he looked side-to-side, "This old place is a tinder-box, so be quick, book-boy, or I'll burn it down. We need to go, they are coming."

Jake's face twisted as he pondered who could be coming. *Hadn't they already come?*

He looked around his room considering the worst possibilities. He pulled on a shirt from the floor and sighed putting his hands on his hips, "Cleveland, eh? Only, if we're going to the Rock and Roll Hall of Fame."

"That's the spirit. You can even go to Canton for the Football Hall of Fame," Frank said from the hallway. "Now step! I'll be waiting impatiently."

"Wait up! I'll need cash," called Jake.

There was an inhuman roar as Frank turned past the large crucifix. He grunted, "You can take the cash in your wallet and credit cards. Outside now!"

Looking around to see the house filling with smoke, Jake hustled up the hall to get his money clip, shoes, coat, keys, and wallet. He looked up to his bloody Lord shaking his head in disbelief, Jake smiled at the personal realization that he had lost his mind before snatching two ten-thousand bindles of hundred-dollar bills from the pool table by the scale.

Jake exited the house and locked the front door. He passed his hand over the door three times and chanted a quiet spell. When he turned to face the street, he saw Dante the cabbie standing in an open car door.

When Dante saw Jake, he shouted, "Hurry up, m'man. We gotta go, if you're gonna catch your flight."

Jake was pleased to see him and hurried down as he called back, "Hey Dante! How was your date the other night?"

Dante smirked sideways before returning to his driver's seat and projected his voice saying, "I'll tell you about it on the way. Now let's get the fuck outta here!"

Jake climbed into the backseat and Dante stomped the gas driving up the street. Looking back at Jake, he said, "You better buckle up, I need to hurry. And I don't care what you think of my driving, if you bang on that glass, I will whip your ass." Dante's laughter echoed through his open window while he fished a cigarette from the pack in his front shirt pocket.

AT THE TOP OF THE STREET, the driver of a dark late-model Chevy Caprice turned the ignition and followed in pursuit of the cab. Inside the vehicle was a black man and a red head, both in suits.

"Agent Dixon thinks she told him we were coming, Agent Clapp," said Agent Dixon with a head nod to his partner, who had accelerated the government-issued sedan to tail the cab.

"Please don't start talking about us in the third-person, Dixon," said Clapp. "I need to drive in the first-person."

About the Author

Jim Leyshon lives alone with his guitars in Golden, Colorado (proper), keeps up on his line drawing and watercolors, washes dishes to maintain a schedule and pay his rent, wrestles with moving to the desert or near the surf, and has a head filled with dreams of working in a Hollywood writing room. He writes in local cafes and churns his next lines in alleys as he smokes knowing the world and his writing would be better off without cigarettes. Buy his books and he'll quit!

Printed in the United States
By Bookmasters